"I Needed Love So Badly..."

His arms suddenly reached out and caught me. Both hands pulled me to his body and his mouth was on mine before I could turn my head to avoid the kiss.

I whimpered and tried to push him away, but his grip tightened and kept me close. In spite of myself, I began to weaken. I felt the strength to resist him ebbing slowly away. It had been so long—so long—since a man's arms held me that tightly. So many months since a man's body pressed against mine with such urgency. I needed love so badly. If only . . .

We will send you a free catalog on request. Any titles not in your local book store can be purchased by mail. Send the price of the book plus 35¢ shipping charge to Belmont Tower Books, Two Park Avenue, New York, New York 10016.

Titles currently in print are available in quantity for industrial and sales promotion use at reduced rates. Address inquiries to our Promotion Department.

WINTER ROSE

Barbara Daniels

BELMONT TOWER BOOKS • NEW YORK CITY

A BELMONT TOWER BOOK

Published by

Tower Publications, Inc.
Two Park Avenue
New York, N.Y. 10016

Copyright © 1978 by Tower Publications, Inc.

All rights reserved
Printed in the United States of America

WINTER ROSE

Chapter 1

It's funny how time and memory never seem to use the same calendar. They're forever playing little tricks on one another. Just this morning, for instance, while I lingered over the newspaper and a second cup of coffee, my eye suddenly caught the date at the top of the page and I realized with a start that a whole year had somehow slipped by since last August. It was a year to the day since Bob, Tracey, and I drove in to New York together for the start of that two-week cruise on the *Ocean Queen*, though in my mind it was all still as fresh as yesterday. And yet, so much else has happened between then and now I could just as easily believe that ten years have passed instead of one. Time and memory . . .

I'd never seen Tracey as excited as she was that afternoon. Ordinarily she tried to act as grown-up and sophisticated as any twenty-year old college junior could be, but that day she was just like my pigtailed little girl again. "How much farther, Daddy?" she kept asking, leaning over the back of the front seat to peer anxiously through the windshield ahead.

"Five miles less than the last time you asked!" Bob would tease, and when she groaned and tugged on his arm to insist he tell her the distance he'd laugh and say, "Keep your shirt on, Princess! That ship's not going anywhere until we get there."

Bob was right, of course. Allowing for even the worst of traffic tie-ups, he'd left plenty of time for the drive in from Maplewood. New York was almost in sight; there wasn't a chance in the world that we'd miss the sailing. And yet, something deep inside of me kept hoping that we would. Some secret little voice kept wishing that at the last minute something would happen to prevent our making it on time. Some enormous traffic jam just around the next curve, perhaps; or two sudden flat tires; or an engine conk-out that would keep us from getting to the pier before the ship sailed.

"Oh, *look*!" Tracey exclaimed, as we started down the final approach to the Lincoln Tunnel. "Look, Daddy! Look, Mother! Look over there on the other side of the river! There it is! There's the boat!"

"The *ship*, honey," Bob laughed. "When a boat's as big as that one is, it's called a ship."

"It's beautiful," Tracey sighed. "It's just the most beautiful boat—I mean *ship*—I've ever seen in my life."

It *was* a majestic sight. The ship stood out against the New York skyline like a gleaming white fortress, glistening in the sun, as tall as the dark skyscrapers behind it. Thick columns of smoke billowed from its twin jet black funnels and what looked like a thousand flags flapped and fluttered in the summer breeze.

"Oh, Mother! Just *look* at it!" Tracey said, craning her neck to catch a last glimpse of the waiting ship as Bob steered around the final curve before the tunnel entrance. "I just can't believe we're actually going to be *on* it! Aren't you excited, Mother?"

"Of course I am, dear," I said with a smile, and it wasn't entirely a lie. My stomach had been jumping with nervous anticipation from the moment I'd opened my eyes that morning, and the closer we got to New York the more it jumped. I'd have to have been awfully world-weary and blasé *not* to be excited about spending the next two weeks aboard the *Ocean Queen*. Back home in New Jersey I was the envy of all my friends. For weeks I'd tantalized them with the full-color brochures that promised fun-filled days and romantic nights on the most glamorous and luxurious cruise liner afloat. Yes, I was excited. But the kind of excitement I felt that August afternoon while Bob drove through the long, white-tiled tunnel toward Manhattan was nothing like the kind of excitement I'd felt when he first told me about the cruise.

I'd known something was up as soon as I met his train at the Maplewood station that night in June. A long day's work in the city and an hour's ride on the commuter-clogged Erie Lackawanna usually took its toll of him and showed on his face and in his walk. But that night he had a definite spring in his step as he hurried down the platform toward the car, and the gleam in his eyes made him look like a kid with a secret he was bursting to tell. He gave me a wink through the windshield as he went around the front of the car and opened the door on the driver's side.

"Scoot over, honey," he said as he got in. "I feel like driving myself tonight." Usually he was too tired to do anything but slump in on the passenger's side and mutter a few half-hearted comments to me about watching out for other traffic and slowing down for stop signs while I drove home.

"What's got into *you* tonight?" I asked, as I offered my cheek for his customary home-from-work peck.

"What do you mean?" he said.

"Well, you just seem so—"

He didn't let me finish. His hand touched the side of my face and gently turned my head. His mouth met mine in a long, lingering kiss that left me as surprised as it left me breathless. It had been a long—*too* long—time since Bob last kissed me like that. The first thing I could think of to explain such a sudden change in him was that he'd got a promotion or a raise.

"Hell, no!" he laughed when I asked him. "What makes you think that?"

"Well . . . you just—" I shrugged and let my voice trail off as I gave him a foolish smile. How could I say, in so many words, that I wasn't used to having a husband who acted like a lover?

"Hey," he said as he started the car, "you got anything cooking in the oven for supper?"

Now *that*, I thought, was more like the Bob Lawrence I knew and was used to; asking what was for supper and what was on television.

"No," I said. "I was going to make spaghetti and a salad tonight. It'll only take a few minutes to fix."

"Forget it," he said. "We're going out to eat."

At first I thought he was mad because dinner wouldn't be ready to put in front of him as soon as we got home, or because the meal I'd planned wasn't to his liking. I remembered how a number of times in the past he'd pushed away his plate, shot me a dirty look, and snapped, "Get your coat; we're going out to eat. I need a decent meal in me tonight, not this slop." But when I glanced over at him there wasn't a trace of anger or annoyance on his face. In fact, he was still grinning that mysterious, cat-that-ate-the canary grin.

"How come?" I asked.

"Why not?" he said. "Couldn't you go for a nice

thick steak? Or how about one of those giant lobster tails at the Blue Grotto? Yeah, that's it; we'll go there. I'm in the mood for some seafood myself." At the next corner he turned right, away from home and in the direction of the restaurant.

"Oh, Bob, no," I protested. "Not right now. Not the way I look. My hair's a mess and I'm not wearing any make-up and this dress . . . If we're going somewhere like the Blue Grotto, at least let's go home first so I can do something with myself."

"Forget it," he laughed. "You look sensational just the way you are." His hand reached across the seat and took mine, squeezing it hard. "As always."

"Liar," I said with a smile in spite of myself.

When we got to the Blue Grotto's parking lot, I insisted that Bob wait a few minutes while I did a fast repair job in the rearview mirror with a comb, compact, and lipstick. But I was still grateful when we went inside that the hostess seated us at a dimly lit table for two in a far corner.

Bob ordered a double dry martini for himself and a Manhattan on the rocks for me. When the drinks came and he'd placed our dinner order, he raised his glass to propose a toast.

"What shall we drink to?" he asked.

"I don't know. Isn't this your party? You decide."

He thought for a moment, then clinked his glass gently against mine. "Okay. Here's to adventure and romance."

"I'll drink to that!" I laughed. We sipped our drinks and Bob lit a cigarette. "Well?" I said after a few minutes of watching him smoke in silence. "Aren't you going to tell me now?"

"Tell you what?"

"What this is all about, of course. What's the big deal?"

He shrugged and smiled. "There's no big deal. Can't I take my wife out of the kitchen once in a while if I feel like it?"

"Oh, *you*! I'm going to hit you in a minute. Come on now; tell me. What's this all about? The suspense is killing me."

He looked at me with all the innocence of a little boy who swears he hasn't been in the cookie jar, but whose face is smeared from ear to ear with chocolate. "Honest," he said. "I just thought you'd like a night out for a change."

"Oh? And that toast about adventure and romance . . . ?"

"What's wrong with wishing for a little adventure and romance?" he teased.

"Nothing," I said, and looked down at my drink. Nothing in the world was wrong with wishing for adventure and romance. But wishing for something and having it come true were two very different matters.

"Ahh, here comes the salad," Bob said. "I hope those lobsters won't be far behind. I'm so hungry I could eat one raw."

I didn't press him any further for a reason behind all this. Maybe, I thought, it wasn't a special occasion after all. Maybe it was just the way he'd explained it: he just felt like taking me out for a change. Things hadn't been going very well between us lately—in fact, things hadn't been going well between Bob and me for quite some time—and maybe this was his way of trying to keep a bad situation from getting any worse. Maybe he thought that by doing something out of the ordinary, by breaking the dull routine our marriage had somehow fallen into in the past several years, we could make an abrupt shift of gears and start heading in a different direction.

Maybe.

And maybe *that* was just wishful thinking on my part, too, I thought. Maybe he'd just decided on the spur of the moment that he'd rather have lobster tail than spaghetti for supper.

While we ate, we talked about the kind of things we'd grown used to talking to each other about after twenty years of marriage. I told him that on my way home from leaving him at the train station that morning I'd heard a knock in the car's engine and it had cost sixteen dollars to get the spark plugs tuned or scraped or whatever it was they'd done to them at the service station. Then Bob told me about a man who'd had a heart attack on the PATH train from Hoboken to New York that morning, and how the twenty minute delay in getting him off at the first stop had made everyone late for work. I mentioned that the grass in the back yard was starting to look like it needed a trim and the lawn mower still hadn't been fixed since it broke down last September; and he told me that he'd read in the *Times* on the way home that they were thinking of raising the cab fare in Manhattan again. We talked without stopping, from the salad straight through to the dessert and coffee, but if someone had offered us a million dollars to repeat the conversation I don't think either one of us would have won the money. We talked to each other only because total silence would have been so much worse, but it was the kind of talk that no one really listened to.

When we'd finished our after-dinner liqueurs and were ready to go, Bob signalled the waitress for the check. He took out his wallet and handed her his American Express card. "This is for you," he said, and reached back into his jacket pocket for a large white envelope. "And this is for you, Kay." He handed me the envelope across the table.

"What is it?" I asked.

"Why don't you open it and find out?" That Cheshire cat grin returned to his face as he watched me tear open the envelope and then—because I didn't understand what they were—stare blankly at the sheaf of papers inside it. "It's a twentieth anniversary present, honey," he explained. "Two tickets to adventure and romance. I've booked us a two-week cruise on the *Ocean Queen*. We sail from New York on August sixteenth, and the way I figure it we should be sipping our anniversary champagne on the high seas, somewhere between St. Thomas and Martinique."

"Oh, Bob . . ."

My eyes began to brim with tears as I stared at him across the candlelit table. I'd never expected anything like this. I'd have been willing to bet he didn't even realize our twentieth anniversary was coming up in August, and certainly never would have guessed that he'd plan anything so wonderful to celebrate the occasion. My heart was suddenly so full of love and unexpected happiness that it was all I could do to keep from crying.

"Surprised?" he asked.

I gave him the best smile I could manage as I dabbed at my eyes with the napkin.

"Happy?"

I nodded my head quickly. I couldn't trust my voice. I was sure that if I tried to talk I'd only break down in tears and make a public spectacle of myself.

Bob reached across the table and gently squeezed my

hand.

"Let's get out of here and go home, okay?"

"Okay," I said, answering the pressure of his fingers on mine.

We were almost home before I managed to get full control of myself again. There were so many conflicting emotions running through me that in one moment I felt like crying and in the next I felt like laughing until my insides ached. Bob would never know, and I would never be able to explain to him, how deeply moved I was by the surprise he'd planned. It was the most wonderful thing to happen between us in more time than I wanted to remember. And yet, the trip itself really had very little to do with the way I felt. It was still too new an idea for me to accept as reality. What had touched the deepest chords of response in me and set off the strongest rush of emotion was the fact that he had cared enough to plan *anything* for our anniversary. It didn't have to be a cruise on the *Ocean Queen*. It could have been a weekend in Atlantic City for all that mattered. The important thing was that he'd cared enough to do *something* to let me know he still loved me.

If only a man could understand how much a thing like that means to a woman, I thought. If only he knew that love isn't something that should be taken for granted. A woman needs to be reminded every now and then by the man she loves that she's still wanted, still needed, still loved by him. And for the longest time I'd lived with the fear that Bob had grown tired of me.

I'd tried to tell myself that I was being silly; that after twenty years of marriage I shouldn't expect candy and roses from him every time he walked in the door. That kind of thing was for kids, still flushed with the joy and wonder of discovering love for the first time. I was thirty-eight years old now; I ought to be looking at love in a different way than I did when I was eighteen. But regardless of a woman's age, it's hard for her to live with a man and see indifference where once there was love. To feel that in his eyes she's become part of the furniture, something that comes with the house.

The wonderful trip Bob had planned for us, though, made all my fears and doubts about his love for me seem silly and groundless. I felt as happy and nervously excited as a new bride when we went upstairs to bed that night. I was sure he was going to make love to me, something that he hadn't done for such a long time I'd begun to feel he never would again.

"D'you mind if I get in the shower first, honey?" he asked. "I haven't been out of these clothes all day and I feel like they're starting to grow on me."

"Go ahead," I said. "I'll just take a quick one when you're done."

I watched him undress, and in my mind I could still see the body of the boy he'd been when we first made love that June night so long ago. Bob took good care of himself. The years may have thinned out his hair a little and turned its coal black color to salt-and-pepper, but his body was as lean and muscular as it always had been and time had given his boyish good looks a rugged, no-nonsense masculinity that made him even more attractive at forty than he'd been in his teens.

"And what about *you*?" I thought, as I studied my reflection in the dresser mirror while Bob showered. "How have *you* held up, Kay old girl?"

I turned from side to side in front of the mirror, trying to be as critical of what I saw as possible. If I'd been looking at another woman's body instead of my own, I might have said that her breasts were starting to sag a little and she could stand to lose an inch or two around the middle. But since it was my own body, my mind quickly found excuses for the flaws. Even as a young girl, I rationalized, I'd needed the support of a bra, and if my waist were any smaller it would make my big-boned hips all the more pronounced.

On the whole, I had to admit that I looked pretty good for my age, too. People I met for the first time were always amazed when I told them I had a twenty-year-old daughter. "You don't look old enough," they'd say, and I have to confess that I secretly agreed with them. My hair was more honey than blonde now, but that was only natural. All blondes got darker with age. And though a few worrisome lines and wrinkles had begun to creep in around my eyes and neck, my complexion was still as taut and firm as a girl's. I felt pleased with myself.

When Bob came out of the shower, he got right into bed. "I'll only be a few minutes," I promised, as I hurried into the bathroom. I brushed my teeth and took a quick shower. When I'd finished drying, I dabbed a few drops of Chanel behind my ears and between my breasts and then, on a crazy impulse, I put a little of the perfume between my legs, too. I wanted to smell good all over for Bob when we made love.

I'd brought one of my best nightgowns into the bathroom with me, but on second thought I decided not to wear it. I'd only have to take it off when I got into bed with Bob anyway, I reasoned, and by going to him naked and ready he'd be sure to know how much I wanted and needed his loving.

My heart fluttered with nervous anticipation as I opened the bathroom door and stepped into the bedroom. Bob had turned off all the lights but the one on my side of the bed and lay under the covers with his back to me.

"Honey?" I murmured. "I'm all done." I wanted him to see me nude in the doorway before I went to him. "It wasn't that long, was it?"

He made no answer.

"Bob?" I felt disappointment starting to nibble away at my excitement as I moved slowly across the room. "Are you awake, honey?"

There was still no answer from him.

I turned down the covers on my side of the bed and flicked out the light. As I got into bed with him, I heard Bob make a faint murmuring sound, but even when I wriggled up close enough to press my body against the solid warmth of his back, he gave no sign that he was awake.

For some time I lay motionless against him. My mind was reeling again. I suddenly felt confused and nervous and more than a little frightened. I'd been so *sure* he wanted to make love to me. Wasn't that what everything else had been leading up to all evening? The dinner out . . . the candlelight and drinks . . . the loving glances he'd given me across the table . . . the wonderful surprise . . . Was this how it ended? The same way all our nights together seemed to end these days? Together . . . but further apart than if an ocean lay between us?

"Bob?" I slipped my arm around him and softly kissed his shoulder. "Honey?" He stirred slightly, but made no move to roll over or acknowledge me behind him.

My pride told me to forget it. To kiss him goodnight and go to sleep myself. It wasn't right for a woman to beg a man to love her. But the need within me was too strong to be denied. I couldn't just turn away and pretend that it really didn't matter.

"Bob?" I shook him gently.

"Huh?" He made a snorting sound and turned his head. His eyes blinked open and looked at me from the depths of sleep. "What's the matter?"

I wriggled even closer to him, pressing my breasts against his bare back. "Didn't you forget to kiss me goodnight?"

His forehead wrinkled with annoyance. "Awwh, for Crissake. Is that what you woke me up for?"

I fought hard to keep the smile on my face as panic and desperation nipped at my stomach. "You know I can't sleep without my goodnight kiss," I murmured.

"Dammit, Kay, I was sound asleep!" he barked.

"Well . . . ?" I said. "You're awake now, honey. How 'bout a nice kiss?"

He shrugged his shoulder free of my arm and started to move away. "Go to sleep, huh?" he grunted. "It's late."

I forced myself to go on with it, throwing all my pride and self-respect to the wind. "Bob? Honey? Let's make love," I whispered. My hand moved slowly down from his chest to his belly. "Please, honey? It's been so long . . ."

"Do you know what time it is, Kay?" he snapped. "Do you know what time I've got to get up for work in the morning?"

"*Please*, honey . . . ?" I felt like a whining pup begging scraps from the table, but I couldn't help myself. The more rebuffed I felt, the more desperate I was to have him love me. It was more than a physical need by then. A little voice inside my head kept screaming, *"He doesn't love you! He doesn't love you! He doesn't love you!''* and I knew there was only one way I could prove the voice was wrong.

"*Please,* Bob. . .?"

He pulled my hand away from him and pushed it aside. "What the hell's the matter with you tonight?" he demanded. "You're acting like a bitch in heat."

"I need you, Bob," I said in a half-choked whisper. "I *need* you. Is that so wrong?"

He sighed as though I were trying his patience beyond all endurance. "Do you really think that after the day I've already put in today I've got the strength left for *that?* For God's sake, Kay, be reasonable. I'm not a machine you can turn on and off whenever you need a job done, you know."

"I'm sorry," I said. "It's just that . . . you haven't . . . I bit my lip before I started to cry. There was nothing more I could say; I'd humbled myself as much as I could. I needed him desperately, but I couldn't force him to love me against his will. A meaningless, mechanical act performed as a duty or guilty obligation on his part would have been far worse than nothing at all.

I rolled over and buried my face in the pillow, hoping I could hold back the sobs welling up in me until Bob was asleep. I felt as though all the wires that held me together inside were coming unstrung and in a very few minutes I was going to fall apart completely. I understood how people who experience nervous breakdowns must feel just before it happens, because at that moment I felt dangerously close to one myself.

Bob turned over and put his hand on my arm. His lips lightly touched the side of my neck. "I'm sorry," he murmured. "I didn't mean to growl at you like that. It's just that it's been such a long day and I'm beat as hell. I would if I could, but—I'm just too tired. You can understand that, can't you, Kay?"

I squeezed my eyes tightly shut to hold back the tears as I nodded. I felt so ashamed of myself. I hadn't even considered his feelings. Of course he was tired. He got up with the sun every day and worked hard all week to pay for our beautiful house and new car and to give Tracey everything she wanted at college. Wasn't that a way of proving his love for me, as much as anything he might have done in bed? I wanted to believe it, but that nagging voice inside me kept insisting that a man's responsibility to provide for his family was one thing, and proving his love was quite another.

"I know how you must feel," he continued, "but his just isn't the right time for it. I'm too keyed-up about all the work that's got to be done before the new Chicago office opens. It's all I can concentrate on right now. It's rough on both of us, I know, but that's one reason why I booked this cruise. By the time August comes and everything's been settled in Chicago, we'll need some time for ourselves. We'll have two whole weeks on that beautiful ship to get to know each other again and have fun together, the way we used to. It'll only be a little while longer, honey. And then we'll be able to make all the good, sweet loving we want to, as often as you like. How does that sound?" He bent his head and kissed my neck again, squeezing my arm at the same time in a reassuring gesture. "Hmmmmmm? Doesn't that sound good?"

"It sounds wonderful," I answered softly. And it did. But for the longest while after Bob moved away and went back to sleep, I lay awake and stared at the shadows on the ceiling, wondering whether or not I'd be able to keep my sanity until then.

I made the next few weeks pass as quickly as possible by throwing myself completely into preparations for the cruise. Once my mind was adjusted to the fact that it was actually going to happen, there seemed a million things that needed to be arranged beforehand.

I spent two full weeks just shopping for a wardrobe for the trip. It had been so long since I'd last bought resort clothes that I needed everything, from a new bathing suit to evening dresses for those glamorous nights at sea the brochures promised.

There were dozens of little matters about the house that needed to be settled before we left, too. Although Tracey would be home from college for the summer by then and able to look after things while Bob and I were away, I knew I'd have to leave little reminder notes for her about everything. Our daughter had never been obliged to do much for herself before. As our only child, she'd been shamelessly pampered and spoiled by Bob and me all her life, to the point where even though she would be earning a degree from Emerson in another year, she still didn't know how to run the washing machine by herself or set the oven temperature so a ten dollar roast didn't turn into a ten cent lump of charcoal.

Finally, though, everything that needed to be taken care of had been taken care of and all that remained was to count the days until our departure. The closer it got, the more excited I grew. Although the cruise was sure to be a once-in-a-lifetime adventure, the real excitement of it for me was knowing that Bob and I would be together in such a romantic setting for two whole weeks. It was sure to have an effect on our marriage. It would be like a shot in the arm. A second honeymoon, except that we'd never really had a *first* honeymoon to speak of. That weekend we'd spent at Bob's uncle's cabin in the Poconos right after we were married wasn't quite the fond memory a young bride looks back on for the rest of her married life. Especially since the whole time was spent with seven of Bob's relatives, and he and I had barely a minute to ourselves.

But I was sure this trip would more than make up for all that. It would give us the chance to know each other again. To rediscover all the little things we'd forgotten over the years and rekindle the romance that once had burned with such a strong flame, but in the past few years had cooled to little more than an ember. Those two marvelous weeks at sea couldn't help but make us fall in love all over again. Maybe, I thought as I gave full rein to my wildest secret fantasies, as a result of the cruise Tracey might even find herself no longer an only child. There was no reason why Bob and I *couldn't* have another baby. We both were certainly still young enough, and the notion of being a new mother all over again appealed to me more than I dared to admit. Of course Bob would have to have some say in the matter, too, and maybe the idea of being a brand-new daddy at forty wouldn't be as attractive to him as I secretly hoped. But it was something to keep in mind. Something to talk about while we dreamily snuggled in each other's arms aboard that beautiful, romantic ship.

And then, without any warning, all my hopes and dreams were suddenly shattered in a million pieces. A week before the day we were scheduled to sail, Bob came home from work and announced that he couldn't go. I stared at him in stunned disbelief, hoping against hope that he was only teasing or playing some sort of cruel practical joke on me. But as I listened to him going on and on about needing to go to Chicago at the last minute on company business, I realized with a dull ache in my heart that he wasn't joking.

"It's those damn idiots they hired out there in the first place," he said. "They don't know their ass from a hole in the ground. If that new office is ever going to get on its feet, somebody who knows what he's doing has got to go out there and show them how to run things."

"Are you the only one who can do that, Bob?" I asked.

"No, of course not. But I'm the one old man Winthrop asked to go."

"Didn't you tell him about the cruise . . . ?"

"Oh, sure!" he snapped. "I'm going to tell the president of the company, the first time he lays some really heavy responsibility on my shoulders and gives me the chance to show what I can do, that I'm sorry, but his multi-million dollar problems will just have to wait, because I'm going on a boat ride with my wife."

"It's just for two weeks, Bob," I said, still hopeful that something could be done to salvage the dream falling apart before my eyes.

"Do you have any idea how much money it's costing Winthrop for every *minute* that Chicago office doesn't open? Christ, Kay, in two weeks the whole company could be bankrupt if somebody doesn't get things humming out there."

I swallowed hard. It was obvious that in Bob's mind business came first. I understood, of course. He'd worked and sweated for fifteen years to get where he was now on the ladder of success, but it still wasn't high enough. He had his eye set on rungs further up and saw this as his big opportunity to leap forward. I couldn't blame him. Not really. Every man wants to make the most of himself. But understanding Bob's ambitions didn't make them any easier for me to accept. Not, at least, in that particular set of circumstances.

"All right," I said softly, "I guess we won't be spending our anniversary sipping champagne at sea after all. We'll just have to postpone the cruise until you're finished with your work in Chicago." He suddenly dropped his glance from mine and looked down at the rug. "Bob . . . ?" I said, knowing by the look on his face what the answer to my question would be even before I asked it. "You *can* trade in our tickets for a later date, can't you?"

He shook his head. "No way. It's impossible. I called this morning and tried to change the booking, but it's too late for either a refund or an exchange."

"Then what are we going to do?"

Bob shrugged. "I guess you and Tracey will have to go together."

"Me and—?" I stared at him in dumbstruck surprise. I didn't know whether to laugh or cry. Did he honestly think, after all the planning and dreaming I'd done about the two of us together on the cruise, that I'd even consider substituting Tracey for him? "Bob, you've got to be joking. I wouldn't think of going without you."

He shot me a hard, almost defiant look. "What do you suggest then? That we just kiss five thousand bucks goodbye? Watch it go down the drain, like it didn't matter?"

"Five thousand—?" Again my mouth dropped open. "I had no idea the trip would cost that much!"

"Not *would* cost," he said. *"Did* cost. Past tense, Kay. Everything's been paid in full, in advance. Either you and Tracey use the tickets and we at least get our money's worth, or the ship sails with one empty cabin that cost the Lawrence family bank account five grand."

I felt a sick sensation rippling through my stomach. We'd gone through too many lean, hard years in the past for me to even consider throwing away that much money for nothing . . . and Bob knew it.

"Maybe we could find another couple to buy the tickets from us?" I suggested.

"Like who? You name anybody we know who could afford it in the first place and who could take it on such short notice in the second place, and I'll pick up the phone right now and give them a call. Who, Kay? Tell me who. Who've you got in mind?"

I shrugged my shoulders helplessly. "Nobody."

He softened his tone a bit as he took my hands in his. "Look, honey, I know this is a big disappointment for you. It is for me, too, and I'm damn sorry about it. If there was anything I could do—"

"I know, Bob," I said. "I know."

"It won't be so bad. At least you're getting to *go*. Look at me. I'll be stuck in Chicago, up to my neck in paperwork and screwed-up accounts, while you and Tracey are having the time of your lives."

"It won't be the same without you, Bob . . ."

"Awhh, like hell!" he laughed. "Why, you and Tracey will probably have such a great time together you won't even miss me."

"Want to bet?" I said. I tried to smile, but I felt like crying.

And I still felt like crying a week later, as Bob drove out of the Lincoln Tunnel and turned right, toward the piers. *Two tickets to adventure and romance,* I thought. There was no way of knowing what sort of adventure I might find on that gleaming tower of a ship coming into view, but one thing was certain. Without Bob along, there'd be precious little romance in store for me on the

Ocean Queen.

Chapter 2

The pier was like a beehive buzzing at the height of summer activity when we arrived. Chaos reigned supreme. A thousand different people were trying to do a thousand different things all at once, and everyone was somehow in someone else's way. Porters. Redcaps. Taxi drivers. Dock workers. Customs officers. Crew. And a steady stream of passengers, most of them looking as confused and helpless in the midst of it all as we three were, who shuffled uncertainly toward the three covered gangways leading onto the *Ocean Queen*.

A bedraggled woman with three small children in tow and a little man laden down with suitcases who followed close behind them stopped alongside us. "Is this the right line for tourist class?" the woman asked, looking for all the world like she'd just pulled the big ship into port all by herself.

I gave her a sympathetic smile. "I'm afraid I really don't know. Does it make a difference?"

"Oh, it sure does," she sighed. "One line's for first class and one line's for tourist and I don't know what the other line's for. But if you get in the wrong one, they don't let you on the boat. We just spent an hour-and-a-half waiting in that line over there, and when we finally got to the front the man told us it was first class boarding only. Some democracy we live in, huh? We've been saving up for three years to take the kids on this trip, and now that we're finally here we can't even find the right way to get on the boat."

I looked around for a sign that might help her, but there were too many people pushing and shoving and waving to friends in the loading area for me to see more than a few feet ahead. "I'm sorry," I said with a helpless shrug, "but I can't tell what line this is either."

"Well, thanks anyway," the woman said. "I guess we'll find it sooner or later. Have a good time now."

"You, too," I said with a smile.

The woman tightened her grip on the three children and forged ahead, with the little man carrying the suitcases trying to keep pace behind her. "Don't cry now, Lucy," she said. "We'll be on the boat pretty soon and then you and Tommy and Mike are going to have such a good time with Daddy and me. Just wait 'til you see . . ." Her voice trailed off as they moved away and soon was lost in the babble of the swirling mass of humanity around us.

"Is *that* the kind of people we'll be travelling with, Daddy?" Tracey asked with a look of disdain.

"Oh, of course not, Princess," Bob said. "Didn't you hear her? They're in tourist class; you're in first. There's a strict segregation between the two classes on board ship. You'll probably never even see them again."

"Well, that's a relief," Tracey sighed. "That woman looked like Tugboat Annie, didn't she?"

Bob laughed hard. "I think she *is* Tugboat Annie, honey! That's why she's having so much trouble finding the right gangway. She's looking on the wrong boat. The one she wants is that little scow out there in the river!"

"Oh, Daddy!" Tracey giggled.

I looked at my husband and daughter with annoyance. What a couple of snobs you two have become, I thought. There was a time not so very long ago when the Lawrence family wasn't much better off than those poor people they were having such fun mocking. Just because we had a little money now and were able to travel first class, it didn't make us better than anyone else or give us the right to look down our noses at people less fortunate. And who was to say that family *was* less fortunate than we were? Money isn't everything. In terms of loving one another and working hard because they wanted to share experiences together, they were probably a lot richer than we were. For two cents I would gladly have run after the woman and given her *our* tickets, so that she and her family could enjoy the cruise to the fullest in first class luxury. I couldn't help feeling they deserved it far more than Tracey and I did.

"You two stay here," Bob said, "and I'll go round up a porter to handle the bags and take us to the cabin. There's no reason why *we* should run around here like bewildered refugees. We've paid for first class service, and that's what we're going to get."

While Tracey and I waited, she pointed out the enormous crates of food and supplies that were being loaded into the storage hold further down along the side of the ship. It looked like they were loading up for a voyage that would last to the end of time.

The quantity of food that would be consumed by the ship's thousand or so passengers during the fourteen day cruise could have fed the entire population of a small town for a month. Anything and everything a person's imagination and appetite could desire was ready and waiting to be served. While we were at lunch a few days later, one of the ship's officers gave our table a rundown on the actual statistics, and it staggered the imagination.

There were forty-five thousand pounds of meat listed on the *Ocean Queen's* manifest at the start of the cruise, he told us. Sirloin steaks. Filet mignon. Prime beef ribs. Tenderloin. Brisket. Leg of lamb. Veal steaks. Pork chops. Pork loin. Baked and Virginia hams. Sweet and hot sausages. Salami, bologna, spiced ham, and every variety of cold cuts, as well as twenty types of cheese.

There were four thousand pounds of turkey and five thousand pounds of chicken on board. A thousand pounds of duck, three hundred pounds of guinea hen, and a mere two hundred pounds of pheasant to be served under glass.

For the seafood lovers, the chefs had waiting five tons of trout, striped bass, red snapper, swordfish, salmon, halibut, turbot, lobsters (with and without their tails), shrimp, crabmeat, and Nova Scotia lox. And, for the more exotic connoisseurs, five hundred pounds of fresh frog legs.

Two tons of potatoes were waiting in the hold to be boiled, mashed, French fried, baked, and roasted. A thousand pounds of carrots and enough lettuce to make a salad for every man, woman, and child in St. Louis. The vegetable lockers overflowed with fresh peas, beans, beets, mushrooms, cauliflower, tomatoes, corn, spinach, Brussels sprouts, broccoli, and turnips. There were fifty cases of eggplant. A hundred cases of asparagus. Three hundred pounds of artichokes.

For fruit lovers, six thousand pounds of bananas were slowly ripening. A hundred crates of honeydew melons. Eighty crates of cantaloupes. A ton of watermelons. Strawberries, grapes, apples, plums, peaches, pears, oranges, and cherries.

Five hundred cases of Scotch were loaded onto the Ocean Queen at the start of every cruise. A thousand cases of imported French champagne. Gin, rum, vodka, bourbon, and brandy. Enough red and white wine to float the ship itself in. The glittering, mirror-backed shelves in the main lounge bar were stocked with eighty-five different liqueurs. Ten brands of international beer were on tap, as well as the full-day's production of a Coke and Pepsi bottling plant.

The ship's bakery turned out five thousand rolls a day, plus bread to feed an army and enough tempting cakes, pies, doughnuts, croissants, and pastries to make even the most weight-conscious passenger swear off his diet.

If nothing else, a cruise on the *Ocean Queen* promised to be a gastronomic trip to paradise.

When Bob returned, he brought not one but two porters with him. They loaded our suitcases onto their luggage carriers and led us straight through the herd of people still waiting to board the ship and up the gangway. A distinguished looking man in a white uniform dripping with gold braid waited to greet us at the head of the ramp.

"Good afternoon, Mrs. Lawrence," he said. "It's a pleasure to welcome you and your daughter aboard the *Ocean Queen*." He glanced quickly at the passenger list on the clipboard he held. "You're in Stateroom D, Boat Deck. Mr. Taylor, the ship's Second Officer, will meet you there in a few minutes and will be happy to give you a tour of the ship before we sail. We hope you have a very pleasant cruise. If you have any problems whatsoever, please don't hesitate to come to me immediately. My name is Mr. Gerard; I'm the ship's purser."

"Thank you, Mr. Gerard," I said, returning his smile. "That's very kind of you."

"Not at all, ma'am," he said with a crisp nod. "It's a pleasure to be of service. We're only sorry that you won't be sailing with us, too, Mr. Lawrence."

That makes two of us, I thought, as I turned to follow Bob and Tracey behind the porters.

I'd seen pictures of some of the *Ocean Queen's* cabins in the brochures, but they hadn't prepared me for the opulent splendor we were shown to. Stateroom D was magnificent. It was really more like a suite of rooms at the Plaza or the Waldorf-Astoria than a cabin on a ship. I had always imagined cramped quarters, bunk beds, and little round portholes, but nothing could have been further from reality. Stateroom D consisted of two spacious, hotel-sized connecting rooms.

The first was a sitting room, furnished with exquisite good taste. Deep blue wall-to-wall carpeting. Two powder blue velvet love seats and several occasional chairs. A highly polished mahogany writing desk. A chrome and glass coffee table. A console color television and radio. Air conditioning. A bar unit with a built-in refrigerator. Square windows as wide as any at home, commanding impressive unobstructed views to the outside. Floor-to-ceiling drapes that could be drawn closed for absolute privacy.

The second room was a large bedroom with two separate double beds. Twin dressers. An easy chair. The same plush, deep blue carpeting as the sitting room. Enormous, walk-in closets. Large windows that promised stunning views of the sea and ports of call.

A full-sized, spotlessly clean bathroom with shower and tub was easily reached from either the bedroom or the sitting room.

"Well," said Bob, when we'd completed our tour of the suite, "what do you think?" He had such a pleased, self-satisfied grin on his face that you'd have thought he had personally designed and decorated everything himself.

"Oh, Daddy, it's wonderful!" Tracey enthused. "I never dreamed it would be this grand! I love it!"

"How about you, Kay?"

"It's beautiful, Bob," I admitted.

"For five thousand bucks, it ought to be!" he laughed.

"Who sent all the flowers?" I asked. There were three huge bouquets of fresh-cut flowers in the sitting room and another glorious spray in the bedroom, on the nightstand between the two beds.

Bob shrugged. "I don't know. I guess they come with the package."

"Oh." I had hoped that he might have sent them. "The champagne, too?" A silver champagne bucket with a bottle of expensive Dom Perignon champagne chilling inside it stood on the bar counter, alongside a tray of delicious looking canapés and cocktail sandwiches.

"Yeah, I guess so. It looks like the royal treatment starts as soon as you come on board. Should we open it and have a bon voyage toast?"

"Yes, let's, Daddy," Tracey said, avoiding my glance. She knew how I felt about her drinking liquor, but made little secret of the fact that she indulged quite a bit while she was away at school.

Bob went over to the bar unit and began searching for a corkscrew, but just when he'd found it and was about to open the champagne bottle there was a knock on the door. I opened it and found a handsome young man in a crisp white uniform standing outside.

"Mrs. Lawrence?" he said with a friendly smile. "I'm Michael Taylor, the Second Officer. Is everything satisfactory?"

I was charmed immediately by the warmth of his smile, which seemed such a sharp contrast to his crisp, precise British accent. "Everything's just fine," I said. Then, stepping back to open the door wider, I asked, "Won't you come in? We were just going to have a champagne toast."

"Thank you, ma'am," the young officer said. As soon as he came in, I saw Tracey's eyes light up. She smiled and unconsciously brushed back her long, shoulder-length blonde hair.

"I'd like you to meet my husband, Bob," I said, "and our daughter, Tracey." The two men shook hands. "Tracey will be taking my husband's place on the cruise, Mr. Taylor," I explained.

He turned toward my daughter and his smile broadened. I saw the same flicker of interest in his eyes that I'd seen in hers a few moments earlier.

"I'm sorry you won't be sailing with us, Mr. Lawrence," he said, "but I must say you've provided a most beautiful substitute."

"Why thank you, sir!" Tracey said as she offered him her hand. "I'm glad to be here. I think I'm going to have a wonderful time."

"We'll do all we can to see that you do, Miss Lawrence," the young man said.

As I looked at them holding hands, I couldn't help wondering just how far he would go to insure that such an attractive and desirable girl as Tracey enjoyed herself. Shipboard romances and all that. I vowed to keep my eyes open for any monkey business during the next two weeks. I wasn't about to allow my daughter to become one more conquest on what I was certain must be a long list of them the handsome young officer already had made.

"You've got a beautiful boat, Mr. Taylor," Tracey said.

"Thank you," he answered with a smile, still holding her hand. "But we like to think of her as a ship."

"Oh, really?" Tracey said, fluttering her eyelashes as though she'd never been told the difference between a boat and a ship before. "How interesting."

"Uh-huh," I thought. I knew for sure now that I'd have to keep my eyes open *wide*. I was surprised by what a flirt my daughter had become, and I was certainly experienced enough myself to recognize a wolf when I saw one. Even a wolf in Second Officer's clothing.

"If you'd like," the young man said, as he finally let go of Tracey's hand, "I'd be happy to show you and your parents around the ship. The *Queen's* awfully big, and you might get lost if you don't know where you're going."

"That would be super," Tracey bubbled. "Mother? Father? Would you like to come on a tour of the ship with Mr. Taylor? Or," she added slyly, "would you rather stay here and have some champagne by yourselves while you say goodbye in private?"

Not on your life! I thought. I glanced down at my wristwatch. "There's plenty of time before sailing," I said. "We can drink our toasts and say goodbye to Daddy after Mr. Taylor's shown us *all* around. And, by the way, we'd like to thank you for the champagne, Mr. Taylor. It was very thoughtful."

"The ship's pleasure, ma'am," he said with a polite nod. "Whenever we can be of service, just call." I was sure I saw him dart a quick glance at Tracey when he said that, and equally sure I saw the hint of a smile on both their faces. Love—or something that went by the same name—was definitely in bloom.

As we left the stateroom, Bob took my arm and held me back for a moment. "What did you thank him for the champagne for?" he demanded. His tone of voice was clearly one of annoyance.

I looked at him for a long moment, too surprised by the question to answer immediately. "Why—because it's polite, of course. Why else?"

"You don't think he sent it personally, do you?"

"Well of course not. But—"

"Look, Kay, we've paid five thousand bucks for this cruise. That means you and Tracey are entitled to be treated like royalty for the next two weeks."

"So . . . ?" I was still confused by his attitude.

"*So*, don't go around acting like everyone's doing you a favor. Try to act a little dignified for a change, huh?"

I flinched as though he'd struck me. "Even dignified people have good manners, Bob."

"You know what I'm talking about," he said in a harsh whisper. "You always let people walk all over you. Try putting the shoe on the other foot for once. Be assertive. Make these flunkies do what *you* want, and don't be thanking them for it all the time. Remember, it's their job to serve you. You're the paying customer, and you don't have to be grateful for anything they do for you."

I sighed, and as we hurried to catch up with Tracey and the young ship's officer I promised Bob that I would try to be as assertive and dignified as possible. But that would never include being rude or impolite, as far as I was concerned.

Ours was one of eight deluxe staterooms on the Boat Deck of the *Ocean Queen*. Four were on the port side of the ship, and four were on the starboard side. There were seven passenger decks in all, and the Boat Deck was third from the top. Mr. Taylor began our tour there.

The eight staterooms were near the bow of the ship. Beyond them, running the whole length of the rest of the Boat Deck, were the two first class nightclubs. The first and largest was called the Queen's Lounge, and the name was very appropriate. It looked fit for royalty indeed.

To the left of the entrance doors, just inside the red-carpeted lounge, was an enormous, L-shaped rosewood bar, with at least three dozen high-backed stools covered in black suede spaced along its length. To the right were several long, comfortable couches and chairs done in silver velvet grouped around low, rosewood drinks tables. Beyond this more intimate area was the main section of the lounge. At least a hundred tables, covered with starched white cloths, were grouped around a U-shaped dance floor and a stage where, Mr. Taylor informed us, variety acts would perform twice nightly.

We walked through the Queen's Lounge and out one of the far exits, then all the way down the outside deck to the stern of the ship. About three dozen deckchairs, and perhaps half as many small table groupings, were set up outside the second nightclub for the enjoyment of passengers who wanted to bask in the sun during the day or watch the moon rise and count the stars at night.

The smaller lounge, called the Piccadilly Club,

looked warm, cozy, and comfortable. Done entirely in red, white, and blue, it was obviously meant for those who wanted to have a quiet drink at a candlelit table and hold hands while they listened to the tinkle of familiar tunes played at the piano bar, or dance cheek-to-cheek on the small round dance floor in the center of the table groupings. It was a lovely little place. The perfect setting for shipboard romance. But I was glad Mr. Taylor didn't linger long there. Without Bob, I was sure I'd never spend any time in it and being there, thinking of all the lovely, romantic nights at sea we wouldn't have together, only made me sad.

We took an elevator (which Mr. Taylor charmingly called "the lift") up one level to the Bridge Deck. This was where the Captain ran the ship from the Wheel House, he explained, and where most of the lifeboats were located. Aside from another grouping of deckchairs in the stern and a small steam room and sauna, most of this deck was off-limits to passengers.

Another level up in the elevator brought us to the Sun Deck, at the very top of the *Ocean Queen*. This was where the sun was worshipped with unashamed devotion. An enormous, Olympic sized swimming pool was ringed by hundreds of deckchairs that spread out in concentric circles and stretched all the way back to the stern. Toward the bow there was a pool bar with stools and a half-dozen tables, where one could linger over a cool Tom Collins without losing a minute's tanning time in the overhead sun. Beyond this, at the very front of the ship, was an indoor casino with a tiny bar, dance floor, and gaming tables where betting passengers could nightly lose their money at roulette, blackjack, and poker.

"Well, there you have the top half of the *Queen*,"

Mr. Taylor said, when we'd walked through the casino and back to the bank of elevators. "Now I'll give you a quick tour of what's below your stateroom level."

With Tracey clinging close to the young officer's side, and Bob and me tagging along behind, we went down three levels to Five Deck. The main first class dining room was located here, in the middle of the ship. I peeked through the entrance doors and saw that the tables already had been laid for the first dinner to be served shortly after sailing. They looked as elegant as any I imagined might be set for a banquet in Buckingham Palace.

The rest of the first class cabins were also located on Five Deck, as well as a lounge where movies were shown several times a day, another small bar and grill, the ship's library, a cozy reading room with little desks for writing postcards and letters to the folks back home, and another open area in the stern for deckchair sunning.

The next level down, Four Deck, was the start of the tourist class section. Mr. Taylor said there were bars and the main dining room for tourist passengers on this deck, but since we would never be eating or drinking in them he didn't bother to include them in our tour. Instead, he showed Tracey and me where we could get our hair done in the ship's beauty salon; where we could buy duty-free watches, cameras, perfume, and souvenirs of our stay on the ship in the shopping arcade; where we could book shore excursions for the various ports of call in the next two weeks; and where the ship's purser, doctor, and recreation director were located, in the event we needed any of their various services.

"And that, folks, concludes your Taylor Tour," the young man said as he led us back to the elevators. "I'm sure that now you'll remember exactly where everything is on the *Queen* and you'll never be the least bit lost."

"Oh, yeah!" Tracey laughed. "I don't even remember where our cabin is!"

Mr. Taylor smiled. "You'll get used to things sooner than you think," he said. "In a day or two, the *Queen* will be just like home to you. You'll be able to get around blindfolded."

"I doubt that very much," Tracey said. "I'll probably have to send out an S.O.S. for you every time I want to go to breakfast!"

"I'm on call whenever you need me, Miss Lawrence," he said, and I could have sworn I saw him give her a quick wink just before the elevator doors slid open. As soon as they did, the family we'd seen on the pier tumbled out, looking every bit as harried and confused as they did before.

The woman's eyes lit up the instant she saw Mr. Taylor's uniform. "Are you an officer?" she asked hopefully.

"Yes, ma'am," he said with a polite nod. "How may I be of service?"

"Oh, thank Heaven!" she sighed. She looked as relieved as a snowbound skier spotting a St. Bernard coming over a rise. "We're lost!" she said with a nervous laugh. "Hopelessly and completely lost! Our cabin is on Two Deck—number 2076?—but we just can't seem to find it. We've been up and down in this elevator so many times the kids are starting to get seasick, but every time we've come to the wrong floor. Can you help us? *Please . . . ?*"

"Of course," Mr. Taylor said, "I'll be glad to show you to your cabin."

"Oh, but . . ." Tracey looked at me and then at him with irritation. "I thought you were going to come have some champagne with us . . . ?"

"Tracey," I said, "I'm sure Mr. Taylor has a lot of other, more important things to do before the ship sails."

"I'm afraid I do, Miss Lawrence," he said.

Tracey shot an openly hostile look at the confused woman and her family, then sunk into one of her sullen moods as we all got into the elevator together.

"We'll take the Lawrences up to their deck first," Mr. Taylor told the woman, "and then we'll go down to Two Deck and get you and your family settled in, Mrs. — ?"

"Jacobs," she said. "Our name is Jacobs." As the elevator rose toward the Boat Deck, she turned to me and asked, "Were you and your family lost, too, Mrs. Lawrence?"

"No. We were not lost," Tracey growled.

I wanted to slap her for being so openly rude to the poor woman. She was just trying to be friendly. "Mr. Taylor was giving us a quick tour of the ship, Mrs. Jacobs," I said. "But I'm sure we'll still be lost ourselves when we try to find things on our own later on."

"It's a beautiful boat, isn't it?" she said.

I smiled and nodded. "Very."

"It's called a *ship*," Tracey muttered, but if Mrs. Jacobs heard her she didn't respond. The elevator stopped at our deck and the doors opened.

"Well, here you are," Mr. Taylor said. "Back where you belong, safe and sound."

"Thank you very much for showing us around, Mr. Taylor," I said.

"My pleasure, ma'am."

"Try to come up for some champagne when you can," Tracey said. "There's plenty; I'm sure we'll have some left."

"If I can," he promised.

"Goodbye," Mrs. Jacobs said. "Maybe we'll see you later."

"I doubt it," Tracey said as she brushed by the woman. "*We're* in first class."

As soon as we were back in our stateroom, I let my daughter have it. "I'm really annoyed with you, Tracey! I never thought I'd see the day when you acted so rudely to anyone."

"Oh, *Mother*," she sighed.

"Don't '*Oh, Mother*' me. You behaved like a spoiled snob, and I'm embarrassed and ashamed of you."

"For what? What did I say that was so terrible?"

"It's not what you said, it's how you said it. That poor woman felt bad enough, and I'm sure you made her feel even worse."

"She's a stupid old cow," Tracey swore, "and I hope she and her whole family fall overboard."

"*Tracey!*" I was truly shocked.

"Well . . . If it wasn't for her, Mr. Taylor would be here right now with us."

"Drinking champagne, instead of helping passengers who really need him?"

"Well . . . why not?" she insisted. "We're paying a lot more than they are. Why shouldn't he spend his time with us instead of them?"

"Because it's his job to look after *all* the passengers," I said.

Before Tracey could answer, Bob stepped in. "Hey! Hey, you two! Is this how you're going to start the cruise? Jumping down each other's throat?"

"Well if this is an example of how she's going to act for the next two weeks," I vowed, "I'd just as soon pick up our suitcases and go home right now. I couldn't stand being cooped up with a selfish little snob for that much time."

"Oh, *Mother*," Tracey groaned.

"Aren't you over-reacting just a little, Kay?" Bob said.

I sat down and fussed in my purse for a cigarette. Maybe he was right. My nerves *were* on edge and maybe I was making more of the situation than actual circumstances called for. Maybe I was grasping at straws in the little time left before the ship sailed, looking for any excuse to keep from going without Bob. Maybe I unconsciously resented Tracey for being there instead of him, and that was being very unfair to her. It wasn't her fault that things turned out as they did, and I shouldn't take my frustration out on her by blowing the incident with Mrs. Jacobs all out of proportion. After all, I knew Tracey had a crush on Mr. Taylor. It was only natural for her to be disappointed when he had to leave.

"I'm sorry," I said. "I didn't mean to start such a big fuss. I just thought she acted rudely to that woman and I wanted to tell her how I felt about it."

Tracey sat beside me and put her hand on my arm. "I'm sorry, too, Mother. I guess I was a little miffed because she came along right then and took Mr. Taylor away. You know the temper I've got. Sometimes I just can't help acting the way I feel inside."

"Just like your father," I said with a faint smile. "It must run in the family."

"I didn't mean to upset you. Honest. I wasn't being rude on purpose. If you'd like, I'll apologize to her if we see them again."

"No," I said, "that won't be necessary. I think it's best if we just forget the whole thing ever happened."

"Then you forgive me?"

"Oh, I guess so," I said, as my smile blossomed.

"Okay," Bob said, "thank God *that's* settled. Now that we're all friends again, how about that champagne?"

By the time we'd each had a few glasses of wonderful French champagne, the incident was completely forgotten. We laughed and joked and toasted everything under the sun. When the deep, rumbling blasts of the *Ocean Queen's* horn sounded to signal all visitors ashore, the three of us were quite giddy. I had a little trouble keeping my balance when I stood up.

"I guess it's that time," Bob said. "You girls going to come wave goodbye to me from the deck?"

"Are you kidding?" Tracey laughed. "I've got a whole purse full of streamers to throw at you!"

We all walked out to the Boat Deck railing together. Bob said there was no sense in our going down to the gangway with him, since the whole area undoubtedly would be a madhouse of visitors going ashore and other passengers saying goodbye. He told us to stay where we were and he'd try to find a place on the pier where we could see him and wave goodbye when the ship pulled out. He took Tracey in his arms and kissed her on both cheeks.

"So long, Princess," he said. "Keep an eye on that temper of yours now, so you and your mother don't start scrapping again. Hear? I want the two of you to have a wonderful time together, with no fighting."

"Don't worry, Daddy. Everything's going to be fine." She sounded like she had a lump in her throat when she kissed him again and said, "I wish you were coming with us."

"So do I, honey. I really do." Bob turned to me then and took me in his arms. "Well, this is it, I guess."

"Yes, I guess so." I had a lump in my throat, too. "I'll miss you, Bob."

"And I'll miss you." He kissed me long and hard. I didn't want to let him go when he pulled away. "There's the second warning," he said, as the ear-splitting roar of the horn sounded overhead. "I'd better get going." He kissed me again, a quick goodbye kiss. "So long, honey. Take care of yourself."

"You, too, Bob." I had tears in my eyes.

He started toward the stairs leading down to the lower decks, then stopped and called back to us, "You two send me lots of postcards from the places you'll be seeing, hear?"

"We will," Tracey yelled.

As he started to go down the stairs, I suddenly realized that in all the confusion and turmoil of the past week I'd never thought to ask him where he'd be staying in Chicago. I ran after him, calling his name as though my life depended on it. He was halfway down to Five Deck before he heard me and stopped.

"Where are you going to be? What hotel in Chicago?" I yelled. "We can't send you any postcards if we don't know where you'll be!"

"Jeez, I don't know for sure," Bob called back. The ship's horn blasted for the third time and I could feel the rumble of the engines beneath my feet as the *Ocean Queen* prepared for sailing. "Miss Blair made all the arrangements. The Regency, I think. Maybe you'd better just send them to the office, and I'll get them when I'm back."

"Bob—! Can't you remember—?" It seemed desperately important to me that I knew where he'd be for the next two weeks.

"I got to go now, honey, or I'll have to swim back to the pier in another minute! So long!" He blew a kiss in the air, gave me a quick wave over his shoulder, and was gone.

"What was all that about?" Tracey asked, when I went back to the rail.

"Your father never told me what hotel he'll be staying at," I said. "If we have to reach him for anything, if something happens, we won't know where he is."

"It doesn't really matter, Mother," she tried to assure me. "What's going to happen?"

I didn't know. But somehow, not knowing how to get in touch with Bob if I needed him made me feel all the more alone. It took all my will power to keep from running down those stairs, too, and off the ship. I really didn't know what I was doing there in the first place without him.

"Look, they're throwing off the ropes now!" Tracey said, pointing over the rail and far below where dockmen were casting off the mooring lines. The rumbling of the ship's engines made the deck feel like we were standing atop a volcano about to erupt. My heart was thumping with fear. This is it, I thought. We're sailing now. There's no turning back.

"There's Daddy!" Tracey squealed. "Oh, look! There he is!" She began to jump up and down and wave both arms like a madwoman. "*Daddy!* Up here! *Daddy!*"

"Where is he? I don't see him."

"Down there, by that woman with the big red hat! See? He's waving to us now!"

I still didn't see Bob. My eyes frantically searched the sea of faces on the pier below the ship, but it was like trying to spot someone you knew in the crowd at Times Square on New Year's Eve. Everyone was waving to everyone else and throwing streamers and confetti in all directions. I felt the ship start to move and I panicked.

"Where's your father?" I demanded, shaking Tracey so roughly that she gasped in surprise.

"Down there!" she said, pointing. "Right below us now. By that big pole and the woman with the red hat."

At last I saw him. My eyes were blurred with tears, but I could see him returning our waves and moving slowly through the crowd to follow the ship as it backed away from its berth and out into the river.

"Here," Tracey said, thrusting something into my hand, "throw some streamers down to him."

I tossed a fistful of the paper over the rail.

"He caught it!" Tracey cried. "Mother, look! Daddy caught your streamer!"

I looked down, and to my complete amazement I saw Bob holding onto the other end of the bright green streamer twined around my fingers.

"Bye, Daddy!" Tracey yelled.

"Goodbye, darling," I whispered under my breath. "I love you." There was no point in yelling. He couldn't have heard through all the commotion anyway.

The ship lurched and I staggered forward for an instant. As my hands clutched the rail for support, I lost hold of the streamer. I watched it fall down to the muddy water below, and it seemed as though the last connection between Bob and myself had been broken. I was completely on my own now.

With another loud blast of its horn, the *Ocean Queen*

moved slowly and majestically out into the Hudson and turned toward the sea. For better or worse, we were underway.

Chapter 3

Tracey and I stayed out on deck until long after the ship had sailed past the Statue of Liberty, under the Verrazzano Bridge, and out of the New York harbor. The ocean air smelled good. Clean, and salty-fresh. We watched in silence as the land slowly vanished from sight in a summer haze settling over the water. The faint hum of the engines vibrating through the wooden deck and the almost indiscernible roll of the enormous ship as it headed south cast a near-hypnotic spell over the two of us. When Tracey finally spoke, the sound of her voice startled me. I'd almost forgotten she was there beside me.

"Mother?"

"Yes, dear?"

"You really love Daddy, don't you?"

I had to laugh in surprise. "Why, what a question!"

"You do, though, don't you?"

I looked back at the ocean, feeling the breeze of the sea cool and comforting on my face. "Of course I do. I love him very much."

"I don't think I realized just *how* much you love him until this afternoon. Until just a little while ago, when I watched you waving goodbye. You were crying."

"Well. . ." I felt a little foolish and embarrassed that she'd seen. "It's the first time I've ever gone anywhere without your father since we've been married."

"But he's gone away without you. Lots of times."

"Yes, but that was different. It was always on business. And I had you and the house to take care of, so it really didn't seem like we were apart."

"Do you hate me for being here instead of him?"

Her question made me flinch. "Darling, of course not!"

She wasn't convinced. "Maybe you don't hate me—not exactly—but you'd still be happier if Daddy were here instead of me. Wouldn't you?"

I couldn't lie to her. She was old enough and wise enough to discern what I was feeling, even if I didn't put it into words. "Well . . . of course I wish your father could have taken the trip with me the way we planned. And I'm sorry that things worked out the way they did. But since they did, I can't think of anyone I'd rather have take his place than you."

"Honest?"

"Of course, Tracey." I reached out and squeezed her arm. "I love you as much as I love your father, and I always will."

"Even if I act like a selfish little snob sometimes?"

"Oh, please!" I laughed. "Let's not bring *that* up again!"

"You were right, Mother. I *was* rude to Mrs. Jacobs. And I did it on purpose. I really wanted Mr. Taylor to come back to the cabin with us, and when he couldn't—because of her—I was so mad I just couldn't help myself. All I could think of was hurting her because Mr. Taylor would be with her instead of with me. I mean," she said quickly, "with us."

"You don't have to explain," I said, smiling. "I saw that look in your eye as soon as he came in. And I saw the same look in his eye, too."

Her face brightened. "Did you really? Oh, that's wonderful! Then it wasn't just my imagination. He does like me!"

"I'm afraid so," I sighed.

"I didn't think there was anything wrong in the way I acted, until I saw how upset you were when the ship sailed. And then I started to think how I'd feel if you treated me like I treated Mrs. Jacobs, because I was here instead of Daddy. I mean, it's almost the same situation, isn't it?"

"Not quite, honey. But I think I know what you mean."

"You really *don't* hate me for coming between you and Daddy, do you?"

"How many times do I have to tell you?" I said with a little laugh. "N-O! *No!* I don't hate you at all."

Tracey suddenly put her arm around my waist and hugged me. It was the first time she'd done anything like that since she was a little girl, and it surprised me.

"We *will* have a good time on this cruise, Mother," she promised. "Wait and see. I won't give you any reason to be sorry that I'm here instead of Daddy. Any more reason, I mean, than the obvious one."

"Okay," I laughed. I made a silent vow at that moment to stop moping about Bob and make the best of the situation. I couldn't let Tracey feel for the next two weeks that I resented her presence, and that's just what she would feel if I didn't force myself to have the best possible time. "Now why don't we go inside and start thinking about all those clothes we've got to unpack?"

"I've got a better idea," she said with a devilish smile. "Why don't we do that *after* we finish the rest of the champagne?"

"You know," I said, putting my arm around her as we headed back to the stateroom, "that *is* a better idea!"

The next few hours were wonderful ones. Tracey and I polished off the bottle of Dom Perignon and nibbled at the delicious little sandwiches and canapés between rounds, laughing and teasing one another in ways we hadn't done since she was a child. In the years she'd been away at school we seemed to have drifted apart from each other, not having as much in common as we did when she was my little girl at home. I felt I had her back now. We were friends again.

When we finally got down to tackling the job of unpacking our suitcases, we took great delight in showing off the new clothes we'd both bought for the trip. Tracey and I were the same size, and we both promised to share with the other everything we'd brought.

"This bikini would look marvelous on you, Mother," she said at one point.

I looked up from the dresser drawer I was filling with underwear and burst into giggles. "You've got to be kidding! *Me?* Wear *that?*" She was holding what looked like little more than two bra cups joined by a pair of strings and a patch that burlesque strippers wear between their legs.

"Why not?"

"I'm not sure I even approve of *you* wearing a thing like that!" I laughed.

"What's wrong with it?"

"Well . . . just . . . *look* at it! And just look at *me!*"

"You've got a terrific figure, Mother," she persisted. "I'll bet it would look stunning on you. And the color's just right for your eyes. It's almost the same shade of blue."

"It would look great with the red I'd be blushing all over, too, I'll bet! No, honey, I'm afraid your mother's too bashful even to let *you* see me in a thing that scandalous."

"We'll see," she said with an impish smile. "Maybe a few days of sea air will give you a little more courage. If you do change your mind, I'm leaving it right here in the bottom drawer."

"Thanks just the same, but I think that's right where it should stay."

A little while later, while we dressed for our first dinner at sea, Tracey had another idea.

"Mother, wouldn't it be fun if we pretended we're sisters?"

"What?"

"Why not? No one on this boat—*ship,* excuse me—no one here knows us. Instead of you introducing me to everyone as your daughter, why don't we tell them we're sisters instead? The Lawrence sisters. Two beautiful young liberated women on the high seas, looking for romance and adventure!"

"Tracey," I said, putting down my eye liner for a moment and turning to look at her, "I am neither young, beautiful, *nor* looking for romance and adventure. I'm a full eighteen years older than you are, and I *am* your mother."

"You don't look that much older," she insisted. "And you only sound like my mother when you get that tone in your voice. Like you're ten feet tall and you're looking down at me, I mean. If you just acted natural, no one would ever guess we're not sisters."

"But why would we want them to believe such a thing?"

She shrugged. "Why not? It might be fun. Who knows? If some tall, dark, handsome man thought you were available, he might even make a pass at you."

"That would definitely not be my idea of fun," I said flatly.

"Why not? Wouldn't you like to try it, just for fun?"

"No. Definitely not. And knowing as you do the way I feel about your father, I'm shocked that you could even consider such an idea."

"Oh, *Mother*," she sighed. "I didn't mean that you should actually *do* anything with another man. Of course I know you love Daddy. But I'll bet *he* flirts with other women when you're not around."

Something so chilling suddenly ran through my stomach when she said that, I thought for a moment I was going to be sick.

"What do you mean?" I demanded. "Are you telling me your father's been with other women?" It made my skin crawl just to voice the suggestion aloud. I'd never once thought of Bob with anyone else but me. Never even considered the idea.

"Of course not, Mother. But Daddy's a good-looking guy. I'm sure lots of other women have given him the eye from time to time. And I'll bet he gets a kick out of flirting with them, too."

"Tracey! Stop it!"

The teasing smile on her face vanished in an instant. My hands were suddenly trembling and my face had completely drained of color.

"I—I didn't mean anything, Mother," she said softly. "Gosh, I'm sorry. I really didn't mean to upset you so much. I was just trying to—"

"Let's not say anything more about it, shall we?" I said firmly. "Your father loves me in the same way I love him, and there never will be anyone else for either of us." But even as I said it, I couldn't help wondering why the idea upset me so much . . . or why I felt such a compulsion to deny it so vehemently.

"All right, Mother," Tracey said. "I won't mention it again." She dressed quietly for several minutes, but when I'd finished my make-up and we were finally ready to go down to Five Deck she couldn't resist having the last word. "I still think it would be fun to pretend we're sisters, though."

"Oh, you!" I said with a laugh. "Let's go to dinner, before I throw something at you!"

The dining room was ablaze with lights and humming with activity when we arrived. The main chandelier glowed with the brightness of a thousand candles. Soft music from a piano and strings floated lazily over the tables. The room itself had looked beautiful when I'd seen it empty a few hours earlier, but now, filled with happy, laughing people all dressed their best, it was magnificent. We paused at the door and waited for the maître d' to seat us.

"Isn't this exciting?" Tracey whispered.

"It certainly is." I felt like we'd been invited to a very special, very wonderful party.

"Ah, yes. Lawrence," the maître d' said when we'd given our name and he checked the seating plan. "You'll be at table number eleven throughout the cruise, with the Wagner family. If you'll follow me, please, I'll show you to it."

"I hope the Wagners don't turn out to be like the Jacobses," Tracey murmured, as we followed the dining room captain past table after table of chattering people.

She didn't have a thing to worry about. The three

people already seated at table eleven looked as gracious and dignified as anyone could want. When we arrived, the two men rose from their chairs and remained standing until we were seated. The older of the two spoke first.

"Hello," he said. "It looks like we'll be sharing most of our meals together for the next two weeks, so we might as well introduce ourselves. My name's Henry Wagner." He was about fifty. Average height, a little on the paunchy side, with glasses and silver grey hair. He turned toward the woman on his left. "This is my wife, Florence."

"Hello," she said with a smile. "It's nice to meet you." She looked a few years younger than her husband. She, too, wore glasses and her curly hair was streaked with silver.

"And this is our son, Jeff."

A tall, extremely handsome young man with curly black hair and a Mark Spitz moustache nodded his head and flashed a smile of brilliantly white teeth. "Hi," he said. "Are we ever glad to see you two!"

"Oh?" I said.

"We were afraid they were going to stick us at a table full of kids," he explained.

"So were we," Tracey said, and I saw the same sparkle of interest in her eyes when she looked at Jeff Wagner that I'd seen earlier when she met the young Second Officer. "I can't stand the little monsters, can you?"

"Well," the young man laughed, "I'm always reminded of what W. C. Fields said about kids. Someone asked him if he liked children and he answered, 'Oh, yes. Yes, indeed. Especially roasted.'"

We all laughed at his clever imitation of the famous

comedian, though his mother seemed clearly embarrassed by the remark.

"Where would *you* be today if your father and I had felt that way about children?" she said, slapping him playfully on the shoulder.

"I don't know," he said with a shrug. "I guess I'd still be twinkling in Dad's eye."

We all laughed again and then I introduced myself. "My name's Kay Lawrence," I said, "and this is—"

"I'm Tracey Lawrence," she said, cutting me short. "I'm her sister." She bit her lip and looked away as I shot her an angry look.

"Well, it's really a pleasure to meet you two young ladies," Henry Wagner said. "Is this your first cruise on the *Queen*?"

"Yes, it is," I said. "Yours, too?"

"Goodness, no!" Florence Wagner laughed. "This must be our eleventh or twelfth sailing. We've come on this cruise so many times in the past years I've lost count."

"Every year since she was built," Henry said. "We just love this old tub. Best afloat, for my money."

"This is the first year they've brought me along, though," Jeff said.

"And that's only because he did so well last year in school," his mother said proudly. "We thought we'd encourage him to do the same this year. Jeff's a second-year law student at Harvard."

"Really?" I looked at him in surprise. At first meeting, I'd thought he was older. "What a coincidence. Tracey goes to college in Boston, too. Emerson."

"Oh?" The young man eyed her more carefully. "What year?"

"I'll be a senior this fall," she said.

"And what do you do, Kay?" Florence asked.

"Oh, I just keep house for Tracey's father," I said. When they all looked strangely at me, it took a moment before I understood why. "I'm afraid Tracey was having a little fun with you before. We're not sisters. I'm her mother. My husband was supposed to take this cruise with me to celebrate our twentieth anniversary, but at the last minute he was called to Chicago on business. Tracey's filling in for him."

"What a pity he couldn't make it," said Florence. "This ship is such a perfect place to keep the romance of marriage alive and well. That must be why I've stayed with this old goat all these years."

"And me with her!" Henry laughed, but it was obvious they were only teasing each other. Even on such short acquaintance, I could tell they were very much in love.

"If you hadn't told us, though," Florence said, "I never would have guessed you weren't sisters."

"You *see*, Mother?" Tracey said. "That's exactly what I told her, but she's got this idea in her head she's some kind of old fogey."

"*I* wouldn't say so," Jeff murmured.

"Me neither, son!" Henry laughed.

"That's very kind of you both," I said, "but I see no reason for pretending I'm something I'm not."

"Well, you are a beautiful woman," Florence said. "And you've got a beautiful daughter, too."

We both smiled, then looked at each other and started to blush. I knew that Tracey was going to like the Wagners as much as I did.

We all ordered drinks before dinner. I disapproved of Tracey having more liquor after all the champagne she'd already drunk that afternoon, but I didn't countermand the order when she asked the waiter for a vodka gimlet. If she was old enough to handle so much drinking, I reasoned, then she was likewise old enough to handle the hangover I was sure she'd have the next morning. Experience, after all, is the best teacher.

The dinner menu was so vast I felt swamped by the possibilities. "Are we really supposed to order all this?" I asked the Wagners. The dinner consisted of juice; fresh fruit cup or shrimp cocktail; hors d'oeuvres; soup; a fish course; and choice of fifteen entrees. That was in addition to a salad, fresh buttered rolls, and dessert!

"Well," Henry laughed, "you could *order* it, but I wouldn't recommend that you *eat* it all. At least not until you're sure you've got your sea legs."

"We usually have something light the first night out," Florence advised. "Soup, a salad, and the chicken breasts are what I'd recommend."

"That sounds fine," I said. "I think that's just what I'll have, too."

Tracey was attracted to the veal scallopine, and once again I let her have her own way without a word. I just hoped she wouldn't be up half the night running back and forth to the bathroom if the sea turned rough.

"Do you have any other children, Kay?" Florence asked while we ate.

"No, just Tracey."

"We just have Jeff, too," she said. "When he was growing up I often thought it might be nice for him to have a brother or sister, but I don't know. Children can be a handful."

"They certainly can," I laughed, giving Tracey a playful glance. "Even one."

"Oh, *Mother!*" she groaned.

"It's nice to have them," Florence continued, "but it's nice when they're grown, too, and a man and wife have some time for themselves again. You seem to miss so much together while you're busy raising a family."

I nodded and went on eating without answering.

"I think the best years of our marriage have been since Jeff went away to college."

"Hey, thanks a lot!" he laughed.

"Oh, you shut up and eat your dinner. Kay and I are talking woman-talk. She understands what I mean. Don't you, Kay? I'm sure you've found the same thing to be true with your marriage, now that your daughter's such a young lady and on her own."

"Yes, you're right." I smiled the best smile I could manage, but it was difficult. If only things between Bob and me *were* the way Florence meant. But since Tracey left home, it seemed we'd drifted further apart than ever.

"Well, when *I* get married," Tracey said, "I'm not going to have *any* kids. At least not until I feel I've lived my own life to the fullest. I don't want to wind up like—" She abruptly cut herself short.

"Like what, dear?" Florence asked.

Tracey shrugged. "Like—*some* women."

"Oh, yes, I know just what you mean," Florence agreed. "I feel so sorry for all those poor girls who get married too young and start having babies right away. They never give themselves a chance to find out what life is all about. By the time they do, it's usually too late. They're too old to get any kind of job once their children are grown, and all they have is an empty house and a husband who usually doesn't need them any more. It's so sad."

"But it's not always like that, is it?" I said. "Surely if

two people love each other enough to marry very young, they can hold onto that love when they're older."

"I doubt it," Florence said. "What you're talking about isn't really love. It's puppy-love. Or, if you'll forgive my frankness, s-e-x. *That's* what usually makes them marry before they know what they're getting into. And that's not what you and I know as real love."

"Oh?" Henry chuckled. "What is it then?"

"It's lust," Florence flatly declared.

"What's wrong with that?" Henry said with a grin and a wink toward his son. "Good old lust never hurt anyone."

"Maybe so, but it's not enough to hold a marriage together when it's the only thing it's based on. Don't you agree with me, Kay?"

"Oh, of course."

"You mean there's some other reason why we're still together?" Henry teased.

Florence put down her coffee cup and gave him a slow, withering stare. "How would you like to swim to St. Thomas?" she challenged.

"I never knew you were such an advocate of Fem Lib, Mom," Jeff Wagner said.

"Oh, God, yes!" Henry laughed. "She burned her bra years ago!"

"He thinks he's being funny," Florence muttered.

"Are you really committed to the 'cause,' Mom?"

"Do you want a serious answer," she asked her son, "or one your father can make another joke about?"

"A serious one. I'd really like to know how you feel about the Equal Rights Amendment and all that."

"Oh, oh!" Henry groaned. "Look out now, folks! You've got her wound up on her favorite subject, Jeff!"

"I'm definitely in favor of E.R.A.," Florence declared.

"Why, Mom?"

"The mere fact that you can even ask why is the answer," she said. "You men are all alike. You seem to think women are asking for something so outrageous, just because they want to be treated as equals to you. We shouldn't have to *ask* for something so basic. It should have been our right centuries ago."

"See? I warned you!" Henry smiled.

"Throughout history men have considered women to be inferior to themselves in every respect. It's about time they started realizing that we're human beings, too, and if it weren't for us, where would *they* be? I've never heard of any man who didn't have a mother."

"Or a father," Henry put in. "Don't forget that we fathers had some part in it, too."

"A very, very small and insignificant part, my dear," she said with a patronizing smile. "With the use of artificial insemination, women could continue the human race all by themselves, long after the last man has been blown to Kingdom Come. But I'd like to see just one man—any man—use his so-called superiority and technical knowhow to give birth to a single child."

"You'd better not let Anita Bryant hear you say that," Henry chuckled. "She's against that kind of experimentation, you know."

Florence looked at me and sighed. "My husband is playing the clown for your benefit, Kay, as I'm sure you're aware. If he was really such a thick-headed dunce, I'd have left him twenty years ago."

"Oh? Is that so?"

"Of course!" she snapped, with the first trace of genuine anger I'd seen in her since the conversation began. "And if I were the namby-pamby drudge you profess to admire, you'd have left me, too. What man could be happy with a woman who has so little respect for herself that she lets him walk all over her and doesn't stick up for her own rights and try to pursue her own ambitions to the fullest? You can get *machines* to keep your house clean and cook food for you. Who wants to love a machine?"

"Yeah, but there's one thing we can't get a machine to do," Henry said with a nudge and a wink, "and that's where you women have us over a barrel. And you know it, too. That's why all this equal rights stuff is so much hot air. A woman can get anything she wants from a man, just by *not* giving him what *he* wants."

"Oh, I give up!" Florence laughed in exasperation. "It's like beating my head against a brick wall! You'd just better pray I never find out you're really serious when you say things like that, Henry Wagner, or you'll live to regret it. Men!" she said with a shake of her head. "Don't you wish we could do without them completely, Kay?"

"Sometimes," I said, but a thought like that had never entered my mind before. I couldn't imagine what I would do if I didn't have Bob to depend on.

The conversation turned to lighter matters after that, and before we knew it the dining room was all but deserted. We'd enjoyed getting to know each other so much that we hadn't even noticed the other passengers around us had finished eating and gone off to other parts of the ship.

"Well, I guess it's about time we let these poor waiters close the place up, don't you think?" Henry said.

I glanced at my watch. It was almost eleven. "I had no idea it was so late."

"See how time flies when you're having fun, Mom?" Tracey joked. But there was more truth in her remark than she could ever realize. The Wagners were a delightful family and in their company, for the first time in a long, long time, I *had* been having fun. The curious part of it was... Bob didn't have anything to do with it. I'd enjoyed myself completely without him. In fact, since we sat down at the table hours earlier, I hadn't as much as given him a thought.

"We're going up to the Queen's Lounge for a peek at the show and a drink or two before we turn in," Henry said, as we all left the dining room. "Won't you and Tracey join us, Kay?"

"Thanks," I said, "but I think we've had enough for one day. We're going to turn in."

"Oh, *Mother!*" Tracey sighed. "So soon?"

"Come on," Florence coaxed. "It's your first night at sea. And they've got a terrific British singer on the bill tonight. Helen McNair. We've seen her a couple of times before, and she's very good."

"Why don't you come with us, Kay?" Jeff said, making the request unanimous.

"I feel like a party-pooper for saying no," I laughed, "but I'm really too tired. It's been a very long day. And I think I'm starting to understand what you meant about getting my sea legs, Henry."

"Feeling queasy?"

"Maybe just a little around the gills."

"Well *I'm* not," Tracey insisted. "You don't mind if I go with them for a little while, do you, Mother?"

My first instinct was to tell her yes, I did mind. But when I looked at her beside Jeff Wagner, her eyes pleading with me to let her enjoy herself a while longer, I didn't have the heart to insist she come back to the stateroom with me. Jeff seemed like such a nice young man. If Tracey were going to get herself romantically involved with anyone in the next two weeks—which at this point seemed very likely, with two contenders already in the running and this only our first day on the ship—I would rather it were Jeff than that Second Officer, Mr. Taylor. To him, she'd be nothing more than this cruise's easy mark; someone to be forgotten as soon as the ship got back to New York. With a boy like Jeff, at least there was a possibility of something more substantial developing between them, especially since they would both be in Boston for school in the fall.

"Please, Mother?" she asked. I half-expected her to start tugging on the hem of my dress, the way she used to do when she was a little girl and wanted something done her way.

"Oh, all right," I said. "I guess I'll look like the villain in the piece if I don't say yes. But no later than midnight."

"You're an angel!" she said, kissing my cheek.

"And no more to drink, do you hear?" I added in a low tone so the others wouldn't hear.

"Whatever you say, Mother dear," she giggled. She was more than a little tipsy already, which worried me, but I trusted that Florence and Henry would take care of her in my absence if she needed any help.

Instead of taking the elevator, we all walked up the outside stairs that led from Five Deck to the Boat Deck. The night was beautiful and there were many couples strolling hand-in-hand along the length of the ship. The sound of jazz drifted out from the open doors of the Queen's Lounge, riding on the crest of happy laughter. For a moment I considered going in with the others after all, but I really was tired and the thought of that big double bed seemed more inviting.

"This is where I leave you," I told the Wagners. "Our stateroom is right down this passage."

"Really?" Florence said. "We're almost neighbors! We're in B."

"Well, you'll all have to pay us a neighborly visit tomorrow then," I said.

"Oh, we'll see you at breakfast before then," Henry said. "Remember, you're stuck with us for every meal from now on. We don't let nice people get away that easily!"

I smiled at him with genuine pleasure. "Thank you for saying that, Henry. You're nice people, too. All three of you."

We said a last goodnight and then they went into the lounge with Tracey. I went back to the stateroom alone. I was bone-tired, but the funny thing was, once I got into bed I couldn't sleep. I tossed and turned for the longest time, but after an hour I felt more awake and alert than when I'd crawled under the covers.

I wasn't used to sleeping in a strange bed, of course, and the faint movement of the ship might have had something to do with it, too, but I knew what the real problem was. Bob. I missed the presence of his body in bed alongside me. By myself, the mattress seemed to stretch endlessly.

I rolled over and buried my face in the pillow, wanting to fight off the feelings of loneliness that were starting to creep through me once again. I chided myself that I was acting more like a homesick teenager away at summer camp for the first time than a responsible, thirty-eight year old woman. But knowing your behavior is silly and being able to do something about it are two different matters. I just couldn't help myself. I missed Bob terribly.

Finally, knowing I'd only sink deeper into self-pity if I stayed alone in the room any longer, I got up and got dressed and went out to the deck. I thought a few minutes of fresh, crisp sea air might act as a tranquilizer. I walked toward the stern of the ship, passing the music and merriment coming from the Queen's Lounge along the way. All those people inside were having such fun, and there I was, acting like the poor boy at the party.

Get hold of yourself, Kay, I thought. For God's sake! If you're going to mope around like this for the rest of the cruise, you shouldn't have come in the first place. Was the five thousand dollars that important? Better to have lost it completely and gone to Chicago with Bob than to put yourself through hell for two weeks like this.

I approached the windows of the Piccadilly Club and heard the soft tinkle of a piano being played inside . . . *When Your Lover Has Gone*.

"Thanks a lot," I murmured under my breath. "That's *just* what I needed to hear right now! Another minute and I'll be the first one on the cruise to jump overboard!"

Glancing through the open door of the intimate little club, I saw that almost all the tables were filled, mostly by couples, saying low, romantic things to each other as they sipped a last drink.

"Damn you, Bob!" I swore, and was surprised by the realization that I'd unconsciously clenched my hands into fists. Sudden, unexpected anger rippled through me as I walked away from the club with its happy lovers and approached the rail at the very end of the ship. Looking down, I saw the dark swirl of the ocean as the ship plowed slowly through it. "Like hell I'll throw myself overboard!" I thought, then wondered where all that anger and resentment had come from.

Bob could have come on the cruise if he'd really wanted to. If it had really, truly meant more to him to be with me for our anniversary than to please Mr. Winthrop by going to Chicago. His job wouldn't have been in jeopardy if he'd told the old man no. There were plenty of others in the company who could have taken his place, and no harm would have come from it. No, Bob went because he wanted to go.

"Face it," I thought, "you just aren't as important to him as his job."

Always striving. Always wheeling and dealing. Always looking for a way to get his feet one step further up that all-important ladder of success. That was what really meant something to him. But for what, I wondered? Why spend so much energy and precious time trying to get ahead, when the end result wouldn't make us any better off or any happier than if he settled for what he already had and learned to enjoy it.

We didn't need another fifty thousand dollars in the bank. We weren't rich by any means, but we were a lot more comfortably off than most people. The house we lived in right now had grown too big for us since Tracey was gone; we didn't need a bigger one. And our car was brand-new and perfectly adequate to suit our needs; we didn't have to have a better one. So why did it mean that damn much to him to get more, more, always *more?* We weren't really happy with what we already had.

The answer had to be that somewhere along the line Bob had transferred all those feelings of love he'd once had for me to his work. That was his true love now. His job. I was just a—a machine. Like Florence Wagner had said a little while ago. A machine to keep house for him and fix his meals. As I'd listened to her talking down there in the dining room, I'd had the uneasy feeling that she was talking about me. If not me specifically, then all the women like me, who'd let their men turn them into inanimate objects they could use or toss aside at will.

Oh, I was mad! If Bob had been there at that moment, we surely would have had the biggest fight of our marriage. How *dare* he treat me like this? What right did he have to promise the most romantic adventure we ever would have had together, then pull the rug out from under me and think the fall wouldn't hurt?

I know I promised to go with you, Kay old thing, but something else has come up. It doesn't matter, though. Tracey will keep you company. Send me a postcard, like a good girl.

"Damn you! Damn you! Damn you!" I raged into the night air.

"I thought that was you, Kay."

The sudden sound of the voice behind me made me jump in surprise. "Jeff. . ." I couldn't tell how long he'd been standing there, watching me beat my fists against the rail and curse the wind.

"I thought I saw you go past the windows of the lounge a couple of minutes ago, but I wasn't sure. Change your mind about turning in early?"

"No, I just found that I couldn't sleep as easily as I thought I would. I hoped the night air would calm me down a little."

"Has it?" he asked, moving slowly toward me.

"Not really. I guess I'm more keyed-up about this cruise than I thought."

"Can I buy you a drink?" he offered. "That might do the trick."

I glanced toward the Piccadilly Club and then at the young man's handsome face. For a moment I half-considered taking him up on it, but second thought made me decline. Sitting in there with all those couples holding hands across candlelit tables was definitely *not* the right thing for me. Not that particular night, at least.

"I don't think so, Jeff. Thanks, anyway."

"Are you sure? It looks like a nice little place."

"Maybe some other time."

"Is that a promise?"

I was a little surprised by the question, as well as the earnest way he'd asked it. As though he really *wanted* to have a drink with me.

"Of course. I never welsh on a raincheck."

"Would you like to sit and talk for a while? It's a beautiful night."

"I think I'd better turn in now, Jeff." I moved away from the rail before he stepped any closer. "It's time I collected Tracey, too. She's played Cinderella long enough for one night."

"Oh, Tracey's already in your cabin. Mom and Dad took her back a little while ago."

"Then I'd really better go. She's probably wondering what happened to me."

"May I walk you back?"

Again I was surprised by the unexpected question and the look I saw on his face. I tried to make my voice sound as light and casual as possible. "Sure. Why not? You're going my way anyway, aren't you?"

"You know," he said, as we started down the deck together, "I'm really glad that Mom and Dad brought me with them this time. I wasn't looking forward to it at first, but now I think this is going to be the best vacation I ever had."

"I'm sure we're all going to enjoy it, Jeff."

"I'm really glad they put you and Tracey at our table, Kay."

"So am I."

"And you know what else I'm glad about?" he said, as we approached the door to my stateroom.

"What's that?"

"I'm glad your husband *didn't* come along."

His remark completely startled me for a moment, until I realized that he must have meant he was glad because Bob's cancellation meant Tracey was able to take his place. Or *did* he. . .?

"Well, I'm disappointed he couldn't make it," I said, "but who knows? Maybe it will all be for the best in the end."

"I hope so," he said. "In fact, I'm sure of it."

As he stepped nearer, I opened the door and told him, "Goodnight, Jeff. I'll see you in the morning."

"Okay." He smiled a radiant smile and gave me a quick wink. "Sleep well, Kay."

Chapter 4

"Now that was all *that* about?" I wondered, as I closed the cabin door behind me. For a moment there, I could have sworn Jeff was going to try to kiss me. That look in his eye had seemed so unmistakable. If I'd hesitated just another few seconds before opening the door and saying goodnight . . .

Oh, brother! I thought. You must really be tired. Your imagination's starting to run away with you.

It was silly of me even to consider such a thing. He was just a kid. Barely older than my own daughter. Why in the world would a boy like that—young . . . handsome . . . virile—be attracted to someone like me? He surely could have his pick of all the desirable girls on the ship. Girls his own age. And yet . . .

"Mother? Is that you?" Tracey called from the bedroom.

I forced my mind back to reality. Too much champagne and sea air, I thought. That's what was putting such crazy notions in my head.

"Yes, dear, it's me."

"Where've you been?" Tracey was sitting up in bed, running a brush through her long, golden blonde hair. The same color hair that mine had been, when I was her age. God, it seemed so long ago. Was I ever really as young as she? It felt like I'd lived an eternity since then.

"Oh, I just went out for a little stroll on the deck," I said.

"By yourself?"

"Well of course!" I laughed. "I wasn't looking for company; I was hoping it would make me sleepy. I tossed and turned for an hour after I left you and the Wagners, but I couldn't fall asleep."

"Were you thinking about Daddy?" she asked, giving me a sympathetic look.

"I guess so."

"You're not going to be like this all through the cruise, are you, Mother? If you are, you're going to have a miserable time."

"I know, honey," I said as I slipped out of my dress. "I guess I just miss him a lot tonight because it's the first night. I'm sure I'll feel better in a little while. I just need some time to make the adjustment."

"I hope so. It would be a shame if you didn't enjoy yourself. I had a ball tonight!"

"Did you?" I put on my nightgown for the second time that night and got under the covers. The bed felt just as empty as it had before, though, being in it alone. "I'm glad you had a good time."

"Boy, did I ever!" she laughed. "It felt like my birthday, Christmas, and New Year's Eve all rolled into one! That English singer the Wagners wanted you to hear is really terrific. She reminded me of Shirley Bassey. She's got the same gutsy sound to her voice, you know? You'll have to come and hear her tomorrow night."

"I will, if I'm feeling more up to it than I did tonight."

"When she finished her act, this great group came on to play. They had an incredible sound! I mean, I never expected to hear music like *that* on this boat. I figured it would be mostly Guy Lombardo stuff, but was I ever wrong! That bunch could rock!"

"Oh? Did you dance?" I pictured her and Jeff together on the dance floor and the image pleased me. They made a nice couple.

"I sure did! I could have danced all night, as the song goes, except this jazz band came on afterwards and the Wagners decided it was time to call it a night."

"Is he a good dancer?"

"Terrific! I really had to work to keep up with him."

"He's nice, isn't he?"

"He sure is!" she said with a sly grin. "He's better than nice."

"You like him then?"

"Mmm-*hmmmmm!*"

"I'm glad. His parents are nice, too, aren't they?"

Tracey gave me a blank look. "Huh?"

"Jeff's parents. You like them, too, don't you?"

"*Jeff* . . . ?" She put down her hairbrush and started to laugh. "Is *that* who you're talking about?"

"Well of course. Aren't you?"

"No! I was talking about Michael!"

"Michael?" I sat up and looked at her. "Who's Michael?"

"Michael Taylor."

"You mean *Mr*. Taylor? The Second Officer? You were dancing with *him*?"

"Mother, really!" Tracey giggled. "You didn't think I meant Jeff, did you?"

"Why not? Didn't he ask you?"

"No." She began brushing her hair again, pulling the brush down with quick, almost angry strokes as she talked. "As a matter of fact, *I* asked *him*. And from the look he gave me, you'd have thought I asked him to drop his pants in public. 'I'm afraid I don't dance to that kind of music, Tracey,' he said with his nose up in the air. *That kind of music*. It was great, Mother. Really together. I don't know how anyone could have resisted it. Even the Wagners were swaying and tapping their feet to the beat. But not Jeff. I guess for him, anything later than the *Blue Danube* is just loud noise."

"I'm surprised. I thought you two would have so much in common."

"So did I," Tracey said. "At first. I mean with that moustache and all, I figured he'd really be a together guy. But as soon as you left, I found out what a bore he actually is."

"Oh? How so?"

"All he wanted to talk about was you."

Me?" I felt an uneasy sensation ripple through me. Was I right about that look I thought I'd seen in Jeff's eyes after all? *Was* it me he was interested in, and not Tracey? It seemed too implausible a notion to be true, but as she went on it became more and more of a possibility.

"Why on earth would he want to talk about *me*?" I asked.

"Who knows? But every time I tried to start a conversation with him about something interesting, he kept changing the subject by asking me questions about you."

"What kind of questions?" I asked hesitantly.

"Oh, how old you are for one thing."

"Did you tell him?" I asked, and immediately wondered why it should matter whether she had or not.

"No, of course not. I told him it was none of his business. A woman's age is a personal thing."

In spite of myself, I was relieved. "What else did he want to know?"

Tracey shrugged. "How long you and Daddy had been married. If you were happy together. Whether you came to Boston to visit me during the school term. Whether you came alone, or if Daddy came with you. Where you stayed. What you did by yourself while Daddy was away on business. Thing like that."

Dear God, I thought, *it's true! He's trying to find out whether it's safe to move in on Bob's territory!*

"Maybe he's just not good at small talk," I said, clutching at straws. "Maybe he's shy and it was easier for him to talk to you about me than about yourself. Some men are like that, honey. Maybe that was his way of getting to know you; by talking about your parents."

"Or maybe he's got a crush on you," she muttered.

My heart froze in my chest. Was it so obvious that even she could see it?

"Oh, Tracey!" I said, forcing a laugh through the tightness in my throat. "That's ridiculous!"

"I know it is. What could he see in *you*?" The brush stopped in mid-air and she turned with a guilty, stricken look on her face. "Oh, Mother, I didn't mean that the way it sounded."

"I just meant that he couldn't possibly see anything in you since you're already married and — well — so much older. You're not available, but I am. And all the while we sat there, he just kept asking me those dumb questions. Like he was trying hard to be polite, but underneath it all he was really so bored he couldn't wait to get rid of me. It made me so damn mad!" She resumed her brushing, and after a few moments said, "Maybe he's gay."

"Tracey!" I had a quick vision of those piercing blue eyes staring at me in the dim light outside the Piccadilly Club. That smile and the quick wink when he said goodnight at the stateroom door. "I hardly think so."

"He could be," she said thoughtfully. "You can't

really tell these days. They're not all mincing fairies any more." She seemed to be mulling the idea over in her head. "You know, I never even thought about that until right now. But I'll bet that explains it. He probably *is* gay."

"Honey, I think you should put that idea right out of your mind," I insisted. "Just because Jeff might not be interested in you personally, it doesn't mean he wouldn't be interested in some other woman . . ."

"How can you tell?" she argued. "If he's normal, why *shouldn't* he be interested in me? Michael doesn't seem to think I'm so bad. At least I know that *he's* a real man. When he came over and asked me to dance, I jumped at the chance. He's a doll, isn't he, Mother?"

"He's very handsome, yes. But I hope you're not planning to fall in love with him."

"Who knows?" she said with an impish smile. "Maybe I will."

"I wish you would do me a favor and not have anything more to do with him for the rest of the cruise, honey."

She looked at me in surprise. "Why? He's a gorgeous hunk of man; you said so yourself."

"Yes, but you can't base a relationship on good looks alone. There's got to be something more to it than that."

"Who's talking about a relationship?" she exlaimed. "The cruise only lasts two weeks, and I don't expect to ever see him again after that."

"You don't?"

"No, of course not!" she laughed. "I'm only talking about a shipboard romance. Everyone has one when they're on a cruise like this. It's part of the package. I know that Michael probably picks up a different girl every time the ship sails from New York, but what does it matter? As long as they have as good a time as he does, who cares? And since he's bound to pick up somebody on this cruise, too, why shouldn't it be me? I'm willing."

"He'll probably try to go to bed with you."

"Yes, I know that."

"And will you let him?"

She hesitated for just a fraction of a second before answering. We were entering territory that had never been openly discussed between us before. "Yes, I guess so. Sure. Why not? It wouldn't be the first time I've gone to bed with a man just for fun."

I felt like I'd just been punched hard in the stomach. "Tracey, my *God!* What if you got pregnant?"

"Pregnant!" She laughed like it was a joke. "Mother, *really*! I've been on the pill for the past three years!"

"Oh, Jesus." I was sure I was going to throw up.

"Why do you look so shocked? Cindy Robinson was fitted for her first diaphragm when she was fourteen!"

I couldn't believe what I was hearing. Cindy Robinson? That sweet little girl from down the block, who used to come and play with Tracey in her sandbox?

"Does *her* mother know that?"

"Who do you think made the doctor's appointment for the fitting?"

My head was reeling. I was trying hard not to show by the look on my face how stunned and upset I was by Tracey's casually flippant attitude toward all this, but I guess I didn't do a very good job of it.

"Don't look so horrified, Mother!" she laughed. "I'd almost think you believed I was still a virgin!"

The matter of Tracey's virginity had never before been in question in my mind. Until that moment, I'd always thought of her as still my little girl. Unblemished. Untouched. Intact.

"Oh, my God!" she gasped, staring hard at me. "You *did* think I was a virgin! Mother, how could you? I haven't been since high school!"

"I don't think I want to hear any more of this," I said. My throat felt dry and raw and tight, like I'd been smoking too much.

"Why not? Now that the cat's out of the bag, why can't we discuss sex openly and freely, like two adult women?"

"Because we're not just two women," I said. "I'm your mother and you're my daughter."

"That makes a difference?"

"Of course it does!" I snapped. "I no more want to hear about *your* sex life than I'd want to tell you about *mine*."

"I don't understand your attitude, Mother."

"I'm not asking you to."

"Are you embarrassed?"

"Let's drop the subject, Tracey. It's late and I'm tired and it's time we both got some sleep." I turned out the light over my bed and settled down beneath the covers. My heart was thumping like a triphammer in my chest. All that time I'd thought she was still pure and innocent. All those boys in their souped-up convertibles who'd stopped outside the house to pick her up for a date. How many of them had laid their greasy little hands on her? How many had pawed my baby—my little Tracey—in their back seats? How many had she let go all the way with her . . . *just for fun?*

"Didn't you ever talk about sex with your mother?" she persisted.

"No, I didn't."

"Maybe you should have."

Maybe so, I thought. But if I *had*—or if I'd known as much as you did about sex and birth control and everything else when *I* was in senior high school—I might not be having this discussion with you right now. Because you might not *be* here.

"Didn't you ever want to?"

"The subject is closed, Tracey."

"But can't we just—?"

"Please turn out your light and go to sleep. I refuse to listen to anything more about it."

"All right," she said with a heavy sigh. "But you can't blame me for trying."

No, I thought, but it seems like there's a lot I didn't know about until now that I *could* blame you for. *On the pill for three years!* Three *years?* She was only seventeen years old three years ago! And God knows how much earlier than that she'd been doing it *without* the pill! What if she'd got herself pregnant? What would she have done then?

The same thing you did, a little voice inside me whispered. And people who live in glass houses shouldn't throw stones.

But I felt certain that wasn't true. Abortions were a dime a dozen. Why pay for a mistake, when it could be disposed of so easily? What would it matter if a human life was lost in the process? An inncoent, unborn life which, given the chance, might grow up to be Tracey Lawrence or Cindy Robinson. As long as they could go on having fun, without a care in the world for the consequences, they would never feel responsible for any mistakes made along the way. Just wipe them out and start all over again.

How could Tracey honestly expect me to discuss sex

with her, when our fundamental attitudes on the subject were so vastly different? I would never be able to understand how she could talk about falling in love and going to bed with someone like Michael Taylor *just for fun*, knowing in advance that it would only last for two weeks. The only man I had ever fallen in love with in all my life was Bob Lawrence, and I'd known from the start that it would last forever.

Florence Wagner might well call what I had felt for Bob puppylove or s-e-x, or say that I was too young to know that what I took for love was really lust, but she'd be wrong. No love was ever stronger or more genuine.

I had loved Bob all my life. As far back as I can remember. We grew up together on the same street, and though he was two years older than I we were inseparable as kids. All through grade school he was my best friend and I was his. He helped me with my homework when I needed it, and I helped him with his chores. There was nothing I wouldn't do for him, not even playing show-and-tell doctor under his back porch, which we did a number of times until his mother caught us at it one afternoon and we were both severely spanked by our parents for doing something so nasty. "The part of you that's under your panties is bad," my mother told me, "and God will send you straight to Hell if He catches you showing it to little boys or letting them play with it." At six years old I believed her, and since I didn't want God to send me to Hell, Bob and I didn't play show-and-tell again. Not, at least, until many years later, when we were both much older and had a lot more to show.

When Bob reached the stage that all boys go through for a while and eventually grow out of—that stage in their development when they feel that all girls are stupid and they only have time for each other's company—we drifted apart for several years. They were miserable years for me. I could never understand what I had done, or *not* done, to lose his friendship. I would stand at the edge of the baseball diamond after school, with tears running down both cheeks, and watch him playing ball with his new friends, never knowing why he didn't want to play catch with *me* any more or let me field pop flies for him. Or I would go up to him during lunch break when he was with a gang of other boys in the school yard and wonder why he always joined in with them when they started teasing me about my freckles or throwing stones at me to make me go away. He never came to watch television at my house any more or asked his father to take me with them when the Lawrences went up to his uncle's cabin in the Poconos for a weekend. I was thoroughly devastated.

And then a strange thing happened. I finally entered that stage of development all *girls* go through for a while, when *boys* seem stupid. I woke up one morning and found blood stains inside my pajama bottoms, and suddenly it didn't matter in the least whether or not Bob Lawrence liked me. I was too filled with awe and wonder of the miraculous changes occuring inside my body to care.

By the time I started caring again, Bob was in high school. He'd gotten over his dislike of girls with a vengeance. At sixteen, tall, dark, and handsome, he was the school Romeo. Other girls followed him everywhere, and wrote his name on little slips of paper they kept in heart-shaped lockets around their necks. Some of them wrote his name in other places, too, like on the walls of the girls' lavatory. I was too young and too naive to understand most of the things they wrote there about him, except that he was supposed to have something big and knew how to use it. Whatever that meant.

Bob was glad to be friends with me again, but I was in my early teens by then and I didn't want to be just friends. I was in love with him now, and wanted him to love me, too. But as far as he was concerned, I was still just plain old Kay, the kid from down the street. He was too busy handling the adoration of the girls his own age to notice that I was growing up. And I was too shy to tell him how I really felt. I worshipped him in silence from afar for five years.

I tried out for an open position on the cheerleading squad in my freshman year so I could be close to Bob during all the football and basketball games he captained. When the opening went to a senior girl instead of me, I was crushed. I cried myself to sleep every night for two weeks.

The next year, Bob's last in high school, I tried out for the squad again and this time I made it. I was in Seventh Heaven—until I found out that by then Bob was going steady with the squad captain, a girl named Rosalie DeMarco. I prayed every night that she would break both legs while doing a split on the gym floor, or, better still, that God would send *her* straight to Hell, since it was common knowledge among the other cheerleaders that Rosalie was playing show-and-tell with Bob every night in the back of his father's Chevy. But if my prayers were heard, they weren't answered. Bob and Rosalie (both legs intact) were still together by graduation, and that summer he enlisted in the service and was shipped overseas to Germany.

I didn't see him for two years after that, though scarcely a day went by that I didn't think about him.

The next time we met, I didn't recognize him. I came home from school one afternoon near the end of my senior year and found a solider in our living room, having coffee and pie with my mother. I figured that he was probably an old Army buddy of my father's, waiting for Dad to come home from work, and I thought nothing more of him as I started up the hall stairs to listen to some records in my room.

"Kay?" my mother called after me. "Aren't you going to come in and say hello to Bob?"

"Bob who?" I thought, but I stopped in mid-flight and went back down to the parlor.

"My God!" the tall, handsome solider said with a whistle, as he looked me up and down and then all over again. "Are you *Kay*?"

My eyes popped as wide as saucers and I felt an instant lump swell in my throat. "*Bob?*"

"I never would have recognized you!" we both said at once, then broke into helpless laughter. We sat on the couch together and started talking about old times and what we'd each been doing in the past two years. We stopped only long enough to catch our breath before rattling on some more.

When my mother had finally listened to enough without being able to get a word in edgewise and went out to the kitchen to start fixing supper, Bob leaned back in the couch and gave me another long, slow, up-and-down examination with his eyes.

"What happened to those freckles you used to have?" he asked.

"I grew out of them."

"Oh, yeah?" He studied me some more. "While the freckles were growing out, it looks like something else was growing in. I don't remember your sweaters being that tight."

I started to blush, feeling the color move straight up my neck and into my cheeks. My whole face turned bright pink. "You never noticed much about me during those last years in high school," I said, "because you were always busy with Rosalie DeMarco. This is an old sweater. I bought it in your junior year."

"Maybe so," he grinned, "but I'm willing to bet money that it never fit you like that until recently. And who the hell is Rosalie DeMarco?"

I could have died happy right then and there.

Bob took me to the movies that night, and after the show he drove his father's car out to Sutter's Lane and parked under the shadows of a big old oak tree at the side of the road. The first time he kissed me, I thought I would faint. It seemed that I'd been waiting all my life to feel the warmth of his mouth against mine and the pressure of his arms holding me close. Our embrace tightened and I found myself making low, whimpering noises deep in my throat while his hands caressed my body. I let him touch and softly caress my breasts through my blouse for a few minutes because if felt good and I'd already let a few other boys do as much on previous dates. But when Bob's lips parted and he tried to wriggle his tongue into my mouth, I had to push him away. No one had ever kissed me like that before, and it scared me.

He was home on leave for a month, and we saw each other almost every night of it. Sometimes he took me to the movies or the drive-in; sometimes we stayed home and watched TV in our living room with my family. On Friday nights we usually drove over to the Jolly Ranger in Lewiston for cheeseburgers, fries, and a shake; but twice that month I surprised him by cooking dinner at home. He said I'd make some guy a good wife one day, then teased me by adding, "If you're not so heavy-handed with the salt shaker!"

In early June, Bob and I went to my senior prom together. It was the happiest moment of my life when we walked through the arch that night and entered the decorated school gym. You could hear the murmur of excitement run from one end of the gym to the other as everyone wondered who the handsome soldier in full dress uniform with me was. I felt as proud as a queen when Bob escorted me down the ramp and onto the dance floor. Next to him, the other guys at the prom in their rented tuxedos looked like so many little boys playing dress-up in their fathers' clothes. He was the only *real* man in the place.

No matter what else we did during that month Bob was home, we almost always ended our evenings parked alone somewhere in his father's car. I slowly got over my fear of letting him put his tongue in my mouth, and soon I even got to like it. We kissed that way a lot. I let him do other things, too. It made me shiver inside when he slowly unbuttoned my blouse or lifted up my sweater, unfastened the hooks on my bra, and exposed my breasts. His hands felt like warm velvet when he stroked them, flesh against flesh, and when he bent his head to softly kiss my nipples and suck them tenderly between his lips, I felt such pleasure I wanted to scream.

I wasn't as willing to give him the freedom to touch me between the legs. Perhaps it was the memory of my mother's warning when we were kids still haunting me, but it seemed far more wrong and sinful for me to let him touch me below the waist than above it. I let him slide his hand up the inside of my thighs a few times, but as soon as I felt his fingers trying to reach under the elastic of my panties, I tensed and made him stop.

I really didn't like touching him, either. The first time he took my hand and put it down on his lap, I swallowed so hard I almost choked. I finally understood what those writings I'd seen on the lavatory walls meant, and they weren't lies. He wanted me to hold him, but I couldn't do it. And when he coaxed me to undo his zipper and reach inside (*"Just touch it,"* he begged. *"Just lay your hand against it, honey. Please?"*), I couldn't do that, either. It was too frightening.

The night before Bob flew back to Germany, though, he was determined to have his way. The month had gone by so quickly. It seemed like only the day before he'd been standing there in our living room like a vision from a dream, and yet in another few hours the dream would have to end. The thought of losing him again filled me with panic and sorrow. I wanted to hold onto him as long as I possibly could, and in that state of high anxiety I gladly would have done almost anything he asked. But that night Bob had no intention of *asking* for anything. He knew exactly what he wanted from me, and in one way or another he was determined to get it.

He drove the car to the far side of Rainbow Lake a little after midnight, turned off the ignition, and doused the lights. "Let's get out and walk down by the water," he said, already opening the door on his side.

I followed him to the lake's edge and sat beside him in a bed of moist, soft grass. It was a balmy night in June, with a moon overhead that cast a cool silver light. When Bob took me in his arms and started to kiss me, I knew at once what he was going to do. The look in his eyes was unmistakable.

My heart began to trip with fear as his hand reached

under my skirt and he rolled me over on my back. He came down on me at once, pinning me to the grassy bank by the weight of his body.

"Bob?" I whispered timidly. "Wh-what are you going to do?"

"What I've been waiting all month to do, honey," he murmured. The tip of his tongue wriggled into my ear, then ran a crazy zig-zag path down the slope of my neck. He quickly opened my blouse and burrowed his face between my bra cups. "God, I want you!" he said, his voice hoarse with need. "I want you so bad, Kay."

I made a whimpering sound and tried to pull his hand out from under my skirt. His fingers were kneading. Probing. Tickling back and forth against the smooth nylon.

"No, Bob. No," I moaned.

"*Yes*, baby. *Yes*, honey. Yes, yes, *yes!*"

His fingers became more urgent. His mouth was nipping at my bra like he wanted to pull it away with his teeth. His hand was moving back down my thighs, trying to bring the panties with it.

"Bob, please! Please stop. I'm not ready."

"You're as ready as you're ever going to be," he insisted. "I'm going to make something happen tonight that we'll both remember for a long, long time after I'm gone tomorrow."

"Uhhnnnn . . ."

"You want it to happen, too, baby," he whispered, his breath hot against my ear. "You *know* you do. You *know* you want me to."

"Oooohhhh . . ." My head rolled from side to side in the smooth grass, trying to escape his lips.

"I know why you're afraid," he coaxed. "But you don't have to worry. I understand. I'll be gentle. I swear it, Kay. I'll be so gentle that after a while you'll beg me to be rough."

His mouth captured mine and his tongue thrust deeply inside. His fingers tugged and pulled and jerked until at last he'd stripped the panties from me and bunched up my skirt. His tongue battered mine while he yanked open his shirt and shrugged it off. His chest was covered with thick whorls of jet black hair, matted flat with anxious sweat.

He stood up and kicked off his shoes. He opened his belt and pulled down his fly. His pants and shorts dropped and he hopped on first one leg and then the other until he'd freed his ankles from them and tossed them aside.

I opened my eyes and looked up at him. He towered above me in the silver moonlight, naked and menacing. A low groan of fear gurgled deep in my throat as he settled slowly down on top of me.

"No . . .," I whimpered. "No, don't. Please, don't."

"*Shhhhh!* It's going to be all right, baby. In another second, everything's going to be just fine."

"No. Please. I don't want this to happen."

"Yes you do. You know you do. *Shhhhh!* It's all going to be . . . just . . . fine."

"*Noooooooooooo!*"

"Mother! What's the matter? Mother, wake up! What's wrong?"

I opened my eyes with a start. Tracey was standing beside the bed and she was shaking me with both hands.

"Mother, *please* wake up!" she cried. "What's wrong?"

I shook my head in confusion. Was I dreaming? Of course. I must have been. But about what? And why had I screamed like that? My ears were still ringing with the echo of that shrill cry.

"It's all right, Mother," Tracey said, stroking the mat of damp hair away from my forehead. "You've just had a nightmare, that's all. And boy, when you have one, you really *have* one! The hair on the back of my neck is still standing on end! When you screamed like that, I thought the ship was sinking! What in the world were you dreaming about?"

"I—don't remember." My mind was still clogged with sleep. I closed my eyes again, trying hard to call back the dream.

"And *you* were the one who warned *me* about drinking too much!" Tracey laughed. "Just wait 'til I write Daddy a postcard about *this*!"

Daddy. Bob. Of course! Suddenly it all came rushing back to me. I'd been dreaming about the night before Bob went back to Germany. The night he made me pregnant up at Rainbow Lake. I remembered it all now. The moonlight . . . the sound of lapping water . . . the strong body on top of mine . . . the hot mouth nuzzling my neck . . . the momentary pain . . . the glint of those piercing blue eyes looking down at me.

But why had I screamed? Something still wasn't right. I hadn't screamed at all that night at the lake. There'd only been a quick stab of hurt and then it had all been wonderful. I closed my eyes again to bring back the dream. The heat of his body . . . my sobs of joy . . . his eyes shining with pleasure . . . the sweat on his chest . . .

"Oh, my God!"

"Mother, what?"

I shook my head quickly. "Nothing," I whispered. Suddenly I remembered. I knew why I'd screamed in my sleep, but I could never tell Tracey. "I'll be all right now, dear. Go on back to sleep."

"Are you sure?"

"Positive."

It was the eyes. I remembered those bright, piercing blue eyes looking down at me while I twisted and writhed on the damp grass in the throes of absolute pleasure. But Bob's eyes weren't blue; they were brown. And the man I had dreamed was making love to me wasn't him at all.

It was Jeff Wagner.

Chapter 5

Tracey and I both slept late the next morning. It was almost ten by the time we got out of bed. We took turns in the shower, then leisurely dressed and went down to breakfast. I had to keep reminding myself there was no reason to rush, but it wasn't easy. I kept glancing at my watch for the time. After all those years of getting up with the sun to get Tracey dressed and fed in time for school and Bob off to work, it was hard to adjust to a slower pace. Ingrained habits die slowly, I guess. Even now that Tracey was away at college, I still got up when Bob did and drove him to the station each morning. So I couldn't help feeling a little bit guilty about sitting down for breakfast on the Ocean Queen at eleven o'clock.

"What a couple of lazy slobs we are," I whispered to Tracey as we crossed the room.

"Yeah! Ain't it grand?"

There were quite a few other late-risers in the dining room when we arrived, but our table was empty. The waiter said the Wagners had been down for breakfast about nine, and had left word that they would either see us for lunch or we'd run into each other later that morning somewhere on the ship. I was just as glad they weren't there. After last night's disturbing dream, I wasn't looking forward to seeing Jeff quite so soon.

I had as hard a time making a choice from the breakfast menu as I'd had with the dinner menu the previous night. There must have been well over a hundred selections to choose from, and a night's sleep and the fresh sea air had given me a ravenous appetite. Everything sounded good.

I finally decided on tomato juice, croissants, a mushroom and herb omelet with a side order of Canadian bacon, and coffee. Tracey chose the eggs Benedict and asked if she could have a Bloody Mary to go with it, but I flatly rejected the idea.

"Why can't I?" she whined. "The liquor's *free*, Mother. It's part of what we paid for."

"That doesn't mean I'll let you become an alcoholic, just so we get our money's worth."

"Oh, *really*. One Bloody Mary?"

"You'll order straight tomato juice and like it."

She ordered it, but she didn't like it. She put the glass down after one sip and didn't touch it again. "It tastes better with vodka in it," she muttered.

The meal was delicious. While we enjoyed it, we skirted around the edges of our conversation just before bed, without actually going into its details again. I would just as well have forgotten the whole thing, but Tracey brought it up.

"Did you remember anything about that nightmare?" she asked.

"No, dear," I said, as I buttered a piping-hot croissant with fresh creamery butter. "I doubt if I ever will. It's best forgotten."

"I hope that talk we had last night wasn't the cause of it."

"Oh, I'm sure it wasn't."

"In the shower this morning I was thinking a lot about what I said. I probably shouldn't have told you as much as I did, but I guess I was a little drunk and once I started talking I couldn't stop. I'm really sorry if some of the things I said upset you."

"It's all right, honey. There's no real harm done. I'll just have to start thinking of you as a woman now, instead of my little girl."

"Will you still love me as much as you did before I told you all those things?"

"Of course I will!" I was taken aback by the question. It seemed that her insecurities about being loved were as great as my own. We both needed constant reassurance. "I'll always love you!"

"Even though I do some things you don't approve of?"

"Well, no mother ever wants to see her babies get hurt, no matter how old they are. That's why we're always telling our children what to do. We think we know best. But you're a woman yourself and I can't force you to do everything my way. You're old enough to make your own mistakes and learn from them, without any interference from me. I may not like it that way, but it doesn't mean I'll ever stop loving you just because you live your life the way you choose."

"If that's the case," she said with a smile, "where's that waiter? I think I'll have that Bloody Mary after all!"

"Tracey, don't you dare call him! It's not good for you to start drinking this early in the day."

"Oh, *Mother!*" she laughed. "Can't you see I'm just teasing?"

I blushed with embarrassment. "I guess it will still take some time before I stop clucking over you like a mother hen. It's hard to get used to the idea that you're all grown up. But I'm trying."

After breakfast we decided to stroll around the ship

for a little while and see how much we remembered from Mr. Taylor's tour. We went down one level to Four Deck and browsed through the shopping arcade. I bought a pretty gold charm of the *Ocean Queen* for my mother to put on her charm bracelet, and some English tea towels with colorful pictures of London on them for myself. Tracey picked up a slew of postcards for us to write to the folks back home when we found time, and pondered over an expensive crystal paperweight with a model of the ship inside as a gift for Bob. But in the end, she decided to wait and see what we might find in the islands when the ship called at its various ports in the days ahead.

While we were paying for our things, I heard a familiar voice behind me and turned to see Mrs. Jacobs with her three children in tow.

"Hello," I smiled. "Not lost again, I hope."

"Oh, hi," she said. "No, this time I know where we're going. I hope! Tommy, leave that alone!" she snapped, as one of her little boys picked up a scale model of the ship and began to swing it back and forth through the air like he was sailing it.

"Look, Mom, it's just like the boat *we're* on."

"Yes, I see. Now put it down before you break it."

"Can't I have it, Mom?"

"I want one, too, Mom," the other little boy chimed in.

"Put it down, Tommy. You can't have it."

"Why?"

"Why, Mom? Why?" the second boy echoed.

"Give it here," she said, taking the model from the child's hand. Before she put it back on the shelf, I saw her turn it over and glance at the price ticket. "Kids," she sighed. "I swear. They want everything they pick up."

"Look at the dolls over there, Mom!" the little girl said. Her big round eyes glistened as she stared at the showcase. "They got crowns on their heads!"

"Don't you start begging for things now," Mrs. Jacobs scolded. "Stand here and be quiet for a minute while I talk to the lady."

"Can't I just *look* at the dolls, Mom?" the little girl pleaded. "Huh, Mom? Huh? Can't I just *look* at them?"

"No! I told you to stay her and be quiet." She rolled her eyes as she looked back at me. "First she wants to just look, then she'll want me to buy her one."

"They're very pretty," I said.

"Yeah, but . . . " She shrugged, and I understood what she meant. Pretty . . . but expensive.

"Where's your husband today, Mrs. Jacobs?" Tracey asked.

"Oh, Walt's down in the cabin. Sick as a dog."

"Oh? I'm sorry to hear that," Tracey said. I could tell she was trying her best to make up for her behavior yesterday. "Was it something he ate?"

"No, I don't think so. It's probably the movement of the boat. He's got a delicate stomach, you know, and it was pretty hard to sleep last night with all those engines going full blast and that rocking back and forth all the time."

"Really?" I said. "I'm surprised. We didn't notice a thing."

"Well," Mrs. Jacobs said, "it's probably a lot different up where *you* are. Us, you see, we're way down in the bottom of the boat. Right over the engine room. It's not the same as up top."

Neither Tracey nor I knew what to say.

"Well, come on, kids," Mrs. Jacobs said, rounding up her two boys as they edged toward the model ships again. "I promised I'd take them swimming," she told us, "but they don't understand why it's got to be in the pool, when there's so much ocean water all around. If I don't keep my eye on them every minute, they'll be jumping overboard to find out for themselves. Come on; let's go," she said, herding them all together. "See you later."

"Goodbye, Mrs. Jacobs."

"Bye," Tracey called. "I hope your husband's feeling better soon."

"Oh, he'll get used to it. You get used to a lot of things in this life, you know?"

When they were gone, Tracey went back to the gift counter and called the sales clerk. "I'd like you to wrap up two of those ship models over there," she said, "and send them to the Jacobs family's cabin. I'm not sure what the number is, but it's down on the last deck. The name is Walt Jacobs; they're travelling tourist." She opened her purse and got out her wallet. "Oh, and send one of those Queen Elizabeth dolls over there, too, will you?"

"Would you like to include a gift card with your name, Miss?"

"No," Tracey said. "That won't be necessary." She paid for the things and came back to me. "Now, why don't *we* go for a swim, too?"

"You know, honey," I said, "sometimes I'm so darn proud of you I could cry."

"Oh, *Mother!*" she groaned.

It was a gloriously bright and sunny August day; ideal weather for lolling around the edge of a pool or basking in the sun in a comfortable deckchair with a cool drink by your side. Apparently, almost everyone else on the

Ocean Queen thought so too. There were so many people crowding the Sun Deck when Tracey and I arrived in our bathing suits, that if everyone had suddenly moved to one side or the other, the ship would have capsized like a top-heavy toy. We were lucky to find a couple of deckchairs near the stern, just vacated by a man and his wife who were going down for an early lunch. We spread our beach towels, took off our robes, and proceeded to grease each other's bodies with sun lotion.

"I think I'll go walk around by the pool for a while," Tracey said when we'd finished.

"Going to show off your new bikini?" I teased. I couldn't blame her for wanting to; it looked terrific against the light tan she'd already acquired from sunbathing at the beach back home. But I had to give her credit for having the guts to wear it in public. So much of her body was exposed, it seemed almost pointless to bother covering the rest. From a distance, in fact, it would be hard to tell if she was naked or not.

"Michael said he might come up for a swim this afternoon," she said. "He's not on duty until later tonight. I'm just dying to see what he looks like in a bathing suit."

"Well," I said, "in one glance he'll certainly know what you look like in *and* out of one." I could just imagine that sea-going wolf licking his chops with eager anticipation when he saw her.

"Mother . . . Remember your promise. I'm not a little girl any more."

"I know," I sighed. If there'd still been any doubt in my mind, one look at her in that bikini would have erased it. She certainly *was* a woman.

"I just hope you know what you're doing, honey," I

said.

"I just hope he does!" she laughed, as she padded away toward the pool. I saw heads turning from all directions when she walked by. With her long blonde hair flowing over her shoulders and her hips seductively swaying with every step, she looked like a gorgeous golden goddess. It was hard to believe she'd once worn pigtails and muddy blue jeans and was the biggest tomboy on the block.

But then, there were so many contradictions about Tracey. She was just like her father in that respect. Totally unpredictable. One day she was acting so rudely to Mrs. Jacobs I wanted to slap her; the next she was buying the woman's children presents with her own money and I wanted to cry with pride. Last night she had spoken like a woman of the world; this morning she voiced a little girl's fear of losing her Mommy's love. Reserved and shy at one moment; bold and impetuous the next. Sophisticated to a fault; then corny as Kansas in August. Both hot and cold running from the same tap. Just like Bob.

I fished a paperback book from my bag and settled back to read it, but I lost interest after the first few pages and let it drop. There was too much real life and activity going on all around me to look for it in fiction. How many hundreds of stories could be told if only you knew what all those different people were doing on the same cruise. Maybe, I thought, I'd try my hand at it one day.

I'd never told anyone about it, but in the back of my mind I'd always thought I would like to be a writer. I loved books as a child. I was always reading something, even the cereal boxes at the breakfast table, and often I thought of better endings to the stories I read then the ones that were actually printed. Books were such magical things. They could take you back to the far-distant past or project you forward to the future with a flip of the page. Between their covers were mysterious, far-off cities and distant lands waiting to be discovered and explored. They could make you laugh on one page and cry the next, raise the hair on the back of your neck in terror, or put a lump in your throat with sadness. And if reading books was such an incredible experience, I reasoned, then writing them must be even more so.

I dreamed so often of putting my thoughts down on paper. Creating little worlds of my own to share with others who might one day read them. But for one reason or another, I never found the time to make my dream a reality. All the stories I'd like to tell were still locked inside my head.

There wasn't time to think about writing books after Tracey was born. Taking care of her was a full-time job. I'd lived with my parents the first year Bob and I were married, while he finished his tour of duty in Germany.

Three months after the night at Rainbow Lake, I wrote him a long, hysterical letter to tell him I was pregnant. I didn't beg him to marry me; not in so many words. But I left little doubt that if he didn't, I'd be forced to do "something drastic." That was how I put it. I let him decide just what it might be, with heavy hints in favor of suicide.

I don't know what I would have done if Bob hadn't married me. I would still have had the baby, of course. At that time, abortion was something that only prostitutes did to themselves with coat hangers in order to stay in business. No decent girl would have even considered it. If you got caught, you paid the price. And in a small town like Cranston, the price you paid for being an unwed mother was shame. Everyone in town would know what you'd done. People would talk about you behind their hands when you walked down Main Street. The phone would ring at late hours of the night and strange, usually drunken male voices you'd never heard before would tell you that they'd heard you "put out" and ask if you'd like to "have some fun" with them. Your child would be marked for life. The target of every school yard bully's taunts. *You don't know who your father is—and neither does your mo-ther!* It cost a lot in those days to make a mistake like that.

Bob got a special five-day leave and flew home from Germany again. We were married quickly and quietly in the Cranston Lutheran Church, with only his parents and my parents in attendance. No newspaper report of the wedding was published, because my mother said it would be best for the baby's future if people believed Bob and I had been secretly married before he went back overseas in June. People counted the months between wedding announcements and birth announcements in those days, too.

We spent our "honeymoon" at Bob's uncle's place in the Poconos, but since almost everyone else in the Lawrence family wanted to escape the late August heat by going up to the mountains that weekend too, it was more like a family reunion than a honeymoon. When we arrived, there were already seven others there, and five more Lawrences arrived the next day for a Saturday picnic. We had to sleep on air mattresses on the floor in the living room, along with three of Bob's cousins. In order to make love, we had to hike far into the woods and do it on a bed of grass and leaves, just like the first time. I didn't enjoy it at all. On the one hand, I kept nervously glancing over Bob's shoulder to see if a troop of Boy Scouts on a nature hike was about to burst through the brush, and on the other hand (though Bob swore it wouldn't), I was afraid all activity might hurt the baby. All in all, we had a miserable time.

When Bob got out of the service and came home, we continued to live with my parents for a few months until he was able to find a job and save up enough for an apartment of our own. They were difficult years. He didn't make much at first and we had to watch every penny. Our furniture was all second-hand; our clothes shabby. But we had each other, and that's all that really seemed to matter. We were in love.

I wondered what had happend between those years and now. What went wrong? It seemed that when we had nothing we somehow had everything, and now that we had everything we had nothing. In those first years of our marriage, Bob worked a full-time job during the day, came home for a quick supper, then flew off to night school to learn business administration, but when he finally came home and we got in bed together we made wild, passionate love for hours. I used to sit beside him on the couch while he studied and our hands would be joined like a silent bond of strength between us. Now, we hardly ever touched. And our lovemaking had become little more than a memory. When we did it all, it was more like a routine function that needed to be done every now and then, like cleaning out the furnace. There was no real passion in it any more. Not like the early times. When we finished, I was often left with stronger feelings of unrest and dissatisfaction than I'd had before we started. It seemed that something was missing. Something very, very important had gone out of it. All the physical motions were still the same, but there was no real communion of one with the other on a higher, deeper plane. We were no longer touching each other where it really mattered.

I still felt as much in love with Bob as I ever had, but his feelings for me had imperceptibly changed. It was like he'd grown so used to me that he took me for granted now. I was like a pair of old, comfortable shoes he could slip on when his feet hurt, but wouldn't think of wearing when he got dressed for a special occasion. They were only good enough to wear around the house.

The more successful Bob became at his job, the more he advanced slowly up the corporate ladder, the less important I seemed to be to him. He didn't share things with me like he used to. Never asked my advice on any but the most trivial matters. Where once it was "Do you think I should take a chance on switching jobs, Kay?" it was now "Should we got the garage painted this year or wait 'til next?" The same man who once couldn't wait to come home to tell me everything that had happened to him at the office, now only wanted to know what was for supper and if anything good was on TV.

I just couldn't understand what had happened. I was still the same person I'd always been. It wasn't as though I'd let myself get fat and sloppy, the way some women do after they've been married for a number of years. I hadn't become a shrew by any means. I didn't nag him, didn't spend money outrageously, didn't neglect my housework. And whenever he wanted to make love, I was always willing and eager. I couldn't see where he had any complaints, or why his feelings toward me should have altered so drastically. If he'd loved me once, why didn't he still love me? My feelings for him hadn't changed, so why had his?

" A piña colada for your thoughts, Kay."

I opened my eyes and looked up in surprise to find Jeff Wagner standing beside me, holding out a tall, cool drink. His smooth, muscular body glistened with a sheen of sweat from the afternoon heat.

"Oh, hi, Jeff," I said with a smile. "I was almost dozing for a minute there."

"You look like you could use this," he said. He sat down on the edge of the deckchair beside me and put the drink in my hand.

"What is it?"

"A piña colada."

"A peeny whata?" I laughed.

"Try it," he said. "You'll like it."

I took a hesitant sip from the glass. It was ice-cold, sweet and delicious. "*Mmmmm!* It is good."

"An island specialty," he said. "Three of them are guaranteed to bring out the native in anyone."

"I'd better only have one, then!" I laughed.

"What's the matter? Afraid of letting your hair down?"

"Only when it's unwise to."

"Don't you like to take chances?"

I shook my head quickly and took another sip from the drink. My throat was parched from the heat of the sun and I felt that I could have downed the whole glass in a few sips. It was one of those sneaky drinks that taste so good you don't realize how potent they are until you've gulped a few.

"I do," Jeff said. "I like to take chances constantly. It's the only way to really live and enjoy life."

"For some people, maybe. But not for me. I like to know exactly what's going to happen in advance before I do something. I'm too old to enjoy being surprised by the unexpected."

"But sometimes the unexpected can be pretty wonderful," he said. "And as far as being too old . . . well, that's a laugh." His eyes darted quickly up and down the length of me. "As a matter of fact, I think you were pulling our legs last night when you said you're Tracey's mother. I think she was telling the truth when she said you're sisters."

"Oh, Jeff!" I laughed. "Of course I'm her mother!"

He shook his head. "Huh-uh. No way. I don't believe it for a minute. No one who looks as good as you do in that bathing suit could have a daughter that old."

I felt myself starting to blush. I took another sip of the drink and avoided his eyes. Little flutters of nervousness were starting to run through me. I was pleased by his compliments, but apprehensive of what they might be leading to.

"Tracey's somewhere over by the pool," I told him.

"Oh?" The way he said it, it was like: *So what?*

"You should see how she looks. She's wearing a brand-new bikini that will knock your eye out. I had to think twice about letting her out of the cabin in it."

"I'm sure she looks great," he said, but didn't show the slightest sign of wanting to go see for himself. He moved closer and his bare knee grazed my leg. "She's a beautiful girl to start with, and it's not hard to tell where she gets her looks from."

"Oh!" I laughed. "So you *do* believe I'm her mother, after all!"

"I believe it, but I don't understand it."

I fished into my bag for my cigarette case and lighter, and at the same time I moved my leg away from the touch of his knee. There was no sense in asking for trouble, by encouraging something that wasn't going to happen.

"Let me," Jeff said, taking the lighter from me. He struck it and cupped his hand around the flame. When I moved closer with the cigarette in my mouth, his other hand touched mine to hold it steady while I drew smoke.

"Thanks."

"My pleasure." He gave the lighter back, and as it went from hand to hand I felt like little sparks of electricity were jumping between our fingers.

"How did you sleep last night after I left you?" he asked.

"Fine. No trouble. I guess the sea air did the trick."

"Pleasant dreams?"

Something inside me jumped and my eyes darted to his. It was silly—and perfectly impossible—but for an instant I thought that he knew what I'd dreamed.

"I—don't really remember," I said hesitantly. "I don't think I dreamed at all."

"*I* did," he said with a smile, and once again I had that same uneasy feeling. Was it possible he'd had the same dream?

"Where are your folks today, Jeff?" I asked, wanting to change the subject as quickly as possible. "I'm sorry we missed you at breakfast."

"So am I," he said. He shifted slightly and once again his knee was pressed against my leg. "Mom discovered that some ladies she and Dad met on one of their other cruises are on the ship and she's down in the lounge having a gabfest with them. And I think Dad's gone up to the Wheel House to make sure the Captain's running the ship properly. He'll never get over his days in the Navy, I guess. He says he's got saltwater in his blood."

"My husband was in the Army before we were married," I said. I felt it was important to remind this young man as often as possible that I was a married woman.

"Oh?" he said, and once again it sounded like: *So what?*

"He was stationed in Germany."

"That's a great country," he said. "I went all through there a few years ago. I went over the summer between my junior and senior years at Princeton and toured Germany, Switzerland, and Austria with a backpack. It was a lot of fun."

"It must have been."

"Have you been to Europe often, Kay?"

"Me?" I laughed. "No. Never. I've always wanted to travel and see strange new places, but this cruise is really the first time I've been out of the United States."

"How come?"

"Well . . ." I had to search for an answer. "I guess when you're busy raising a family you don't have time to go off and see the world."

"Mom and Dad did," he said. "They used to travel together every summer. They'd pack me off to summer camp for a few months and then take off by themselves. They've been almost everywhere in the world together. Last year they even went to Red China. Mom said it was the thrill of her life. How come you and your husband never did the same thing?"

"I . . . don't know." I looked down at the half-empty drink in my hand and took another sip. "This is really good. What's in it, Jeff?"

He ignored the question. "If I were married to someone like you, I'd want to take you everywhere."

"Well . . . sometimes it's just not possible. With the kind of job my husband has, he can't take much time off for travelling." But even as I said it, I knew it was a lie. Bob could take as much vacation time as he wanted, but whenever he did, we always stayed at home. Even when he travelled on business, which he did quite frequently in the past several years, he never took me along. "You'd be so bored, you wouldn't know what to do with yourself, Kay," he always said, and I never argued the point. I just stayed behind and waited for him to come back home. *Why*, I wondered? Why hadn't I insisted that he take me with him?

"Hey, you're starting to get pretty pink on this side," Jeff said. "Maybe it's time to turn over and let your back have some sun. Go ahead. I'll rub you with lotion."

I hesitated. "I—think maybe I'll go down and change for lunch instead," I said. "That sun's pretty strong. I might have had enough for one day."

"On this side," he insisted. "But you don't want to look like a zebra, do you? You've got to tan the other side, too."

Reluctantly, I turned over on the towel and Jeff picked up the tube of sun lotion I'd left by the chair. As he started to smooth it over my bare back and shoulders, I felt hot flashes of excitement run through me. He wasn't just smearing Coppertone on me. It felt more like his hand was making love to my body. His fingers were warm and strong, gently massaging the muscles as they moved slowly over my skin.

"Feel good?" he murmured.

I swallowed hard. "Greasy," I said. I couldn't let him know how it really felt.

"Is that all? I always thought I gave a pretty good massage."

"It's . . . okay," I admitted. But deep inside me, I knew it was more than just okay. He'd left me tingling with awakened desires.

When he finished my back and shoulders and started to apply the lotion to the backs of my legs, I stopped him. I wasn't sure what would happen if I let him rub my thighs with those big, strong fingers. They'd been without a man's touch for too long. I was far too vulnerable.

"You don't have to do my legs, Jeff," I said. I turned over for a moment and took the tube from him. "I did both sides before I lay down."

"Okay." He looked disappointed. "If you're sure."

"I'm sure."

He stretched out on the other deckchair and for several minutes neither of us spoke. My mind was racing with all sorts of crazy thoughts, and I guess his was, too. I didn't understand what was happening to me. I knew what it might lead to if I gave Jeff the slightest sign of encouragement, and the idea terrified me. But at the same time . . . it excited me, too. He was such an attractive young man. Lean. Muscular. Extremely handsome. It was only natural for me to be flattered by his attentions. But what I was feeling right then wasn't just the gratitude of an older woman for a young man's flattery. It was desire. The instinctive response of my body to the need for a man.

"Damn you, Bob!" I thought angrily. "This is all your fault." If he hadn't left me so in need of loving for so long, I'd never even be thinking that something might develop between Jeff and me.

But maybe there was really no danger of such a thing ever happening. Maybe I was reading more into the situation than actually existed. maybe Jeff *was* just being friendly, and would have laughed at the thought of anything more than that.

"Jeff?" I said. "Why did you ask Tracey all those questions about me last night?"

"She told you, did she?" He laughed. "Some lawyer I'm going to make! I can't even cross-examine a witness without giving away my motives."

"What were your motives?" I asked slowly.

"That should be obvious. I'm interested in knowing all I can about you."

"Tracey wished you'd have been more interested in finding out about *her*."

"I already know all I need to know about Tracey," he said after a moment's pause. "She's a nice girl, but I've met a hundred other nice girls just like her. They don't really interest me."

What did he mean by that? I wondered for a moment if Tracey's wild suggestion that Jeff was gay might not, after all, be true.

"You like girls, don't you?" I asked.

"No," he said flatly. "I like women. They're much more fascinating."

Before the conversation had a chance to go any further, Tracey reappeared. She was dripping wet.

"Wow!" she laughed. "What a wild sensation it is to swim in a pool that's moving at the same time you are!"

"Hi, honey." I sat up and Jeff did, too. "Are you having fun?"

"Lots!" She shook her wet hair and her breasts jiggled as if they were going to spill right out of the tiny bra cups of her bikini. I knew she was doing it for Jeff's benefit.

"I guess I'm in your chair," he said, standing up.

"No, stay there," she said. "It's okay. I'll dry off in the sun."

"I'm going to go down and change for lunch anyway," he said. "My belly's starting to growl. This sea air really gives me an appetite."

"I guess we'll be going down soon, too," I said.

"Well, see you in the dining room then," he said.

As soon as he was gone, Tracey plopped down beside me with an angry scowl on her face. "Did you see that, Mother?" she sputtered. "He didn't even look twice at me. Every other guy on this boat freaked out when I walked past in this bikini, and that jerk acted like he didn't even notice. He's got to be gay. I'm sure of it now."

"Oh, honey!" I laughed. "I think it's just that he's not as easily impressed as you'd like him to be. You'll have to try something more than a skimpy bikini if you want to get him."

"Who wants to?" she said with a flippant shrug. "My loss is some other guy's gain."

"Don't be too sure of that," I said, as I collected my things. "Some other *woman* just might surprise you."

Chapter 6

"You're going to fall in love with St. Thomas, Kay," said Henry Wagner. It was our third night at sea and we were all relaxing between floor shows in the Queen's Lounge, after yet another incredible dinner a few hours earlier. If I kept eating the way I was, I'd be going back home two dress sizes larger. It seemed every time I turned around on the *Ocean Queen*, food was being served. Whopping breakfasts. Morning bouillon. Five-course lunches. Afternoon tea with cookies and *petit fours* and cucumber sandwiches. Dinners. Sumptuous midnight buffets. And even pizza, offered every night at two o'clock for those who'd worked up another appetite on the dance floor.

"Yes, St. Thomas is our favorite island," Florence agreed. "It's probably the most beautiful in the Caribbean. You'll see for yourself when we arrive tomorrow. We've been going there for years. Even before we started taking these cruises."

"That's because Dad wanted to take advantage of all the duty-free liquor!" Jeff laughed.

His mother slapped him playfully on the arm. "You be quiet. I remember that *you* didn't waste much time heading straight for the liquor stores the last time we were down, so don't talk about your father."

I turned to Jeff. "Oh? Then you've been to St. Thomas before, too?"

"A couple of times," he said. "And Mom's right. It really is a great place."

"Yes, I hear it's quite gay," Tracey murmured, and hid her smile behind her hand when I shot her a dirty look.

"I hope you two brought your checkbooks with you," Florence said, "because you're just going to go crazy when you see the shops in Charlotte Amalie."

"That's really why she's been dragging me down there for years," Henry chuckled. "For the bargains."

"Are things really cheap?" I asked.

"Oh, wait 'til you see!" Florence laughed. "You'll have to pick up another suitcase to carry back all the other things you'll want to buy!"

"Everything from Gucci to Pucci," Henry sighed. "It's all there, and Florence knows just where to find it. I can feel my poor wallet shuddering already."

"Hey, I've got a great idea," Jeff said. "Instead of eating on the ship tomorrow night, why don't we take Kay and Tracey to Cha Cha Town for kalaloo?"

"Oh, yes!" Florence exclaimed. "That's a wonderful idea, Jeff. They'll love it."

"Take us where for what?" I laughed.

"Cha Cha Town for kalaloo," he repeated with a smile.

"Cha Cha Town's the nickname they gave to Frenchtown, Kay," explained Henry. "It's the section of Charlotte Amalie where the French-speaking natives from the island of St. Barts settled. The people who were already living in St. Thomas called the area Cha Cha Town because they couldn't understand a word the French-speaking natives were saying."

"It's one of the most picturesque little spots you'll ever see," Florence said. "There's a breath-taking view from the top of the hill. We'll have to walk up there during the day, so you and Tracey can take lots of pictures. You did bring your cameras with you, didn't you?"

"Of course," I smiled. "What red-blooded American tourist would be caught anywhere without his Kodak?"

"What's kalaloo?" Tracey asked. "Is it some kind of voodoo?"

"No!" Henry laughed. "It's some kind of food, honey."

"Delicious!" Florence swore. "It's like New Orleans gumbo. They make it with salt meat and fish cooked with fresh spinach and okra pods, and serve it with cornmeal balls they call fungi."

"It sounds disgusting," Tracey muttered.

"Oh, honey," I chided. "Don't say that unless you've tried it. It might be very good."

"It is," Jeff said.

"We'll have to have asparagus pudding, too," Henry said.

"Asparagus *pudding*?" Tracey made such a face that we all had to laugh.

"It's a lot better than it sounds, believe me," Florence promised. "Very rich and very tasty."

"It should be quite an adventure for us," I said. "We'd love to go. Wouldn't we, Tracey?"

She shrugged. "I guess so."

The lights in the lounge dimmed and the sound of rock music blared from the stage, as a combo of young, long-haired British musicians began to play.

Henry groaned. "*Them* again? I thought Helen McNair was on the second show bill tonight." He quickly polished off the rest of his drink. "If I'd known these characters were coming on, I'd have turned in an hour ago."

"Don't you like them?" Tracey said. Her fingers were tapping on the table top in time to the music. "I think they're great."

"Well, my dear," Henry said with an indulgent smile, "your eardrums are a lot younger than mine. When they get to be my age, they'll appreciate soft, mellow sounds, too."

Florence laughed and stood up to join her husband. "I'll be turning in now, too, Kay."

"She wants to be up bright and early, so she can catch the first launch in to town," Henry said with a quick wink at me. "When the natives know she's coming, they swim out to meet the ship with sacks of Wedgwood and Chanel Number Five."

"Oh, you!" Florence said, slapping him hard. "We'll see you in the morning for breakfast. Are you staying, Jeff?"

"For a little while," he said.

When his parents were gone and the three of us were alone, an uneasy silence settled over the table. "If you two would like to dance," I suggested, "please go ahead. I'll be all right by myself." Jeff and Tracey exchanged looks like two wary cats on the same back fence.

"Would—uh—you like to, Tracey?" he asked.

She smiled and shook her head. "Thanks anyway, but I think I've already got a partner."

I followed the direction of her eyes and saw the young Second Officer approaching the table. He gave me a polite nod and Tracey a quick wink. "Good evening, Mrs. Lawrence. Are you enjoying the cruise?"

"Yes I am, thank you."

"If you don't mind, I'd like very much to dance with

your daughter."

"I don't mind at all if you *dance* with her, Mr. Taylor." It's what else you've got in mind that worries me."

"Why did you do that?" Jeff asked when we were alone. His thick black eyebrows were knit in an angry frown.

"Do what . . . ?"

"Why did you force me into asking Tracey to dance?"

"*Force* you?" I had to laugh. "Would it have been such an imposition?"

"Frankly, yes. I feel the same way my father does about this kind of music. I'd have felt like a fool out there twitching and shaking my body as though I was having an epileptic attack."

"I'm sorry. I didn't realize."

"Yes, you did," he snapped. "You knew exactly what you were doing, and I wish you'd stop it."

"Stop what?"

"Stop trying to play the matchmaker. It's not going to work. You certainly must know by now that I'm not interested in getting anything going with Tracey. And you must know *why*, too." He reached across the table and took my hand. "You *do* know why, Kay. Don't you?" I tried to pull my hand free of his, but his fingers tightened. "*Don't* you?"

"Jeff, please. We've all had such a wonderful time together these past three days. Don't spoil it. I'd hate to have to tell your parents—"

"What?" he cut in. "Tell them what? That their big bad son is making passes at you and you want him to stop it?"

"If that's how you want to put it . . . yes."

"That won't be necessary," he said. "You don't have to ask my parents to make me stop it. All you've got to do is ask me yourself."

"Let go of my hand, Jeff. Please. You're hurting my fingers."

"Ask me to stop it, Kay. Tell me yourself that you don't want me hanging around you any more, and you won't see me again for the rest of the cruise."

"And what would we do about table arrangements and things like that?" I sighed. "It would be so embarrasing—"

"You don't want to tell me, do you? Because you feel the same way I do. You know that something's happening between us, and you don't want it to stop any more than I do."

"I'm a married woman, Jeff."

"Aren't you forgetting something?" he said with a strange smile. "Isn't that line supposed to be: 'I'm a *happily* married woman'? Or couldn't you force yourself to say it, because you know it's not true?"

I pulled my hand free and snatched up my purse. "I'm going back to my cabin, Jeff. It's late and we've both had a few drinks and I think it's best if we bring this conversation to an end right now."

"I'll walk back with you."

"Please don't," I said, but when I stood up and started for the exit, he was right behind me. We took the elevator up to the Boat Deck in silence and walked down the little corridor of staterooms. When we reached my door, he took the key from me and turned it in the lock.

"Goodnight," I said. I reached for my key, but he held it back.

"I'd like to come in."

"No, Jeff." I shook my head vehemently. "Absolutely not."

He smiled. "I won't try to rape you. I'd just like to talk for a while in private."

"I don't think there's anything more that needs to be said. Now if you'll please give me back my key, I'd like to—"

His arms suddenly reached out and caught me. Both hands pulled me against his body and his mouth was on mine before I could turn my head to avoid the kiss. His lips were warm and surprisingly soft. They parted, and I felt the tip of his tongue trying to force entry to my mouth.

I whimpered and tried to push him away, but his grip tightened and kept me close. In spite of myself, I began to weaken. I felt the strength to resist him ebbing slowly away. It had been so long—*so* long—since a man's arms held me that tightly. So many months since a man's body pressed mine with such urgency. I needed love so badly. If only—

The sound of an opening door further down the corridor made us both jump. Jeff pulled back, and in his haste he dropped my door key on the floor. As he stooped to retrieve it, I turned and saw his mother standing outside their cabin in her robe.

"Oh, that *was* you I heard, Jeff," said Florence. "I thought so. Are you coming in now? I was just going to turn off the lights."

"In a minute," he said. "I was just helping Kay with her lock. It was jammed and I had to force it."

"Is everything all right now?"

"Yeah, Mom. Everything's just fine. It should open easily now." He gave me a smile and a wink that his mother couldn't see and started down the corridor.

121

"Goodnight, Kay," he said. "See you in the morning."

St. Thomas proved to be everything the Wagners had promised, and more. When Tracey and I got up the next morning, the ship was already anchored a short distance from the harbor entrance. Because the *Ocean Queen* was so huge and its hull too deep for the ship to sail all the way in to shore, small motor launches were lowered from the Bridge Deck to the level of the gangway and used to ferry passengers back and forth from Charlotte Amalie, the capital of the Virgin Islands and St. Thomas's largest town. We stood outside on the deck for a few minutes, admiring the view before going down to breakfast.

The mountainous island, lush and brilliantly green, rose before us like an emerald set in the sea. The hills around the harbor were dotted with little pink and blue and lime green houses, from the waterfront all the way up to the steep peaks overlooking the sea. The harbor itself was a cluster of cabin cruisers, sailing skiffs, speedboats, and private yachts; and a number of chartered fishing boats were on their way out for the big ones.

"We'll have to take a picture of this for Daddy," Tracey said.

"Yes," I murmured. "We wouldn't want him to miss it, would we?"

Right after breakfast, we took one of the first launches in to shore. Florence said it would be best if we got our sightseeing out of the way before tackling the shops on Main Street, since most of the town was built on the hills and it would be a nightmare struggling up and down them with our arms loaded down with packages.

We started by taking an aerial tramway a thousand feet up to the top of Flag Hill. The view from the peak was incredible. All of Charlotte Amalie was spread below us like a huge, living map. The colorful harbor, where native fishing boats had their early-morning's catch spread out on the dock for eager buyers; the crooked, winding little streets with their colorful houses; an array of stately courtyards enclosed by high walls; and the bustling market square, where once slaves were sold and now their descendants bartered for vegetables, peppers, herbs, and other island produce.

To the east of the harbor were powdery, white sand beaches. In the distance was the island of St. John and the neighboring British Virgin Islands. And, of course, the magnificent *Ocean Queen* anchored on the calm blue sea just off shore. Tracey and I took pictures of everything, while Henry told us that centuries ago the very hill we stood on had been used by pirate buccaneers as a lookout post to spot the sails of trade ships on their way to other islands in the Caribbean from Europe.

We took the tramway back down to town and spent the next two hours exploring Charlotte Amalie on foot. The Wagners were excellent tour guides. They took us through Frenchtown, where we were to return later that evening for our exotic meal, and our cameras clicked constantly as we wandered through the narrow little paths lined with bougainvillaea, flamboyant trees, and fire-red hibiscus.

We strolled through the ancient Danish cemetery, with tombs made from brightly painted conch shells, and toured the dungeons of Old Fort Christian, where a number of pirates had been ingloriously hanged for their crimes. We passed by Government House, the residence of the Governor of the Virgin Islands, and visited "Quarter B," with its beautiful old staircase that supposedly had come from an old pirate ship.

By the time the Wagners had shown us everything they felt we should see, my aching feet were grateful for the chance to rest at a waterfront café while we lingered over cool banana daiquiris before tackling the duty-free shops.

Rather than tag along with Florence, Tracey, and me, the two men decided they would go off on their own and meet us at five o'clock back at the waterfront where the *Ocean Queen's* launch docked. It was just as well. They must have known they'd be bored to tears hanging around while we women oohed and aahed over the incredible array of merchandise offered in the Main Street stores and boutiques.

"Remember," Henry cautioned before we separated, "you're only allowed to bring back two hundred dollars worth of goodies duty-free." Then, groaning and rolling his eyes in mock exasperation, he added, "*Only* two hundred dollars worth? What am I saying?"

It was easy to see how a person with bargain hunter's fever could spend twice that amount in less than an hour and still not be satisfied. Shop after shop offered such a tempting array of merchandise at ridiculously low prices that I had to use all my will power to keep from going overboard myself.

I really didn't need another watch, though the forty percent discount on such famous names as Lucien Piccard, Piaget, Omega, and Longines made me seriously wonder if I did. I had a harder time passing by the strings of pearls and star sapphire rings at half the price in jewelry stores back home, and by the time Florence took us to the little boutique that specialized in fine

French and Italian kid gloves and handbags, my resistance broke down completely. I started to buy like money was going out of style.

Tracey was just as bad. She picked up two Pringle cashmere sweaters, a Mary Quant blouse, a stunning Dior scarf, and a leather wallet; all for less than a hundred dollars.

We each bought two bottles of perfume for sixty percent less than we would have paid in New York, and when I saw cartons of cigarettes for two dollars and bottles of rum for a dollar-eighty, I surrendered completely.

"Bankruptcy court, here I come!" Henry laughed, when we met him and Jeff at the launch, our arms laden with packages and shopping bags.

"Don't complain," Florence clucked. "I also bought two beautiful Dior ties for you." I'd bought two for Bob myself, and an exquisite Dunhill lighter he'd wanted for months.

"Oh, good," Henry said. "I hope they'll match the barrel I'll be wearing, too, after I've paid for all the other stuff you bought!"

"I notice you two didn't do too badly yourselves," she said. Both he and Jeff were carrying five-quart liquor containers and plastic shopping bags stuffed with cartons of cigarettes.

"A little something to forget my financial woes, my dear," Henry sighed. "That's all."

We took the launch back to the ship and agreed to meet again at seven o'clock in the Wagners' stateroom for a drink before returning to shore for our dinner in Frenchtown. As soon as we were back in our cabin, I kicked off my shoes and flopped on the bed. My legs felt like I'd walked a million miles that day.

"Mother?" Tracey asked while she unpacked her new-bought treasures. "Did something happen between you and Jeff that I don't know about?"

My heart jumped into my throat. "Like what?" I asked as casually as I could.

"I don't know. It's just that for the past couple of days he's been hanging around you like a little puppy, and now all of a sudden you're hardly speaking to each other. What happened? Did he ask for a recipe and you refused to give it to him?"

I sighed under my breath. It was obvious by her flippant attitude that she hadn't the slightest idea about what was really going on.

"Of course not, dear," I said. "Don't be silly. I didn't notice anything different. And I think you're just imagining that he's been hanging around me a lot, because he hasn't been hanging around you. I'm sure he's not really interested in either of us."

"Thank God," she said, but a little too strongly for me to believe she meant it. "Who'd want him to? He's just like all those other stuffed shirts at Harvard Law. You'd think they were all studying to be undertakers instead of lawyers. Their idea of having a good time is showing each other misprints in the *Congressional Record*."

"Oh, Tracey!" I laughed. "I'll bet Jeff's a lot more fun than you imagine, once you get to know him better."

"Then *you* get to know him better," she muttered. "I know all I need to know."

The Wagners had ordered some delicious little hors d'oeuvres from room service, and we nibbled at them with our drinks before taking the launch back to Charlotte Amalie for dinner. It was just enough to whet our appetites. The restaurant they took us to in Frenchtown—or Cha Cha Town, as they insisted we call it—was tiny, quaint, and charming. It was well off the beaten tourist path and the few other diners all looked to be locals to me. Tracey and I decided to let Florence and Henry do the ordering for us, since they'd been to the place many times before and knew all the house specialties.

While we waited for the food to come, we sipped a heavily spiced drink called maubi, which Henry said was the Virgin Island's answer to cider, but was made from the fermented bark of the maubi plant rather than apples. It had a strange but interesting taste. I enjoyed it, but Tracey took only a sip or two and didn't touch her glass again.

"Well, Kay," Henry asked, "now that you've spent a day here, what do you think of our little island?"

"I think it's the most beautiful, charming spot I've ever seen," I honestly said. "I could stay forever."

"We're going to, one day," said Florence.

"Oh?"

"We're planning to move down here permanently when I retire," Henry said. "And the way Wall Street has been acting up these days, that may be sooner than I think."

"It's a wonderful place to retire," Florence said. "Do you know, you can get a cook or a maid or a gardener for only seventy-five dollars a *month*? We've already bought our lot. We'd have taken you to see it, but it's over on the other side of the island, near Magens Bay. There just wouldn't have been enough time this afternoon."

"Not if you wanted to hit all the stores, too," Henry chuckled.

"You'll have to come down and visit us when we've built our house," said Florence. "And bring your husband, too, of course. Who knows? Maybe you'll both like it so much you'll want to buy a lot also, and we'll be neighbors."

"I'm sure Bob would love it here as much as we do," I said. It was a charming idea, but once again I couldn't help feeling a little sad when I compared the Wagners' marriage to my own. They took such pleasure in each other's company and such obvious delight in planning their future. Bob and I didn't think much about what we were going to do together next week, let alone when he retired. For us, the future was an unknown void looming somewhere ahead of us; but for Florence and Henry it was a glorious prospect of shared happiness. If only we could be like that, I thought, and wondered if we ever would. If the time would ever come again when Bob and I were truly a couple.

The meal the Wagners ordered for us was simply delicious. Spicy and hot, but so different from anything I'd ever eaten before that I enjoyed every bite. Tracey, though, only nibbled suspiciously and moved the food around on her plate with her fork, the way she used to do as a little girl when I served liver for supper. The only thing she really seemed to enjoy was the peanut and coconut sugar cake we had for dessert.

"Have you ever seen anyone do a fire dance, Kay?" asked Jeff, while we lingered over coffee.

"Not lately!" I laughed.

"I saw one once," Tracey volunteered. "On the Ed Sullivan Show, I think, a thousand years ago."

"Oh, you've got to see it in person to really appreciate it," he said. "When you're sitting close enough to actually feel the heat of the flames, you know what you're seeing is for real and not a fake."

"Well, the next time I hear of someone doing a fire dance in Maplewood," I said with a smile, "I'll be sure to go."

"You could see one tonight, if you'd like," he said. "They've got a terrific show up at the Bluebeard's Castle Hotel. Fire dance, native music, the whole works. Would you like to see it?"

"Well . . . ?"

"Oh, yes!" Florence insisted. "You and Tracey really should see it while you're here. The show's quite spectacular. Henry and I have gone a number of times, and we've always been thrilled."

"It does sound like fun," I admitted. "What do you say, Tracey? Should we go?"

She quickly shook her head. "I don't think I'd better. I'm not feeling very well tonight."

"Oh, dear," Florence said. "I hope the meal didn't disagree with you . . . ?"

"No, everything was fine," she said. "It's not that. It's—something else."

"What's wrong, honey?" I asked in concern.

"I've just been having—well—cramps all day. You know what I mean, Mother. I think I'd better go back to the ship and lie down."

I knew what she meant, but I didn't understand it. She'd had her last period just days before we left home. It wasn't possible that she was having another one so soon, yet that was clearly the impression she was trying to give.

"Well," I said, "I guess we'll have to catch the show another time then."

"Oh, *you* could still go, Mother," Tracey said quickly. "I'll be all right by myself."

"I wouldn't think of it."

"*Please*, Mother?" she insisted. "I'll only feel worse if I know I'm spoiling your fun."

The urgency in her voice made me all the more suspicious. What was going on in that crafty little mind of hers, I wondered? Why was she so anxious to go back to the ship alone?

It suddenly came to me. Mr. Taylor, of course. If I was safely out of the way on shore and Tracey had our stateroom all to herself . . . Oh, no! I wasn't about to sit back and let *that* happen! I wasn't going to give them not only the opportunity, but the place to take advantage of it, as well!

"If you're not feeling well," I said flatly, "I wouldn't dream of leaving you alone. We'll both call it a night and go back together."

"Oh, *Mother!*" she whined. "There's nothing you'll be able to do to help. I just need to lie down."

"No, dear," I insisted. "I'll go back with you."

"Oh, all right!" Tracey fumed. "Then I'll stay. I'm not going to feel guilty about spoiling your fun."

"But if you're not feeling well—"

"It doesn't matter," she snapped. "I'll stay."

"Why don't you and Jeff go see the show together, Kay?" Florence said. "This is silly. Henry and I were planning to take the early launch back anyway. I can see that Tracey gets settled down and comfortable. There's no need for you to miss the show, and no need for her to stay if she's feeling miserable."

"No, Florence. I really think it's my responsibility. I wouldn't dream of imposing on you."

"Don't be silly!" she laughed. "What imposition is it? I'll be right down the hall if Tracey needs anything, and that's as much as you'd be able to do for her. As she said herself, all she needs is rest. Why don't you stay and see the show with Jeff?"

"Go on, Mother," Tracey said. "I'll be just fine."

Yeah, I'll bet! I thought.

"It looks like you're in the minority, Kay," said Jeff with a sly smile. "Shall we go?"

There seemed no way out of it. With Tracey insisting that she would stay and be miserable unless I let her go back to the ship alone, and Florence insisting that she could take care of Tracey and there was no reason for me *not* to stay, they had forced me into a box. I'd look like a positive ogre unless I said yes.

"Oh, all right," I sighed. "I guess we'll have to."

"Good," Florence said. "I'm sure you'll both have fun."

We all went back to the launch together, and once the others were headed back to the *Ocean Queen*, Jeff looked around for a taxi. I got inside while he told the driver where we wanted to go, then he slipped into the back seat beside me.

"Well, alone at last!" he said with a grin.

It hadn't occurred to me until that moment, but he was right. I'd been so concerned about leaving Tracey alone with Mr. Taylor on board ship, I hadn't even thought of the consequences of leaving myself alone with Jeff on shore. If I had, nothing in the world could have stopped me from going back on that launch, too.

The taxi pulled away from the waterfront with a jolt and started up into the steep hills surrounding Charlotte Amalie. As I stared through the front windshield, I had an uneasy feeling that something was very wrong. But it took several minutes before I realized just what it was.

"Jeff!" I gasped. "This driver must be drunk! He's on the wrong side of the road!"

Jeff laughed. "No he's not. Even though the steering wheel's on the American side of the car, down here they use the British side of the road. Everyone drives on the left."

"Oh," I said. But knowing it was the accepted custom didn't make it any easier to adjust to. Every time we went careening around a hairpin curve at breakneck speed, I was dead certain we were going to run smack into an American tourist in a rented car who didn't know he was supposed to be on the other side of the road.

My hands clenched nervously into fists, and several times I couldn't help squealing under my breath in terror when I saw headlights approaching fast from the other direction. My palms were wringing wet when Jeff took my hand and clasped it firmly in his. I didn't object. I held on to him for dear life as the taxi climbed higher and higher into the mountains.

"Are you sure he knows where he's going?" I whispered anxiously.

Jeff gave my hand a reassuring squeeze. "He knows."

We finally reached the top of the mountain and started down the other side. There were no streetlights or houses now in any direction, and aside from the faint light of the overhead moon it was pitch black. We seemed to drive for miles through the middle of nowhere. I kept looking around for the lights of the hotel, but all I saw was wild, undeveloped land.

At last the driver slowed down and turned off the main road. But instead of turning into a hotel entrance, he took us down a narrow, winding dirt land with overgrown trees on both sides. Suddenly I saw a beach and water ahead. The taxi stopped.

"Well, here we are," Jeff said. He reached across me and opened the door on my side. I got out of the car and the heels of my shoes sunk into sand. There wasn't a hotel or a sign of any other lighted place in sight.

When Jeff had paid the driver and got out of the cab, he came toward me and took my hand. The driver backed slowly up the dirt lane, and as the headlights receded in the distance we were suddenly alone in the dark and absolute stillness of the night.

"Where *are* we?" I demanded.

"At the lot my mother was telling you about. This is where she and Dad are going to build their house."

"But—?" I stared at him with a mixture of horror and rage running through me in equal measure. "You said we were going to that hotel to see the show . . . ?"

"It's not really so hot," he said with a smile. "I decided it would be more fun to come here instead."

Understanding slowly dawned. I jerked my hand free from his. "You *planned* it this way, didn't you? This is where you intended to bring me all along, isn't it, Jeff?"

"Well," he grinned, "not exactly. If Tracey had wanted to come along, I guess we'd be at Bluebeard's Castle right now, watching some fool rub fire all over his body. But the way she's been giving that Second Officer the eye for the past few nights, I kind of figured she'd jump at the chance to go back to the ship by herself. So I didn't plan it this way, no. Let's just say that things worked out as I hoped they would."

I was so mad I was ready to scream. "And just how do you think we're going to get back to the ship before it sails?" I demanded. All the passengers who'd gone ashore that night had been warned that the last launch would be leaving the waterfront at two o'clock sharp. Anyone who missed it would be out of luck. With or without any last stragglers from shore, the ship was sailing on schedule.

"Out here in the middle of nowhere, how are we going to find a taxi to take us back to town, Jeff? Or did you imagine we could *walk* back over those mountains in time?"

"Hey, cool down!" he laughed. "There's no problem. I told that driver to come back here for us in two hours."

"And what makes you so sure he will?"

"Well, the ten dollar tip I promised him, for one thing." He reached out and took my hand again. "Don't worry, Kay. We'll make the last launch in plenty of time."

"Wonderful," I muttered. "And what are we supposed to do here for the next two hours?"

A grin crept over his face. "We'll think of something."

I tensed and tried to pull my hand free, but his grip tightened.

"For starters, why don't I show you around the folks' property? There's a helluva view of the bay from here." He tugged on my arm and started down the dirt lane toward the beach and the water. "Come on; I'll show you."

Reluctantly, I trudged along behind him. I was burning with anger, but the thought of being left alone in the dark in the middle of all those trees seemed worse than what I might face by following Jeff.

It was much brighter when we reached the sandy edge of the bay. The moon glistened on the calm water, casting its reflection back to shore.

"This is where they're planning to put the house," Jeff said, turning with a sweep of his arm toward the brush we'd just come from. "Of course they'll have to clear away most of the trees, but the setting is perfect, don't you think?"

"It's lovely," I said, and it was. But I didn't feel much in the mood to discuss the Wagners' retirement plans at that moment. "Damn you, Jeff," I swore. "Why did you do this to me?" I pulled my hand free once again and dug into my purse for a cigarette. He tried to take my lighter and strike it for me, but I brushed away his fingers. I was trembling with rage.

"Hey, I'm sorry," he said. "But this was the only way I could think of to be alone with you for a little while. If you remember, I wanted to talk last night but you wouldn't let me in your cabin."

I blew a cloud of angry smoke toward his face. "What could you possibly have to say to me that's so important?"

He shrugged and smiled. "Nothing much. Just that I think I've fallen in love with you," he said softly. "That's all."

"Oh, Jeff, don't!" I turned away and started to walk across the sand toward the water lapping up to shore. I'd known in my heart that he was going to say something like that sooner or later, but I'd prayed he wouldn't. "It's too ridiculous an idea even to consider."

"Why?" he demanded.

"Well just look at the two of us, for one thing," I said. "You're just a boy, and I'm—"

"I'm not a boy!" he stated. "I'm a man, Kay."

"All right, maybe you are. But that doesn't make *me* any younger. I'm still old enough to be your mother."

"Oh, Christ!" he spat. "Don't lay *that* on me! My mother's fifty-three years old!"

"And how old do you think *I* am, Jeff?"

He shrugged.

"I'm thirty-eight."

He started to smile. "So? I knew that. I figured if Tracey was twenty, you had to be around forty. As a matter of fact, you're actually *younger* than I thought!"

"And what about my husband?" I said.

"You tell me. What about him?"

"Doesn't the fact that he exists make any difference to you?"

"Not really. Why should it? You don't love him—"

"I *do* love Bob!" I protested.

"Okay, maybe you do," he said. "But is the feeling mutual?"

"Of course it is."

"Like hell!" Jeff laughed. "Don't try to hand me that, Kay. You forget that I'm studying to be a lawyer. I'm trained to look at the evidence and draw a reasonable conclusion from it. And ever since the first night you sat down to dinner with us, I've known something wasn't right between you and your husband."

I was stunned. "How . . . *could* you?"

"By the look on your face, for instance, when Mom started talking about girls who fall in love too soon and wind up in loveless marriages when they're older," he said. "You looked like you thought she was talking about you personally."

"I—I was thinking about a friend of mine," I swore. "A very close friend."

"Sure you were," he said. "The same kind of 'friend' women always seem to have when they call a lawyer's office to ask questions about divorce. They never want the information for themselves; it's always for 'a friend.'"

"I love Bob," I said softly, "and he loves me. You have no right to say that he doesn't, Jeff." I felt my throat starting to tighten and my eyes mist. I puffed restlessly at my cigarette and tried to pull away when his hands touched my shoulders, but his fingers tightened and held me as he moved nearer.

"If that's true," he murmured, "why were you trembling when I kissed you last night? Why are you trembling *now*? What are you afraid of, Kay? Me . . . or yourself?"

"Please let go of me, Jeff."

He took the cigarette from my hand and threw it toward the water. His strong hands turned me around so we faced each other. His lips moved slowly toward mine.

"Jeff, don't. Please don't."

"You're trembling like a leaf," he whispered. "I'm not going to hurt you, Kay. I only want to love you. And you know you want me to."

I swallowed hard. "I . . . *don't* . . ."

"You don't have to be afraid," he murmured. His hand moved slowly up and down my back and it felt like sparks of electricity were shooting through me. "Nothing's going to happen that we both don't want to happen."

Our lips met and I tried to turn away, but his other hand clasped the back of my head and held it firmly in place while his lips sought mine a second time and the end of his tongue flicked over my mouth.

"No . . . Jeff," I whimpered. "No . . ."

His body felt so warm against mine. The strength of his arms crushed me to him and in another few moments I no longer could resist. We kissed long and deeply. My lips opened and his tongue slipped inside. Both his hands moved down to my buttocks and pressed in on them, while he ground slowly against me. I felt his need and I was frightened.

"Stop it. *Please*," I begged. My head was spinning dizzily. My knees felt like they were going to buckle in under me. My heart was thumping like a drum.

To my surprise, he released me and drew back. "All right, Kay," he said. "I'm not going to force you. I want you very much, and I know you want me, too. But I'm not going to rape you." He started to unbutton his shirt.

"Wh-what are you doing?"

"I'm going to let *you* make the final decision. That's the only way it will be any good."

He took off his shirt and spread it carefully on the sand like a small blanket. His strong, muscular torso glistened in the moonlight like polished bronze. He opened his belt and took off his pants. When he started to take down his shorts, too, I turned away and looked out at the silvery water in the bay. I felt so confused and frightened I didn't know what to do.

"I'm waiting for you, Kay," he said softly. I looked over my shoulder and saw him stretched out on the beach. He was naked. His discarded clothes had been neatly arranged alongside him. "When you're ready . . ."

"Jeff, *please* . . ." I whimpered.

"I want you so much, Kay." He held out his arm, his hand waiting to clasp mine and draw me down beside him. "Come. Lie with me. You know you want to."

I shook my head. I couldn't. I just couldn't. I'd never been unfaithful to Bob in all the years we'd been married. That had to mean something. I couldn't just throw away all those years of fidelity for a momentary fling with a boy young enough to be my son. Not . . . *just for fun*.

And yet . . .

I needed so badly to be loved. If only that were Bob on the sand, so strong and ready to give me what I ached for in my heart. If only I could fight that surge of feeling running through me as I looked into Jeff's eyes and saw the fever burning in them.

"Come, Kay," he whispered. "Come to me. Please?"

In spite of myself, I took a hesitant step forward.

"That's right. There's nothing to be afraid of. You know I'll be good to you. You know I'll give you everything you need."

I took another step and my hand slowly reached for his. Our fingers lightly touched and then his grip tightened, drawing me down to the sand. One last hesitant cry of fear rippled from my throat as he drew me into the warmth of his embrace, and then I surrendered myself to him completely.

Chapter 7

Guilt can be such an elusive motion. Like a mischievous imp, it appears and disappears at will. Before you do something that you know is wrong, it skips all around you like a bothersome child; and afterward its taunts and torments give you no peace. But when you need guilt the most—while you're *doing* the thing you know to be wrong—it's nowhere in sight. It vanishes completely, leaving you to your own devices.

I felt no guilt whatsoever while Jeff Wagner and I made love on the beach that night in St. Thomas. Once I lay down beside him and he took me completely, I felt only joyous rapture. I closed my eyes and clung to him with all my strength, while he brought me again and again and again to the very pinnacle of absolute joy, only to draw me back from the edge each time with a little laugh and a murmured, "Not yet."

Earlier that night I had called him a boy, but he had sworn he was a man. His lovemaking left no doubt about who was right. As I sobbed and thrashed under him, my body straining toward fulfillment, I knew without question that a *man* was in total control of me. A tender, loving man, yet one would be hard and rough when it was necessary and who knew that he was the absolute master of the situation.

It seemed that we made love for an eternity. By the

time Jeff's warm mouth pressed close to my ear and he urgently whispered, "Now, Kay! *Now*!" I had become his willing slave. Nothing else in the world mattered in those last delirious moments except the joy he was giving me and the aching need I had for even more. I would have done anything to get it.

"Oh, *yes*!" I gasped.

We clung so tightly together as our bodies fused in total release that the sweat between our skin made a wet, smacking sound when it was finally over and Jeff lifted up and away from me.

He rolled over on his side, still close to me, and panted for breath. We were both so flushed with the exhaustion of reaching absolute pleasure that neither of us could speak for several minutes. I lay on my back, looking up at the brilliant profusion of stars like diamonds in the black velvet sky, and smiled. I was remembering what Henry had said the previous night about falling in love with St. Thomas. He was right, but more so than he would ever know. I had fallen in love with the beautiful little island, but at that moment I would have sworn that I'd fallen in love *in* St. Thomas, too.

Jeff's lips grazed the side of my neck. He leaned closer and kissed his way slowly down to my shoulder blade and then onto the slope of my breast. My fingers curled tenderly through his thick black hair as he kissed a path to my nipple and slipped it inside his warm, wet mouth. He sucked on it gently for a few moments, like a satisfied baby, but his moustache tickled and I made him pull away.

His eyes were shining when they looked down at me. "Happy?" he murmured.

I sighed with contentment. "Mmmmmm. More than I

ever imagined I could be."

"Good." His smile broadened. "I'm glad. That's just how I wanted you to feel." He rubbed his palm slowly up and down my belly. "You're so beautiful, Kay," he said softly. "I can't really believe this is happening. It's too wonderful to be true."

I knew exactly how he felt. It seemed like I was dreaming. So much happiness just couldn't be real.

"So beautiful," he whispered again, as his hand slipped softly between my legs for an instant and applied a gentle pressure that made me moan.

"It's the moonlight," I said. "If you saw me in the sun, with all my sags and wrinkles and—"

He didn't let me go on. "Hey, stop it, O.K.?" His tone of voice had a soft but insistent reproach in it. "Don't always be so down on yourself. I don't like it when you talk like that. You should have more pride and self-respect."

"Jeff," I said with a little laugh, "I know how I look. It's only natural for a woman my age to be critical of herself."

"You look fantastic," he countered, "and I wish to hell you'd get over this age hangup. The way you talk, you'd think thirty-eight was one step from a rocking chair and a hearing aid. You're in the prime of your life, Kay. A woman doesn't even start to achieve her full beauty until she's forty. Why can't you see that?"

I avoided his eyes. "Maybe because I've got such a beautiful daughter who's much younger than I am."

He laughed and shook his head. "Do you think Tracey's anywhere near as beautiful as you are?"

"Don't you?" I asked.

"Of course not. As far as physical looks go, you're just about even. But what puts you miles ahead of her is the beauty you've got inside. That's a quality of beauty she won't even know anything about for years to come. It's not just what you can see in a mirror that makes a woman beautiful, you know. It's the things inside that really count."

"Like what, Jeff?"

"Like sensitivity, for one thing. And wisdom and compassion and caring about other people's feelings, for three more. I could go on making a list all night, but you know what I mean. A woman's inner beauty is made up of all the things that girls like Tracey are too young to have. She's like a kid who uses her body like a new toy. She's not really sure how it works, but she wants to have fun playing with it. She doesn't even suspect what's inside it."

"You sound like a man who's had lots of experience with older women," I said. "Have you?"

"Enough," he answered.

"Oh." I looked away, feeling a sudden and unreasonable pang of jealousy shoot through me. "Then I'm not the first."

His hand squeezed my thigh. "Does it make any difference?"

I tried to be light and flippant, but it wasn't easy. I had an unexpected catch in my throat. "No, of course not. I just didn't realize that you do this all the time. Do you think of it as something like missionary work, Jeff? Converting as many older women as you can to the truth about their inner beauty?" My voice had such a hard, bitter edge to it that I felt instantly ashamed. But the words had already been spoken and I couldn't take them back. Nor could I bring myself to apologize for having said them. They expressed what I was really feeling inside, which was a sort of betrayal and the belief that, somehow, I had been used.

"No, of course not," Jeff said softly. "As a matter of fact, you're only the second 'older woman,' as you insist on putting it, that I've ever been with."

"Oh?" Hearing there was only one other before me made my anger and jealousy subside in an instant. "I'm sorry, Jeff. I didn't mean to say what I did. It's just my insecurity, I guess. I still can't understand what you see in me, when you could have girls like Tracey just by snapping your fingers."

"I've *had* girls like Tracey," he said. "Lots of them."

"Oh?"

"And it was just like being hungry and stuffing myself full of candy. All I got out of it was a bad stomach ache. I really wasn't satisfied. I still needed something more substantial. And that's when Miss Ramsey came along."

"Miss Ramsey . . . ?"

"She was one of my pre-law instructors at Princeton," he said. "I had an affair with her during my junior year. Do you want to hear about it?"

"Only if you want to tell me," I said after a moment's hesitation. I wasn't entirely sure that I wanted to hear about him with another woman.

"I think I should. It might help you better understand the way I feel about you, if you know how I felt about her."

"All right," I said.

"Well, I was a real hell-raiser back in those days. It hadn't taken me long to find out that all the town girls from Princeton were hot for boys from the college. If you had a fast car—preferably a foreign, convertible job like my MGB—and money to spend on them, you could get as much as you wanted. I had a different girl every weekend. I used to drive into town and stop in the parking lot of a hamburger joint where they all hung out every Friday night, and in five minutes there'd be four or five of them buzzing around the car like bees drawn to honey. I'd pick the one that looked best, open the door for her, and off we'd go. Most of them would do anything I wanted. And I mean anything; not just the usual stuff. They were all so damn anxious to please because every one of them wanted to hook a 'Princeton guy' for a husband. Sometimes I'd make them do things for me that I wasn't even really in the mood for, just to see how far they'd go. I never found one who couldn't be coaxed into doing whatever I told her to, no matter how far-out it might be. I could tell you stories about things that went on with girls we smuggled into the frat house that would curl your eyebrows."

"Please, don't," I told him, as images of what Tracey might be doing while *she* was away at school flitted through my mind. "I'll use my imagination."

"Well, anything you can imagine, they did."

"It sounds like every college boy's dream."

"It was," Jeff admitted. "For a while, at least. But then I started to wonder where it was all leading. I mean, sex is great if there's something else behind it. If two people are using their bodies to express deep, intimate feelings for each other, it's the most wonderful experience in life. But with those town girls it was always just sex for its own sake. I'd pick up a girl one weekend and ball the hell out of her, and the next weekend I'd see her driving off with some other guy from school to ball like hell with *him*. It didn't mean any more to them than it did to us. We were just bodies to each other, instead of people. We were bodies that they hoped to convert into husbands; and they were bodies that we used to have fun with. We were like a bunch of look-alike rabbits all hopping around in one big cage. Sometimes I'd pick up the same girl twice, and not even know I'd been with her before until she reminded me. And usually the only reason *she* knew it was because she remembered my car, not me. It got pretty discouraging after a while."

"Yes, I could see how it might." Wasn't that exactly what I'd tried to tell Tracey the other night? There had to be something else in a sexual relationship besides physical attraction for it to have any real meaning.

"I kept telling myself that it would all be different," Jeff continued, "as soon as I met the right girl. I thought that as soon as this mysterious 'she' came along, I'd start to feel real enjoyment from sex again. Because, to tell you the truth, after a while it was all so mechanical that I got as much satisfaction from using my hand as I did from picking up one of those girls. And it was a lot less bother, too.

"Well, I looked and I looked and I looked, but if this girl was in the Princeton vicinity, she was in hiding, because I never found her. It was always the same thing. *What a swell car you've got, Jeff. I'll bet your folks have money, huh? Do you want to have some fun with me?* It was like an old record I kept hearing over and over again. The more girls I picked up, the more alike they all seemed. It got to be like a drug habit I couldn't kick. I was so desperate to find someone who'd make it all meaningful, I went through girls like a sickle cutting grain. Some weekends I had as many as four or five different ones."

"That must have done wonders for your school work," I said.

"Yeah, it did," he smiled. "It sure did. I was almost flunking out by the middle of my junior year, but it didn't seem to matter. I was obsessed with this thing about sex. I couldn't care about anything else until I got that straightened out. And that's when I met Ellen Ramsey."

"You didn't meet *her* at the hamburger stand in town, I'm sure," I said.

He laughed. "God, no! In fact, I'd seen her around campus a number of times, but never paid much attention to her. She was-well, here we go—she was older than I was and at first I wasn't interested."

"How much older, Jeff?" I asked, because I felt I had to know.

"I was nineteen; she was thirty-five."

I did a quick mental calculation. It was the same age difference that existed now between him and myself.

"She was a special instructor," he continued, "not one of the regular professors. It was her job to give special tutoring to guys who needed it, and just about that time there was no one more in need than me. I was failing everything, because I just couldn't give any time to studying. As soon as classes were over, I was hopping in my car for a ride into town.

"Well, one afternoon Mr. Langstrom, my Ethics In Government professor, sat me down after class and laid out some cold, hard facts of life. He said that if I didn't shape up soon and get hold of myself, I'd not only be flunking out of Princeton, but I'd be blowing every chance I had of getting into Harvard Law, too. Or any other good law school in the country, for that matter. He asked what the problem was, but how could I explain? How could I tell him I couldn't study because I had a case of continual hot pants? I made up some excuse about not being able to grasp the material, and he suggested that I spend some time getting special tutoring from Miss Ramsey.

"I didn't like the idea at first. It meant cutting two or three hours every other night from my adventures in town, but after a while I was finding it wasn't so important. I was really starting to enjoy studying again."

"Because of Miss Ramsey?" I said. "She must have been an exceptional teacher, to take your mind off sex and put it back into law books!"

"She was," Jeff said. "She was a great teacher, but it wasn't just that. All my other professors were great teachers, too, and it hadn't made any difference. No, I found out that a person can only learn when he *wants* to learn. And Ellen Ramsey made me want to learn."

"How?" I asked.

"I guess by giving me a sense of my own worth," Jeff said. "She made me feel that I had a good, legal mind to start with, and all I needed was a little help from her to encourage it. She had such confidence in my ability — even more than *I* had at the time — that I started studying again just so she wouldn't be disappointed in me. I wanted to live up to the standards she set, and that's the best encouragement for anyone. If you make someone believe that he really can do something, then give him the chance to prove it, nine times out of ten it'll work. At least it did with Ellen and me. By the end of the semester, I'd pulled all my grades up to the passing level and by the end of the year I was straight-A again."

"But . . ." I looked at him with a smile as his hand moved slowly up and down my leg. "That doesn't explain how you had an affair with her. Surely she didn't go to bed with you as a reward for passing your courses."

Jeff laughed. "No. Nothing like that. In fact, going to bed with me wasn't Ellen's idea at all; it was mine. And she resisted for a long, long time before it eventually happened."

More than I did, I wondered?

"As soon as I got back my respect for myself," he went on, "I started to fall in love with her. It's like that old fable about the statue coming to life and falling in love with its creator, you know? She made me feel like such a worthwhile person, that I began to realize how worthwhile *she* was. I admired everything about her. She had such style and intelligence and, more than that, such a sense of herself as a person. I wanted to learn all I could from her. Not just about law and government, but *life*. She seemed to have all the answers. She knew about music and art and literature that I'd only skimmed through in my English lit classes because it was required reading. After we got through with one of our sessions at her apartment on campus, she'd fix tea and we'd talk for more time than we'd spent in the tutoring session. About a picture she had on her wall, for instance. Or an opera record she put on the stereo. She seemed to glad to share it all with me, too. That was the important thing. She wanted to share everything she knew about life, like a person giving food to someone else who's hungry. I guess it was only natural that I started thinking about sharing her bed, too.

"She was a beautiful woman. Not stunning looking. I don't mean that. Some of the guys I talked to about her didn't even think she was pretty, and maybe she wasn't. Not in the conventional sense. But by the time I wanted to sleep with her, I wasn't looking at just the outside. I was seeing all the beauty she had inside, too, and I wanted her like I'd never wanted any of those empty-headed, spreadlegged girls from town. When we finally did go to bed together, I felt so clumsy and inadequate that you'd have thought it was my first time. I'm sure *she* did," he said with a smile. "And who knows? Maybe it was. At least it was the first time it really counted. When I made love to her, I felt like we were sharing something so much deeper than sex that the movements of our bodies hardly mattered. It was the giving and taking of ourselves that was so fantastic. She made me feel like a man for the very first time. A *real* man, I mean. In the sense that I was communing with a real woman."

"It sounds as if it must have been a wonderful experience, Jeff," I said softly. But I couldn't help wondering how he could compare it to whatever feelings he might have for me. What could I ever teach him about life, when I felt so helplessly naive myself? If anything, it was more like a reversal of the situation he'd described with his teacher, when I thought of him and me together. *I* was the one who knew so little and had so much to learn this time.

"It *was* wonderful," he said. He dug into his shirt pocket for cigarettes and offered one to me, then lit them both before continuing. "It opened my eyes about so many things. I'm a far different person today than I'd ever have been without Ellen. She turned my whole life around and put it back on the right course."

"It sounds like you fell in love with her."

He drew in on his cigarette and slowly exhaled the smoke before answering, "I did. I could have spent the rest of my life with her, if she'd let me."

"What happened?"

"I guess I was too much in love," he said. "I got too dependent on her, and it wasn't good."

"But isn't that what love is?" I asked. "Two people depending on one another for their needs?"

"Sure," Jeff admitted. "To a certain extent. But only when they're both still growing and developing as separate individuals. Only when they're both still giving, as well as taking. And I'd have been happy to stay exactly as I was forever, while Ellen knew that I still had a lot of independent growth ahead of me that I wouldn't do if she allowed the status to remain quo. And she was right, too. As long as I knew I had her to count on when the going was rough, I didn't have to do anything to make it any easier on my own. It was like hiding in the safety of the womb, if you'll pardon the image. As long as I had her to fall back on, I didn't have to take any chances on my own. I didn't have to *dare*.

"She knew this, and that's why she broke it off. When I came back to Princeton for my senior year, after a summer at home thinking about nothing but her, she was gone. She'd applied for a job at William and Mary, and when she was accepted she'd transferred there. I didn't even find out where she'd gone until two months after the start of the semester." He took another long pull on his cigarette.

"I wrote her a long, pleading letter, asking if I could come down and see her for a weekend. She never answered. Then I wrote her a long, angry letter, demanding to know why she'd done such a terrible thing to me. Why she'd broken my heart and ruined my life. Know what she wrote back?"

"What?" I asked.

"Just one sentence. '*So your heart will be stronger and your life your own, dear Jeff.*' That's all she wrote. It took me quite some time to understand what she meant, but now that I do, I know she was right. With the attitude I had then, we'd never have been happy together. I was too dependent. I wanted to take too much from her, without giving anything of myself. I think if we were to meet again for the first time today, though, it would be a different story. I'm ready now for the kind of relationship I couldn't have handled back then."

I couldn't face him as I asked, "And just how do I fit into things, Jeff?"

"You're not that different from Ellen Ramsey," he said. "From the first time I saw you, I knew you were a woman who also had a lot to share with someone."

"But I already *have* someone," I said. "I have my husband—"

He shook his head and smiled. "You know as well as I do by now that I'm talking about something completely different than what you have with him. If you felt completely satisfied with your marriage, if you were getting everything from it that you need, we wouldn't be here together like this right now. You'd have no need of any other man, if the one you're married to completely satisfied you. And you know I'm not just talking about sex. What happened between you and me a few minutes ago was much more than sex. It was sharing, Kay, and that's something you haven't had in your life for some time, I'll bet. Am I right?"

I couldn't answer him in words. I could only nod my head slowly. Long ago, when we were first married, it had seem that Bob and I shared everything in our lives together, but now it was only tangible, physical things. The house. The car. The joint checking account. Things that really didn't matter, because they were outside each of us as people. Those inner, more important things were never shared any more.

Jeff stubbed his half-smoked cigarette out in the sand,

then reached for mine and extinguished it, too. His hand softly stroked my breasts and belly as he moved nearer.

"You're like a winter rose, Kay," he said softly.

"A what—?"

"A winter rose," he repeated. "There's a beautiful flower inside you that wants to blossom, but there's too much cold all around you. The climate isn't right, and you're withering on the bush without ever having the chance to show the world how truly beautiful you are."

"Oh, Jeff." My eyes were suddenly moist with the quick rush of tears.

"Let me help you to blossom, Kay," he said, as he kissed my breasts one after the other and slowly swung his body back onto mine. "Let me show you how beautiful a winter rose can be when it's given the chance to flower."

My arms curled around his back, and when his lips touched mine they were open and ready for the gentle probing of his tongue. My body stirred when he touched me, and my excitement quickened. We were still damp from the heat of our first lovemaking, but I wanted him again as much as he wanted me. I wanted him to make all those beautiful things he'd just said come true. I wanted to flower and blossom, if only I knew how. If only he were truly able to make it happen, I felt I could love him forever.

"Please," I whispered. "Please, Jeff, please."

"I will," he promised.

I closed my eyes, just seconds before I knew he would be mine again, but suddenly Jeff tensed. He pulled back and muttered something that sounded like a curse under his breath. I looked up and saw there was suddenly light all around us. Bright light, from the headlights of a car in the dirt lane leading down to the beach.

"Who is it?" I gasped in fear. I reached for my discarded dress and held it in front of me as my eyes blinked in the blinding glare.

"Well, you were worried about the cab driver not coming back for us," he said. "I guess that ten dollars I promised him did the trick, all right."

"Is it that late already?" I glanced down at my watch. The driver was early, but not by much. Jeff and I had been together almost two hours, but it seemed more like as many minutes. The sound of Tracey's voice echoed in my head. *See how time flies when you're having fun?* But this was more than that. It wasn't just fun.

"Hello, Mister?" a voice called from the darkness beyond the headlights. "Are you ready to go back to town now?"

"All right! All right!" Jeff shouted angrily. "We'll be ready in a minute. Just go on back and wait in the car."

"Okay, Mister," the dark voice called back, and I could have sworn there was a hint of laughter in its tone. "You're the boss."

We got dressed as quickly as we could, and while I was putting on my clothes I felt a heavy shroud of guilt weighing me down. Everything had been so beautiful when it was just Jeff and me alone on the beach. With the stars overhead and the quiet murmur of the sea lapping against the shore, we could have been alone in creation for all it mattered. But now the rest of the world had invaded our sanctuary in the form of a taxi with bright lights and a driver whose eyes had seen us and quickly assimilated what they saw.

I kept my head bent low, avoiding the direct confrontation with those burning lights, while Jeff and I walked hand-in-hand back to the taxi. I felt embarrassed about having the driver see us holding hands, but Jeff's fingers wouldn't let mine go. It was as though he didn't care what the driver or anyone else in the world thought about us; he was determined not to break the wonderful bond between us.

"You're early," he barked when we got into the cab. "I told you to come back for us in two hours."

"Sorry, Mister," the driver said with the same gleeful sound just barely hidden in his voice. I glanced up and caught the reflection of his dark eyes in the rearview mirror. "Sorry, Missus," he said, and the quick wink he gave me made me cringe in shame beside Jeff all the way back to the harbor.

We caught the last launch back to the ship, with five minutes at the most to spare. There were few other passengers returning from shore at that hour, and no one that either of us knew, but I still felt guilty and embarrassed about letting Jeff hold my hand in the back of the little motorboat. Every time someone turned around for a last look at the glittering waterfront in the distance, I felt they were looking at us. I felt that everyone in the world must have seen what the cab driver saw on the beach, and everyone knew what he knew. Jeff was quick to notice the change in me.

"What's wrong?" he asked, a few minutes before the launch reached the *Ocean Queen*. "Why so tense all of a sudden."

"That taxi driver," I whispered. "He—he *saw* us, Jeff. He knew what we were doing."

"So?" he shrugged. "Does it matter that much? You're never going to see him again, so who cares?"

I knew he was right, but somehow I couldn't help feeling that it did matter. Very much. We rode the rest of the way to the ship in silence.

Chapter 8

I'd hoped that Tracey wouldn't be in the cabin when I returned, but as soon as I put my key in the lock I heard her call from the other side.

"Mother? Is that you?"

"Yes, it's me," I sighed, as I opened the door and went in. "Who else were you expecting?" My nostrils prickled suddenly, almost as though in answer to the question. There was a strange scent in the air, and it grew stronger as I walked from the sitting room through to the bedroom. The air bristled with the familiar smell of a man's cologne. I was positive I had smelled it before. But where? On whom? And then I realized. Of course. It was the smell of Mr. Taylor's cologne, deep and musky. It was unmistakeable.

"Did you have a good time?" Tracey asked. She was sitting up in bed, doing her nails.

I shot her a sharp, reproaching glare. "Did *you?*"

"What's that supposed to mean?" she asked, blinking in wide-eyed innocence.

"Tracey, who was in here tonight with you?"

She gave me a blank look in answer.

"Who did you have in this bedroom?" I demanded. As if I didn't already know.

"No one, Mother," she insisted.

"Don't lie to me, young lady. Mr. Taylor was here,

wasn't he?"

"Michael. . .?" She laughed, a bit nervously I thought. "No, of course not! Why would he—?"

I didn't let her finish. "That's why you wanted to come back here alone, isn't it? You weren't fooling me by pretending you had menstrual cramps. I happen to know you had your period last week. The least you could have done would be to invent a better excuse than that."

"Mother—!"

"I *knew* it would turn out like this," I fumed. "I just *knew* it was going to be more trouble than it was worth to come on this trip with you instead of your father. We should have both stayed home and let the tickets go to waste. It would have been better than—than *this*, at least."

"Than *what?*" Tracey protested. "Mother, I don't know what you're talking about."

"I'm talking about you sleeping with Mr. Taylor," I snapped.

"Mother—!"

"Couldn't you have had the decency to do it in *his* cabin? Did you have to do it right here—in the bedroom *I* have to sleep in, too? Did you have to flaunt it in my face, like—like a little whore?"

Her face suddenly crumbled like plaster turning to dust.

"I didn't sleep with Mr. Taylor," she said, her voice cracking with barely suppressed sobs. "Not tonight . . . not ever."

"Then why is the room reeking of his cologne?" I argued. "Don't be a liar along with the rest."

Tracey defiantly wiped the back of her hand across both eyes and confronted me. "The room smells like this because Henry doused himself with cologne he bought in town this afternoon," she spat, "and he came down here earlier with Florence to see that I was all right."

I swallowed hard. "Henry. . .?"

"He admired Michael's cologne the other night in the lounge while we were all watching the show, and asked him where he got it. He couldn't wait to try it out on himself when he bought some. He came down here like the big clown he is and asked if I thought it made him look twenty years younger. Big joke, huh, Mother? Except the laugh's on *you*. It was Michael's cologne you smelled, all right, but it was on the wrong man."

I sat on the edge of my bed, feeling like my legs wouldn't support me any longer if I kept standing. Why had I jumped down her throat like that . . . called her such an awful name . . . for no other reason than suspicion? A smell in the air? I'd never dreamed I could say such things to Tracey, but once I'd started I hadn't been in control of my tongue. It was like I was accusing her of everything I was secretly feeling—yes, I had to admit it—about myself.

"Oh, honey," I began. "I didn't mean—" But she wouldn't let me finish.

"And just in case you're wondering, Mother," she cracked, "Florence was here all the while Henry was showing off his cologne. I didn't sleep with *him*, either."

"Oh, baby—"

She turned away from me, putting her bottle of nail polish back in the bedside drawer with such a clatter I was surprised it didn't break. She was genuinely angry with me, and who could blame her? I deserved whatever righteous indignation she might be feeling.

"I'm sorry," I said. "I guess I shouldn't have jumped to such a conclusion, but—"

"No, you shouldn't have, Mother. All kinds of wrong impressions come from jumped conclusions. For instance, I might wonder why the back of your dress is all covered with sand and jump to the wrong conclusion about *that*."

Dear God! Was it? My heart leaped into my throat, and it was all I could do to keep from brushing my back.

"Of course I *know* nothing could have happened between you and Jeff," she continued. "Knowing the way *he* is, that would be a physical impossibility. I'm sure the sand must have been on the seat in the launch."

"Of course it was!" I said quickly. Perhaps too quickly. Tracey looked over at me and her eyes held a moment's suspicion before discarding the thought.

"I know that. But you walk in here and smell cologne, and right away you're calling me a whore. Well, it might interest you to know that after the talk we had the other night, I'd decided *not* to sleep with Michael, after all. Now I'm not so sure I won't, if he asks me. Maybe I'll even ask him. Why not? After all, why be hung for the crime if you don't enjoy any of the pleasure of committing it?"

"Tracey, please listen to me," I begged. "I'm sorry. I didn't mean to yell at you like that, and I certainly didn't mean to call you a—a whore. I'm just overly tired, I guess. It's been such a long, tiring day and my head is throbbing."

"It's been a long day for me, too," she said, not giving an inch to ease my conscience. "And I think I've had my fill of the Wagner family for quite some time. All day listening to Henry drone on about the history of the island, like he was some kind of authority on it instead of a half-baked tourist himself, and hearing Florence cluck about this, that, and everything else under the sun. I'm fed up with all of them. *That's* why I wanted to come back to the ship alone. I couldn't stand the thought of spending another minute with them. I wish now, though, that I *had* come back to sleep with Michael. Believe me, I won't miss my opportunity the next time."

"Maybe we should both stay away from the Wagners for a while," I said. "They might be getting on both our nerves more than we realize."

"Do what you want to, Mother," she muttered, as she turned off the light above her head. "I don't care."

"Why don't we order breakfast in the room tomorrow then?" I suggested. "The steward said there'd be no problem about it. Should we do that, honey?"

"It really doesn't matter to me *what* you do, Mother," she said. "Now if you don't mind, I'd like to get some sleep."

"Of course, dear," I said. "And once again, I'm very sorry."

"It's all right, Mother," she sighed, but I knew it wasn't. Nor would it be for some time afterward. I'd hurt her more than I realized, and scars of that nature take more than a simple *I'm sorry* to heal them.

I undressed and went into the bathroom for a quick shower. My skin felt gritty with sand and dried sweat, but I didn't feel much cleaner when I came out and crawled into bed. I felt dirty inside, where soap couldn't reach.

I may not have felt much guilt while Jeff and I were making love, but I felt plenty of it now. It danced through my head like a tune you can't get rid of. How could I have let such a thing happen? After all those years of marriage, how could I have thrown myself at the first boy who wanted to take me to bed? *Because Bob doesn't want to,* the voice of self-justification whispered. How could I have thought it would ever lead to anything more than a few minutes of fleeting pleasure—and why would I ever *want* it to lead to anything else? *Because you know your marriage is crumbling,* the voice argued. *It's only a matter of time before it falls apart completely.*

I couldn't let myself believe it. The thought of breaking up with Bob was too horrible to contemplate. What would I do without him? Where would I go? How would I live?

I tossed restlessly in the bed, trying to fight even the idea of such a thing happening from my mind. There wasn't anything really wrong with my marriage. We just needed a little time to make the adjustment to being on our own again, now that Tracey was away at college. *It's been three years; how long will it take?* the voice whispered.

It was only natural that we had problems. All married couples did, but they found some way of working them out. Maybe these two weeks away from each other would make a difference. Absence makes the heart grow fonder, and all that? *Don't count on it,* the voice murmured. *You've been apart before, and it hasn't made the slightest difference.*

Maybe we needed to talk to a marriage counsellor. Someone who could look at the problem in an impersonal, professional way and come up with a solution. *So, you admit there is a problem?*

I closed my eyes and tried to think of all the happy times Bob and I had had together, and what I could do to bring them back. If only I could find that point in the road where he'd turned in one direction and I'd gone in the other, I thought. If only I knew where and when the two paths would converge again and we could continue the rest of the way side-by-side. Like Florence and Henry. *But you've never been like them,* that nagging voice whispered. *How can you expect to return to a situation that never existed in the first place? Face it, Kay, your marriage has failed and there's nothing you can do to make it right again.*

I refused to believe it. For one thing, I could put Jeff Wagner out of my life before anything more happened between us. His presence was only confusing the issue, like a joker thrown into the pack unexpectedly when a serious game of cards was being played. It would serve no earthly good for me to sleep with him again, no matter how great a need I might feel for love. There was only one man in the world who had the right to love me, and that was my husband. No wonder I'd flown off the handle to such a degree with Tracey. I'd seen myself in the way I'd imagined her to be, and the picture hadn't pleased me at all. As I drifted off to sleep, I vowed that what had happened with Jeff that night would never happen again.

Keeping that promise, however, proved far more difficult than I ever imagined. He wasn't about to let me go that easily.

Tracey and I didn't go down to breakfast the next morning. We ordered from the menu in the sitting room's desk drawer and ate alone together. Though I tried to talk and laugh as though nothing had happened last night, Tracey's attitude was decidedly cool. She was still angry with me, and I honestly couldn't blame her. I still hadn't forgiven myself for pawning my own sins off on her, like a two-faced hypocrite.

A little while after we finished eating, there was a knock on the stateroom door and I heard Florence calling my name, but I pretended I didn't hear. I was too embarrassed about Jeff and me to face her so soon afterwards, too.

"Would you like me to roll up your hair and set it?" I asked Tracey. We'd been restlessly pacing the cabin like two caged tigers trying not to get in each other's way.

"No, Mother," she said. "Thanks anyway. I thought I'd go down to the salon and see what they can do with it."

"Oh, why waste the money?" I said. I moved closer and touched her shoulder, but she pulled away. "I always used to do a nice job with your hair when you were a little girl, didn't I?"

"Yes," she said, her voice icy cool, "but remember? I'm not your little girl any more. I think I'd rather let a professional do it."

"All right, honey," I sighed. I'd tried my best to make up with her; I wasn't going to get down on my knees and grovel.

Some time after she went down to the ship's beauty salon, there was another knock on the door. I thought at first it was Florence again and I was determined not to answer until I felt ready to face her without a guilty look in my eyes, but then I realized it must be the steward come back for the breakfast table he'd brought earlier. I hurried to answer the knock, opened the door, and confronted Jeff.

"We were starting to think you'd fallen overboard during the night!" he said with a grin. "Where were you and Tracey at breakfast?"

"We—decided we'd rather have it up here," I said.

He smiled. "Breakfast in bed, hmmmm? Am I too late for some myself?"

I knew what he meant, but I answered him as though he'd asked the question seriously. "Yes, you are. In fact, I thought you were the steward for the dishes."

"Can't I come in anyway?"

I tried to hold back the door, but he forced it open and came into the stateroom. "Jeff, please," I said. "I'm alone and—"

"Yes, I know. I saw Tracey heading for the beauty parlor and I figured we'd have at least an hour." He reached for me and took me in his arms against my will. "Be nice to do it in a bed, huh?" he murmured, running the end of his tongue slowly down my neck. "Not that the sand was so bad—"

"Jeff, *stop* it!" I pushed him away and tried not to look at the startled, uncomprehending expression on his face.

"What's all this about?" he said.

I pulled the sides of my robe tighter together and reached for a cigarette. "What happened between us last night can't happen again, Jeff," I said. I blew a cloud of smoke through my nose and kept my back turned to him. "It was wrong. I'm sorry it ever happened. If I had it to do over—"

"You'd do it all again," he interrupted. "And so would I." His hands tried to turn me, but I wouldn't budge. "Hey, come on," he murmured. "I know what you're feeling. You've got a bad case of morning-after guilt. It's only natural. What happened last night is a big change in both our lives, and I expected you to look at it a little differently in the sun instead of the moonlight. But, Kay, it only *seems* different. Nothing's really changed. We still feel the same way about each other, don't we?"

I took a deep breath, summoning all my courage. "No, Jeff. At least I don't. You caught me with my guard down last night. I was weak and you took advantage of it. But I'm stronger now. More in control of myself. It won't happen again."

"Yes it will." His arms were slipping around my waist, his hands reaching for my breasts through the open front of my robe.

"*Stop* it, Jeff! This can't go any further than it already has."

"Why not?"

"Because I'm not some giddy school girl or some lonely old maid desperately looking for a shipboard romance. I'm a married woman with a daughter who's almost your age."

"Oh, Jesus!" he groaned. "*That* again? I thought we settled all that last night? I told you, your age doesn't make any difference to me. If Tracey were like you, instead of the way she is, I'd gladly leave you alone and start chasing her. But she's not. And no other girl I've met in the past three years *is* like you."

"Don't you mean like Miss Ramsey?" I said.

"Oh, boy," he sighed. "Is that what you're thinking now? That poor little Jeff had a crush on his teacher and he's still not over it, so now he's picking on you?"

"You said it, not me."

"Dammit, Kay, I *love* you!" he swore. "Doesn't that make any difference?"

"Maybe it would if I knew why. . ."

"Does there have to be a reason for everything? Some things just happen because that's how they were meant to be. We've got no control over them."

"We do, if we try hard enough," I said.

"Well, I'm not trying. If you want to think of what I feel for you as an adolescent's crush or a shipboard romance or whatever, then okay. But why not give in to it? The damage has already been done; I've already slept with you. Doing it again isn't going to make the first time any less real, is it? If you want to think of it as a frivolous fling, why not go all the way with it? Why cut it short so soon? Why not let it run its full course?"

"Because someone's bound to get hurt, Jeff," I insisted.

"Who? Surely not you. At least as far as you tell me, you're happily married. You don't want an involvement with me, because you've got your husband and your family responsibilities. Okay, fine. But you still need loving, Kay. There's no way in the world you'll ever make me believe you don't. Not after the way you clung to me last night. So why not let me love you? When this cruise is over, you can go right back to your nice husband and your nice house in New Jersey and forget any of this ever happened. Except, of course," he added, "on those cold, lonely nights when your husband still isn't giving you any love, and you start thinking about me again. But that might be a long while off. Why not have fun while you can, if it's not going to make any difference to your marriage?"

"Because it *will* make a difference, Jeff, and you know it."

"How? If you love him, and he loves you, how could I ever get in the way of it?"

I knew I couldn't answer him, and he knew it, too. It would make a great difference, going back to Bob, if I allowed myself to go any further with this boy. It would be like coming in out of the cold to the warmth and splendor of a hearty banquet, then being expelled again just when you were getting used to feeling full and warm and happy again. No, I couldn't let it continue.

"What about you, Jeff?" I asked. "Even if I did go along with it, wouldn't *you* be hurt when it comes to an end?"

"I'll be hurt as it is, if you end it now," he said simply. "So what difference will a little more pain make? At least I'll have the memory of having loved you a few more times." His hands reached for my breasts again and his mouth nuzzled the back of my neck. "Please, Kay? Let's forget that everything else in the world exists except you and me, here and now. Life is too short for us to deny ourselves happiness when it comes along. We should grab it and hold onto it for as long as we can, because there's precious little enough of it to go around as it is." He kissed me softly, gently, moving his lips down from my neck to my shoulders. His fingers squeezed lightly through my robe, then slipped inside to caress the naked flesh.

I felt myself starting to tingle once again from the nearness of his body and the remembered pleasure he had given me last night. It had to be like drinking seawater, I thought. The more you have, the more you need, but it never really quenches your thirst.

"Jeff, *no*..."

He was opening my robe. Slipping it off my shoulders and letting it fall in a soft puddle of velvet to the floor. He moved slowly around me, his hands stroking my body as if he were soothing a frightened bird that might up and fly away at any instant.

"Something this wonderful shouldn't end so quickly, Kay," he said. "I won't let it end. Not yet."

He bent his head and kissed my breasts each in turn, then began to suck on my nipples with a gentle but insistent pressure that soon had them erecting between his lips. When his hand slid down my body and touched between my legs, I thought I would die with re-awakened need. I wanted him just as badly, just as desperately, as I had last night on the beach. I trembled with desire as his warm, soft lips moved slowly down to my belly . . . and then further.

"*Jeff!*" I gasped in surprise and pulled his head away. My cheeks flushed scarlet with shame and embarrassment. I had never been kissed like that before; not even by Bob. We didn't do such things.

"I'll do anything for you, Kay," Jeff whispered, looking up at me with pleading in his eyes. "Anything you want. Whatever you need. Just tell me, and I'll do it. All I want is to make you happy."

He bent forward and kissed me the same way again. My fingers tightened in his hair, trying to pull him back, but he wouldn't stop. His tongue felt like hot strokes of lightning on my quivering flesh.

After a few minutes, he got back to his feet and took my hand. He started to lead me toward the open bedroom door and the waiting bed.

"Come with me, Kay," he pleaded. "I won't ever make you sorry. You won't regret loving me, I swear it."

I wanted to believe him. I needed to believe him. It was the only thing that made me grasp his hand a little tighter and, after a moment's hesitation, follow him into the bedroom and close the door.

The *Ocean Queen* docked in Martinique two days later. It was a lovely island in its way, with a magnificent harbor and a wide, curving bay backed by lush greenery, but I couldn't summon the same emotional feelings for it as I had for St. Thomas. Perhaps because of Jeff and what had happened there, St. Thomas would always hold a special place in my heart that no other island could touch.

The Wagners and I went ashore to visit Fort-de-France the morning we arrived, but Tracey pleaded a headache and stayed aboard ship. I knew she was still sulking and trying to avoid contact with the Wagners, but it was just as well. She didn't miss much.

With such a romantic-sounding name as Martinique, I had imagined the island would be aglow with native French charm and picturesque locales. Sadly, it wasn't. The capital city itself was something of a shock after the small-town coziness of Charlotte Amalie. Fort-de-France was a bustling, jam-packed, active little metropolis, with little to offer in the way of island tranquility. Most of the buildings were run-down and frowsily decrepit, rather than charming, and there was little to see of any historical significance. The harbor, with its flotilla of sails and yacht masts, was the only impressive sight I bothered to capture with my camera.

We strolled through the crafts museum for a while; looked at a few public monuments—including a statue of the Empress Josephine, who Henry informed me had been born on the island; picked up a souvenir or two just for the sake of having been there; and struggled valiantly to order drinks at a little café from a waiter who quite pointedly and rudely let us know he did not speak English and had no desire to pick up even the few words that would have been necessary to give us courteous service.

"Well," Henry muttered, as we headed back to the harbor, "It's nice to know the French are still the French. No matter where in the world they go, they're still as rude as they've always been."

"The next time we take this cruise," Florence swore, "we won't even bother getting off the ship when it stops here. They can have their island, for all I care." She was clearly as offended by the waiter's behavior as her husband was. They were both ready to take the next launch back to the ship. I would have joined them, but Jeff insisted that I stay ashore and take a tour up into the mountains with him instead.

He had never been to Martinique, and he explained that he wanted to see the site of the famous volcanic eruption that had taken place there just after the turn of the century. He didn't want to go on the tour alone, and since I had never seen it, either, Florence and Henry urged me to accompany him.

"It's worth a look, I guess," Henry conceded, though it was plain by his seething anger that he wouldn't have minded in the least if another eruption were to finish off the rest of the island as soon as our ship sailed.

Jeff and I bought tickets at the local tourist bureau, and in a little while we were headed up into the mountains, past broad pineapple fields and lush fern forests, to see where Mont Pelée had blown its top. On the way, a charming, coffee-colored girl gave all the passengers on the bus some background information on the disaster, first in French and then, for our benefit, in English.

In 1902, she explained, the city of Saint-Pierre had been a bustling, commercial seaport center of some forty thousand inhabitants. It lay beside the sea, at the foot of the volcano, until one morning in May when, quite unexpectedly, it ceased to exist. Mont Pelée had been rumbling and sputtering for some time previously, but so had other volcanoes on neighboring islands and no one was overly concerned about a full-scale eruption. The governor of Martinique had even come up from Fort-de-France to assure the residents of Saint-Pierre there was no cause for undue alarm.

On the morning of May eighth, as the town slowly woke up and began to go about its ordinary business, the volcano exploded. It wasn't lava that spewed down on the town by the sea. Instead, a blazing avalanche of gas and flame engulfed the city in a matter of mere minutes and burned it to cinders. Only one of the dozens of ships in the busy harbor was not destroyed. And of the forty thousand residents, only one escaped—a Negro laborer named Cyparis, who had been in jail at the time. Though he, too, was badly burned, he survived the holocaust and went on to become a prized exhibit in circus side shows as the man who cheated death of its last victim.

After the eruption, the guide explained, there was talk of abandoning the entire island. But in time, people began to resettle on the very site of the disaster and a new Saint-Pierre was born, though nowhere near as large or as commercially important as the first. The volcano, she assured us, was now calm and still, its summit ringed by innocent white clouds.

Hearing about the disaster was one thing, though, and actually touring its ruins was quite another. I felt sick at heart as Jeff and I went through the little museum that had been built as a memorial to those who died. Many of the exhibits were so simple and dealt with the disaster in such basic human terms they were heartrending. Bits of charred clothing; blackened bones from unidentifiable corpses; a child's toy; burnt pottery and household utensils; a trumpet that the severe blast of heat had melted to the shape of a pretzel. After a while I couldn't look at any more and asked Jeff to take me outside. I clutched tightly at his hand as we walked around to the side of the museum and sat on a grassy slope overlooking the sea. He lit cigarettes for us both and we smoked in silence for quite some time before speaking. We had both been profoundly shaken by the experience. So much so, in fact, that I couldn't help wondering if bringing me there hadn't been another of his plans.

"Jeff?" I asked.

"Mmmm?"

"Did you have a special reason for bringing me here?"

He looked at me in surprise. "No. None at all. I just wanted to see what it was like. Now that I know, I'm not so sure I wouldn't have been better off *not* knowing."

"I'm glad we came," I told him. I reached for his hand again and squeezed it hard. "It's made me do a lot of thinking about things I never considered before."

"Oh? Such as?"

"How fleeting life is, for one thing," I said. "All those people, forty *thousand* of them, going about their business, just like always, thinking they had the rest of their lives ahead of them. And then, in less than five minutes, they all were dead. Time had run out for them before they even knew what had happened. They had no time to hug their children and tell them they loved them; no chance to make up with their husbands or their wives for little fights they may have had the night before; no last meal; no final pleasure; just—nothing. One minute they were alive, the next they were facts in a history book."

"It was horrible, yes," he said. I thought he was

starting to see the point I was driving at. "And it could happen to any of us. Any time. Anywhere."

"That's what you meant the other night about life being too short to deny ourselves happiness, isn't it?" I said softly.

He nodded his head. "Think of all these people. How differently they might have spent their last night if they'd only known there wouldn't be another. All the wasted opportunities; all the dreams that never had a chance to come true."

An idea was slowly forming in the back of my mind. An idea for a book, about just the things we were discussing. What it must have been like in Saint-Pierre during those last hours of May, 1902. What a poignant book it could make. I told Jeff that I wished I could write it.

"Why don't you?" he said. I had to look at his face to be sure he wasn't joking.

"*Me?*" I had to laugh. "No, it's too great a story for *me* to ever write. It will have to be told by someone with a lot more skill than I could ever muster."

"How do you know, until you try?" he insisted.

"I just know me," I said. "I know what I'm capable of and what I'm not. When it comes to making beds and fixing breakfasts in a hurry, I'm a whiz. But writing books like that—? Never, I'm afraid."

"There you go again," he said. "Putting yourself down. Have you ever tried to write a book?"

"No."

"Then don't say you can't do it until you've tried. You might fail, of course. We all run the risk of failure every time we set out to do something new. But not even making the attempt is certain failure, isn't it?"

"Okay," I laughed. "You win. As soon as I get

home, I'll buy a portable typewriter and get started!"

"I wish you were serious about that," he said.

"Who knows? Maybe I am."

He put his arm around me and drew me closer. His lips brushed the side of my cheek and his hand squeezed my breast. "Try it, Kay," he said. "I know you can do it. Even if you don't think you can do it, I do. Anyone who has the sensitivity to shed tears over a burnt, broken toy as you did back there in the museum has the sensitivity to tell a story about this place and what happened here. Try it; you'll see I'm right, I'll bet."

I dropped my cigarette and answered his embrace as he drew me to him. At that moment I felt I could do anything. Build bridges. Leap tall buildings in a single bound. Write books. Love him.

Life was so precious, it was a sin to waste even a single moment of it. I hadn't felt truly alive for more years than I cared to count. I'd just existed. Moved from day to day without any real direction or purpose, while time ticked away and there was less and less of my life still to be meaningfully used. If I could only believe that Jeff's faith in me was justified. If I could only make something of myself—

The sudden sound of childish laughter close behind us startled us both. Still in Jeff's embrace, I looked over my shoulder and saw three little children staring at us. For a moment I didn't recognize them. Not until I heard their mother's voice calling them and saw Mrs. Jacobs round the corner of the museum. She looked as startled as I did when our eyes met. For a moment she just stared at Jeff and me, as though she was unable to remember exactly where she'd seen me before. Then a frown creased her brow and she called to her three children.

"Tommy! Mike! Get over here! You, too, Lucy! Do you hear me? Right now!"

"Look at the man and the lady!" one of the little boys giggled. "They're kissing!"

"Yeah!" the other little boy chimed in. "And the man had his hand inside the lady's blouse, too! You should've seen, Mom. He had it in up to *here!*" He measured for her on his own arm.

"Get over here!" Mrs. Jacobs shouted. "Didn't I tell you not to wander off without me?" She dealt each of the children a crack across the back as they filed in around her. "Now go back to the front of the building and wait for me there. Your father's been looking all over for you. Stay right there, do you hear?"

The children scampered around the side of the museum and for a moment Mrs. Jacobs didn't move. She seemed to be gathering her indignation for the torrent of abuse that soon came tumbling out of her. I hadn't even seen the Jacobses on the tour bus, or suspected that anyone else from the ship was within miles of Jeff and me. Now, as Mrs. Jacobs stepped slowly toward us, I shrugged his arm from my shoulders and got to my feet.

"Mrs. Lawrence," the woman began, "what you do with your life is your own business. However, when there are innocent children around, I wish you would have the decency to restrain yourself from making a public display."

"Who is this woman?" Jeff demanded. I motioned for him to be quiet.

"I'm sorry," I said. "I had no idea your children were here, Mrs. Jacobs. But I assure you, I was not making a 'public display' of myself."

"No?" She made a snorting sound through her nose.

"It looked like one from what *I* could see. God only knows what the children saw."

"There was nothing happening," I swore. My throat ached as I talked and I felt so upset I easily could have burst into tears, were it not for the fact that I didn't want to give her the satisfaction.

"Mrs. Lawrence was deeply upset by the exhibits in the museum," Jeff said, as he rose to stand beside me. "I was only trying to comfort her."

Mrs. Jacobs eyed us both with a contemptuous sneer. "By sticking your hand inside her blouse?" she snorted. Then, aping her son, she added, "Up to here?"

"Look, who the hell are you, anyway?" he snarled.

"I'm a decent, respectable woman with a family I care very much about," she said. "Which is more than can be said of *some* people, it appears. My husband and I may not have the money to travel first class, but we know how to behave in public. Which is *also* more than can be said of some people." With a final snort and a last, self-righteous tilt of her head, she turned and hurried after her children.

"What the hell was all *that* about?" Jeff asked. He looked as though he didn't know whether to laugh or explode in anger. "Who *was* that old battle axe?"

"She's a woman from the ship," I said. I felt like someone had just pulled a plug inside me and all my strength had gone down the drain. "Tracey and I ran into her a few times, that's all."

"Then where does she get off, saying things like that to you about behaving in public and knowing how to act?"

"I think it all goes back to some things Tracey said to her the day we left New York," I sighed. "Mrs. Jacobs is just getting a little revenge on the 'upper classes'."

"It's not just that, Kay," he said. "There's got to be more to it. You're trembling, for crissake! That old witch really got to you for some reason."

"Oh, *Jeff!*" I said, as the tears started to fall in spite of anything I could do to hold them back. "Don't you see? She *knows*."

"Knows what?"

"About *us*. She knows I've got a husband back home and now she's got a pretty good idea about you and me."

He shrugged. "So?"

"Oh, God," I moaned. "What am I going to do?"

"Nothing!" he said with a little laugh. "What's the big deal?"

"What if she *tells?*" I insisted.

"Tells who? And anyway, what does it matter?"

It mattered a lot. More than I could ever make him understand, though I tried for several minutes. He just couldn't see it from my perspective. Someone else *knew* about us now. Not just a smirking taxi driver in St. Thomas we would never see again, but a woman who knew my name. Who knew my *husband's* name. Who knew that my daughter was on the *Ocean Queen,* and out of spite for the rude things Tracey had said to her in the elevator the day we sailed just might tell her about Jeff and me.

I felt as if I had suddenly discovered that a gun I'd been playing with was not a harmless toy at all, but a loaded and dangerous weapon, one that now could be used against me at any moment.

Chapter 9

The *Ocean Queen* sailed from Martinique that night, bound for Caracas, and I was never so glad to leave any place behind in all my life. My memory of the island would always be scarred by that mocking, scornful look I'd seen on Mrs. Jacobs's face outside the museum in Saint-Pierre. Even though anything between Jeff and me was really none of her business, as he tried to convince me, I couldn't easily disregard her contempt. In my mind it was symbolic of the scorn and contempt that would be showered upon me by *any* woman who knew I'd been carrying on with a boy like Jeff. Mrs. Jacobs had affected me so deeply because inside myself *I* felt scorn for what I was doing, too. She had only brought to the fore those instincts and feelings I'd been trying to suppress. I'd almost begun to believe that it wouldn't really matter if I had a harmless shipboard romance with him before going home to Bob. But the essence of my belief was the certainty that no one would ever have to know about it. Now someone did know, and the whole thing had been thrust into sordid reality. I wanted to curl up and die.

When Tracey and I came back from dinner, there was a large brown shopping bag outside our stateroom door. Inside it were two model ships of the *Ocean Queen* and a little Queen Elizabeth doll with a crown on its head.

They were the toys Tracey had bought for the Jacobs children and sent to their cabin.

"Look at this, Mother," she said in bewilderment. "They brought back the toys. I wonder why?"

"I really don't know, honey," I said. But I *did* know why, as certainly as if Mrs. Jacobs had included a note that read: *We don't want any charity from your kind. We may be poor, but we're decent people.*

"Maybe she felt funny about accepting them," I said. "It might have looked like we were offering her a hand-out, because we thought she was too poor to buy these things herself."

"Well isn't she?" Tracey asked. "And anyway, if that's how she felt, why didn't she send them back the day they arrived? Why wait all this time? I'll bet the kids even played with the things. Sure they did; look at this doll's dress. It's got a chocolate smear on the hem."

"I don't know why she did it, Tracey," I sighed. "Who knows why people do a lot of the things they do?"

"Well I've got a good mind to go right down to their cabin and find out," she said, and from the determination in her voice I was afraid she would do it.

"No!" I insisted. I must have said it with such a note of urgency that Tracey looked startled. "No, don't do that, honey. Please. It would only make the situation more involved. You tried to do something nice for her children and you were rebuffed. Let's leave it at that. I guess I was wrong when I accused you of being rude to her. It seems that she's the one who doesn't have manners."

"I'll say she doesn't. And for two cents, I'd like to tell her so to her face."

"Please don't," I said. "Why don't you just put those

things in the wastebasket for the steward to throw away, and we'll try to forget all about the Jacobses?"

"All right, Mother," she said. "But the way I'm feeling, it sure won't be easy."

I understood just what she meant.

The day before the ship arrived in Caracas, Florence Wagner asked if she could have a private talk with me in their cabin. From the somber tone of her voice and the way she avoided my eyes when she made the request, I knew it wasn't going to be just a social visit. Something was wrong. But I had not idea just *how* wrong until we were alone and started to talk.

"Kay," she began, "I want to tell you right from the start that I've always tried to live my life by two simple rules. The first is to mind my own business; the second is never to be a meddling mother. Now, having said that, I'm afraid the time has come when I must break both those rules at once, for the good of Jeff and, of course, for you own good, too."

Something froze inside me, like a clock that suddenly stopped ticking. Did *she* know, too? It didn't seem possible, but that look on her face was so intimidating it made me want to immediately beg her forgiveness, whether she knew about Jeff and me or not. I tried hard to maintain my composure, though, as I asked, "What on earth are you talking about, Florence?"

"I'm talking about you and Jeff," she said flatly. "I want to know what's been going on between you two for the past week."

Dear God! She does know! I closed my eyes for a moment and unconsciously squeezed my hands into tight, nervous fists. How could I ever have let myself get into a position like this? The whole world was starting to crumble around me, and there wasn't a thing I could do to stop it.

"I—really don't know what you mean," I said, because I had to. Until I knew the full extent of her knowledge, I had to deny everything. "What could be going on between us?"

"All right," she said with a weary sigh, "I'll put it as bluntly as possible. Whether you're aware of it or not, Kay, I believe my son is falling in love with you."

"*What?*" Somehow, I managed to force a laugh from my throat. "Oh, Florence! You can't be serious!"

"I am serious," she said, "and you don't know how relieved I am to hear you laugh at the idea. Unless you're a very good liar, which I doubt, you probably know less about all this than I do."

I swallowed hard. "What ever gave you the notion that Jeff's in love with me?"

"Haven't you noticed the way he acts whenever he's around you?"

"I—can't say that I have."

"It's like you're the only woman in the world," she said. "He doesn't even notice Tracey, for instance, and I know that under any other circumstances he'd have swept her off her feet by now. Jeff's always been a big ladies' man. When he was in Princeton, he spent so much time chasing girls for a while that he almost flunked out."

"Oh, really?"

"His father and I thought we might have trouble with him on this cruise because of that, but as far as we can tell he hasn't shown the slightest interest in anyone but you. It's not healthy for a boy his age to be so attracted to an older woman. Especially not a *married* older woman like yourself."

"No, of course not," I said.

"And I'm afraid you've encouraged him more than you realize. He might even believe that you're returning his interest."

"But—how could I have encouraged him, Florence?"

"Well, by letting him in your cabin when Tracey isn't there, too, for one thing," she said. "I've seen him going in and out of your stateroom a number of times lately, Kay, and whenever I ask him where he's been he lies and says he'd gone for a stroll on the deck or was playing shuffleboard with some of the other passengers."

"Oh," I said softly. "I didn't realize that." Nor did I realize that she'd been keeping such close tabs on her son's movements in and out of my cabin. I almost laughed at the thought of how sure we'd been that no one suspected Jeff was visiting me regularly now. Except that it wasn't funny in the least.

"He's at such an impressionable age, Kay," Florence continued. "And especially in a situation like this, where people see each other day after day in a setting that's bound to seem more romantic than it really is, it was only natural to expect he'd develop a crush on someone. You know what they say about shipboard romances and all. Well, there's more truth to it than you might imagine. On our previous cruises, Henry and I have seen the most unlikely people develop attractions for each other and we were always amused by it. But this is different. This involves our own son, and we don't want to see him get hurt. No good could possibly come from his falling in love with you."

"No, of course not," I said, choking on the words.

"I'm so glad we agree on that point, Kay," she said. "That's why I wanted to have this little talk with you. I wanted to find out how much you knew about Jeff's crush, and to warn you if you didn't suspect what was happening."

And if I'd told you I did know? I wondered. What would you have done to stop it, Florence?

"Now that I know," I said, "what would you like me to do about it?"

"Oh, nothing drastic, of course. I don't want you to act any differently than you have all along. Just . . . well, be a little more on guard about things you might say to him. Don't let him think you're in any way interested in being more than just good friends with him, as you are with Henry and me. I wouldn't let him see you alone from now on, either, and it might help if you talked more about your husband in Jeff's presence, too. He might tend to forget that you *are* married, you know, and it wouldn't hurt to remind him that the ring on your finger isn't there just for decoration. Perhaps if you mentioned now and then how much you miss your husband and—"

"I think I'll be able to handle it, Florence," I said, cutting her short. I couldn't let her go on any further. I felt like a condemned prisoner being read a final list of do's and don'ts. "I'll be more careful around Jeff in the future; I promise. You won't have anything more to worry about."

"I'm sure of it, dear," she said with a satisfied smile. "We've all had such a lovely cruise up until now; it would be a shame if anything happened to spoil it."

If you only knew, Florence, I thought as I got up to leave. If you only knew!

But thank God she didn't.

That night, Tracey went down to Five Deck to see a

movie that was being shown in the theatre-lounge. At least that's where she *said* she was going. I had a sneaking suspicion that she might really be going to spend the next few hours with the young Second Officer in his cabin, but after the incident in St. Thomas I felt I couldn't question her about it. I'd already done enough damage on that score. I had to resign myself to the fact that she was old enough to know what she was doing. If she was sleeping with Mr. Taylor, it was her own business. Just as the fact that *I* was sleeping with Jeff Wagner was mine. Under the circumstances, I could hardly play the self-righteous mother role with her any longer.

A little while after she left, I heard Jeff's familiar tap-tap tap-tap on the stateroom door. I took a deep breath, summoned up all the strength and courage I had left by then, and went to let him in.

"Hello, darling," he said. As soon as the door was closed, he reached to take me in his arms. I let him kiss me, but didn't respond to the warmth of his mouth as I usually did. I stayed limp in his embrace, giving no encouragement. "Is something the matter?" he finally asked.

I drew away from him and walked across the sitting room. "Yes, Jeff. Something's very much the matter."

"What?"

"Sit down," I said. I sat too, and lit a cigarette with hands I was trying very hard to keep from visibly shaking.

"Oh-oh," he said with a grin. "That sounds ominous. In the movies, whenever they tell someone to sit down it usually means they're about to get hit with some bad news."

"I had a long talk with your mother this afternoon in

your cabin."

"Oh? So that's why she made Dad and me go for a swim. His smile slowly faded as he began to suspect the seriousness of what I was going to tell him. "What did you two talk about?"

"Us," I said.

"*Us?*" He looked at me in surprise. "You mean— you and me? That kind of us?"

I quickly nodded my head. "Yes. She knows, Jeff."

"Everything?"

"No, not everything. In fact, she really doesn't know anything for sure."

"Then what's the problem?"

"She suspects quite a lot. She told me that she's sure you're in love with me."

He laughed. "Well she's right! I am!"

"She wanted to warn me about it, in case I didn't know, and then she asked me not to . . . encourage you."

"Uh-huh." His face became grim. "And I'll bet you promised her you wouldn't. Am I right? That explains the cold shoulder you just gave me at the door. Something tells me we're right back to square one again."

"What else *could* I tell her?" I protested. "I had to make that promise. Especially once she'd told me exactly what she thinks of your 'crush' on me, as she put it."

"What does she think?" he asked. "I'd like to know."

"She said the whole idea was ridiculous, and she believes you'll only get hurt chasing after me. So, she wanted to make sure I'd let you know we were just . . . friends. And she asked me not to see you alone like this any more. She thinks it's bound to give you the wrong idea."

"Damn that woman!" His forehead creased with anger. "You should have told her to mind her own business!"

"How could I, without letting her know for sure how involved we already are with each other?"

"Where the hell does she get off," he swore, "trying to mess up my life like this?"

"She was only doing what she thought was best," I said. "She's your mother, and I can understand how she feels. I'm a mother myself, don't forget. She feels the same way about you that I feel about Tracey. She loves you, and she just doesn't want to see you get hurt."

"So? When I was a kid, she didn't want to see me get hurt, either. But I still fell out of trees and skinned my elbows. I got over it, though, without her help. And I don't need her clucking around me now like a mother hen. I'll take my own chances and handle my own hurts." He sighed heavily. "All right, so you promised her you wouldn't encourage me. So what? It doesn't really change anything between us, does it?"

"Well . . . of course it does!"

"How? Why?"

"I've got to keep that promise, Jeff. I can't run the risk of having her find out how far this thing has already gone."

"Oh, Jesus!" he groaned. "We *are* back to square one again." He got up and came across the room. He knelt beside my chair and took my hand. "Look, Kay, it doesn't make any difference to me if my mother finds out about us or not. In fact, I've got a good mind to tell her myself. *And* tell her to mind her own business and leave you alone."

"Oh, no! Jeff, please don't do that!"

"Why not? Maybe we should clear the air. I'm sick of ducking into doorways and hiding in shadows because we're afraid someone will see us. I want the whole damn world to know that I love you, Kay! I want to sit beside you at a candlelit table in that little club we've never dared to go in, and hold your hand and put my arm around your shoulders and whisper in your ear just how much I love you. I want to hold you in my arms on the dance floor and listen to someone at the piano playing slow, romantic songs we'll remember as our songs for the rest of our lives. I want to be just like all the other people on this ship who are in love and don't give a damn who knows it."

"Oh, Jeff." My fingers tightened around his and I raised his hand to my mouth and kissed it. "That sounds so wonderful. If only it could be that way. But it can't. And it never will."

"Why not?"

"Because I'm *married*. How many times do I have to remind you of that before it finally sinks in? I'm not like Tracey. I don't have the freedom she does. I've already committed my life to another man. I've built my whole world around Bob. My home and my marriage are all I've got. If anything ever happened to destroy them because of us, here and now, I don't know what I'd do. I'd have nothing left."

"You'd have me," he said softly.

"For how long?"

"As long as you needed me, Kay."

I kissed his hand again and felt my eyes misting with tears. "If this were just a shipboard romance that we could enjoy while it lasted, with no fear of the consequences, I'd jump at the chance to do everything you just said. But it's not that easy. It's different for us. This dream can't last forever. Sooner or later, whether we like it or not, we've got to wake up and face reality. When the cruise is over, you'll have to go back to school, and I'll have to go back home to my husband."

"Why?"

"Don't keep saying *why*!" I snapped. "You're starting to sound like a pestering child who's begging for something."

"I *am* begging, Kay. I'm begging for you. Why do you have to go back to your husband?"

"Because that's where I belong."

"No, it's not. Maybe before last week it was, because you had nowhere else to go, but now you've got me. You belong with me, not him."

"Jeff, please," I said, "you're starting to say ridiculous things you don't mean and you'll be sorry for later. Let's just not talk about it any more. If it were possible for us to keep seeing each other, it would be wonderful. But we can't. Not now that your mother suspects so much. It's just too dangerous. I've got to think of myself, and I have too much to lose."

"Like what?" he insisted. "Your big house in New Jersey? Your car? Your furniture? Your trash compacter? What's so important that you're afraid of losing? And don't try to tell me it's your husband, because I know better than that by now."

"I'm afraid of losing my security," I said.

"Your security . . . ?"

"Maybe things aren't as good between Bob and me as they could be, or even as they *should* be, but I know he'll take care of me for the rest of my life. I could never manage on my own. I've got no skills, no talent, nothing but the years I've been married to Bob. With him, at least I know I'll never have to worry about how I'm going to pay the rent or where I'll get the money for food and clothing—"

Jeff cut me short. "Oh, that's just great! That's some rosy future you've got ahead of you, all right! Free rent, food, and clothing for as long as you live. *Wow!* I can see why you'd be willing to sacrifice something as inconsequential as your happiness for all that!

"But I've got news for you, Kay. You can get the same deal at any state prison. All you've got to do is commit a murder and it's yours. Come to think of it, maybe that's just what you're doing. You're murdering yourself by staying with a man who doesn't make you happy, and to pay for the crime you're walking right back into that neat little prison all your own in New Jersey."

"You're talking nonsense now. I've never thought of my home as a prison," I swore, but was it really true? All those countless afternoons I'd spent by myself while Tracey was in school and Bob was at work. When the dishes were done and the wash all dried and neatly folded, when the rugs had been vacuumed and the windows cleaned, when there was no other possible busy work I could find for myself to do until it was time to start supper . . . hadn't it seemed like solitary confinement of sorts? Hadn't I often gone to the windows and looked out at the street and felt that the curtains between the glass and myself were more like iron bars, keeping me locked inside the house because that's where I *belonged*, while all those people outside had the freedom to go and do whatever they pleased? Hadn't I sometimes found myself watching television in the middle of the day because there was nothing else for me to do and wondered why the picture had suddenly gone so blurry, only to realize my eyes were filled with tears for no logical reason at all? Didn't I jump every time the phone rang, and run to answer it with the hope that someone on the other end of the line would ask me out? Out where didn't matter; just out of that house for a few blessed hours.

It was hard to deny that everything Jeff said was true. But even if it was, what alternative did I have? A woman doesn't just walk away from a twenty-year marriage without knowing exactly where she's going. There were too many uncertainties in the world to be faced that easily. Too many dangers. Too many questions without answers. I was too old now to start my life all over again from scratch, too frightened to risk making a mistake I couldn't correct and would always regret. The time for taking dares and risks was when you're young. Tracey's age. Jeff's age. Not mine. I'd already made my choices, and if things hadn't turned out the way I'd hoped they would, I'd have to learn to make the most of what I had. Like my mother used to say, once you've made your bed, you have to lie in it.

I drew a deep breath and crushed out my cigarette. "I wish you would leave now, Jeff," I said. "I don't think there's anything more for us to talk about."

"It was great fun, but it was just one of those things?" he said, his voice edged with bitterness. "No, Kay. I'm sorry. It's not going to end like this. If I have anything to say about it, it's not going to end at all. I'm not going to lose you this easily, just because my mother shot off her mouth when she had no right to. I want you. Not just for this cruise. For always. I want you to marry me."

"Oh, Jeff!" I had to laugh. The idea was so ridiculous I couldn't take it seriously. "Have you been down in the bar too long tonight?"

"If the only reason you have for staying with your husband is security," he said, "then I can make the same offer. I'll see that you have a roof over your head and food on your plate and clothes on your back. It may not be what you're used to right now, but it will do. And once I'm out of law school and in practice on my own, I'll be able to give you everything he can. You'll just have to wait a little while for it, that's all. But in the meantime, I'll be giving you something he's not. And that's love."

I reached for another cigarette, but he stopped my hand and brushed aside the case.

"What do you say? Is it such a bad offer?"

"How can you expect me to give you an answer, when I can't even take the question seriously?" I said. "Are you really asking me to divorce Bob and marry you?"

"That's exactly what I'm asking, yes."

"I can't believe this is happening," I said. "It's all too preposterous to be true."

"Why is it?" he insisted.

"What would people *think*? Your mother . . . your father . . . Tracey . . . my friends . . . ?"

"Who cares what anyone else thinks?" he argued. "Does anyone else's opinion have so much importance that you've got to live your life hoping to win their approval? It's your life, Kay. *Our* life. Our happiness. Let's live the way *we* want to, because we've only got one ride on this merry-go-round and when it's over, it's over. When the music stops, it doesn't make any difference whether you've been a sinner or a saint, you've still got to get off. The only hope any of us have is catching the brass ring while the merry-go-round's still turning."

"But we don't know anything about each other, Jeff. We've practically strangers."

"We weren't strangers yesterday afternoon," he said, motioning toward the open bedroom door. "Not in there."

"That isn't the only thing that matters," I said. "Sex doesn't make a relationship last forever." I'd already made that mistake once in my life; I wasn't about to make it again.

"No, of course it doesn't," he said. "But love does, if it's strong enough. And what I feel when I'm with you isn't just sexual gratification, it's love. Stronger than I've ever felt before."

"Even with Miss Ramsey?" I said with the hint of a smile.

"Ten times more than with her." His hands squeezed mine. "We're so right for each other, Kay. I know it. And you know it, too. We've got so much to give to each other it would take a lifetime before we're half-through. When you feel something so strongly, you just can't give it up. Not for a very, very good reason."

"I—don't know what to say, Jeff."

"This is all so sudden?" he said with a smile.

"All right, cliche or not, it's true."

"No it isn't," he said. "We both knew what it was leading up to, right from the start. You wouldn't have made love with me on the beach back in St. Thomas if you hadn't. You're not the kind of woman who'd have slept with me just for a one-time thrill. You knew something more would happen between us, didn't you?"

"Yes," I admitted. And it was true. I had needed the love of a man and he'd caught me at a vulnerable time. But it was more than that. I could have resisted another man, but I gave in to him because I did feel something stirring inside me stronger than sexual desire. Frightened as I was by his proposal, I suppose I'd expected all along that he would make it eventually . . . and had wanted him to.

"I'm not wrong in thinking that you love me, too; am I?" he asked. I couldn't meet his eyes. "Kay? Do you love me, too?"

I nodded my head slowly up and down, as my eyes flooded with tears. It felt like a great weight had been lifted from my shoulders. A burden I'd been carrying for too long had been dropped, and at last I was able to breathe freely.

"Let me hear you say it. Please? It means a lot to me."

"I . . . love you," I whispered. I touched his cheek and moved my fingertips slowly down his handsome face. We stared into each other's eyes for a long moment, and then I broke down completely. I hugged his head to my breast and clung to him as though my life depended upon it. "I love you, Jeff," I cried. "God help me, but I do love you!"

Chapter 10

I flew back to New York the next day from Caracas, without telling anyone I was going except Tracey and the ship's purser who arranged my ticket. I told him that while the cruise had been delightful so far, I was starting to feel a little seasick and thought it best that I get back on solid ground again rather than continue on with the ship for the final week. He seemed to understand. I told Tracey that I was feeling homesick and missed her father terribly. I said that I wanted to fly back and see if I couldn't join Bob in Chicago, and asked if she would mind being left alone for the rest of the cruise. She seemed to understand, too, and swore she wouldn't mind at all. I was pretty sure I knew why, but I couldn't think about that now. My only thought was that I had to get off that ship and away from Jeff as quickly as possible, before something disastrous happened.

I'd spent a long, sleepless night after he left my cabin, thinking about all he'd proposed, and in the early hours of the morning I'd come to a decision. I could never divorce Bob and run off with Jeff. The whole idea was ridiculous. I must have been out of my mind even to consider it. I had to make every attempt to keep my marriage together. It wouldn't have been fair to Bob, after all those years, just to walk out without giving him a chance to redeem himself. I felt sure that if we just had time to sit down and talk things over, we could reach an understanding. If I told him how I felt and how much more of him I needed than he'd been willing—or able—to give in the past years, he would realize the situation between us had reached a critical stage, and do all in his power to change things. I owed him that much, at least.

As for Jeff . . . well, I knew he'd be hurt at first, but he was young and the young have a remarkable resiliency. In time, he'd be able to adjust. He would get over me. Perhaps, all along, it really had been nothing more than a shipboard romance for him, as Florence said. Once he was back in familiar surroundings at school and immersed in his studies, everything that had happened between us might seem no more real than a very pleasant, half-remembered dream.

And as for myself, I only knew that I had to get away. I was being torn apart by conflict. When I was with Jeff, I felt genuine love for him and wanted to believe everything he told me. I felt such happiness when we were together and he held me in his arms that nothing else existed. But when he'd gone and I was alone with my thoughts, guilt and shame almost sickened me. All of the obligations and responsibilities I had to my husband and our marriage came rushing back and I had to face the cold, hard reality of what I was doing. I felt that I was in a box and the walls were closing in on me from both sides. While there was still time, I had to escape.

I felt an enormous sense of relief flow through me as soon as I was home. There was safety in familiar surroundings. I knew every inch of our house as well as I knew the back of my own hand. Nothing bad could ever happen to me there. It was like waking up from a terrible dream and finding myself once again in the comfort and security of my own bed.

Even before I unpacked my luggage, I called Bob's office in New York. A girl whose voice I didn't recognize answered the phone.

"Mr. Lawrence's office," she said.

"Is this Miss Blaire?" I asked.

"No, I'm sorry. Joan's on vacation this week. Can I help you?"

"This is Mrs. Lawrence," I said. "I'd like to get hold of my husband, but I'm afraid he didn't know where he'd be staying in Chicago. Could you find out for me?"

"In Chicago?" the girl asked, sounding confused.

"Yes, he's there on company business. I'm sure someone in the office knows about it. If you could just tell me what hotel he's at so I can give him a call, I'd appreciate it."

"Hold on, Mrs. Lawrence," the girl said, "and I'll try to find out."

I waited for what seemed an interminable length of time before she came back on the line.

"Mrs. Lawrence? I'm afraid I can't help you. No one here knows anything about Mr. Lawrence going to Chicago on company business. Everyone I asked said he's on vacation this week and last."

I felt a strange, tingling sensation run through the pit of my stomach, but I tried to ignore it. "No," I explained, "you see he was *supposed* to be on vacation. He and I were going on a cruise together, but at the last minute something came up in the new Chicago office and he had to fly out there to take care of it."

"Mrs. Lawrence," the girl said, "we don't *have* an office in Chicago."

"What?" I laughed nervously. My hand was starting to sweat around the receiver and my head had a funny humming noise inside it. "But you must. Bob's been talking about it for weeks. He went out there to help open it."

"I'm sorry," she said. "I'm kind of new here myself. Maybe there *is* a new office in Chicago, but I don't know anything about it."

My patience was wearing thin as my anxiety increased. "Well isn't there *someone* in the office who could tell me where my husband is?"

"I guess Joan would know, but like I said: she's on vacation this week. I'm just answering her phones. I really don't know anything about Mr. Lawrence's business."

"All right," I sighed, "thanks anyway." *For nothing*. I put down the phone. My knees were starting to shake and I had to sit to catch my breath for a few minutes. This was absurd. How could no one in the office know where Bob was? He *had* to be in Chicago. Where else could he be? That stupid girl I'd talked to was just too lazy to get the information for me. That had to be it. If Bob's regular secretary were there, she could have let me know in a minute. Every time I'd talked to Miss Blair she'd sounded so cool, crisp, and efficient. If only she hadn't picked this particular week to take her vacation, too.

I searched my mind for some time, desperately trying to remember the name of the hotel where Bob told me he thought he'd be staying. At last it came to me. I picked up the receiver again and dialled the operator. I asked her to place a long distance, person-to-person call to Bob at the Regency Hotel in Chicago. I was sure that was the name he'd called up the stairs to me just before the *Ocean Queen* sailed.

After an eternity of clicking and buzzing and humming while the long distance connection was made, the operator came on the line and told me there was no Robert Lawrence registered at the Regency.

"But he's *got* to be there!" I said. "Are you sure?"

"I asked the desk clerk to check the register twice, Ma'am," she said.

My mind raced frantically. "Well, maybe he *was* there, but he moved to another hotel. Could you find out if he left a forwarding address when he checked out?"

"One moment please."

I tapped my fingertips nervously on the telephone while I waited. He had to be somewhere in Chicago. Where else could he be?

"I'm sorry, Ma'am," the operator said, "but they have no record of a Mr. Robert Lawrence checking into the hotel at any time in the past three weeks, and no reservation was ever made in that name."

I put down the receiver without even thanking her for her trouble. All right, I thought, what are you going to do now? Start calling every hotel in Chicago, like the wife of the town drunk calling all the saloons to ask if her husband is there? It took me a moment to think of it, but there was one more number I could try. It seemed so obvious when I thought of it, I wondered why it hadn't occurred to me immediately. I called the operator again and asked for the number of Winthrop and Company in Chicago. Of course. It should be a simple matter to reach Bob directly at the new office. If he wasn't there at the moment, they'd certainly know where he was staying and how to reach him.

"Would you spell that name, please?" the operator asked after several moments of silence. When I had, I waited again while she checked the information listings.

"I'm sorry," she said, coming back on the line, "but I see no listing under that name."

An icy fist suddenly grabbed hold of my stomach and squeezed. My voice was shrill with panic as I told her, "You've *got* to have a number! It's a business. It's the branch office of a large corporation."

"Would it be a new number, by any chance?"

I almost laughed with relief. Of course! The office was new; the number probably wasn't in the regular Chicago directory yet. "Yes, it is," I said. "They've just opened a little while ago."

"I'll check the new listings for you, then."

"Would you do that, please?"

She was off the line for a long while, and every second more that it took made me all the more certain of what she would say when she came back on.

"I'm sorry. I've checked all the new telephone listings and we have no record of a Winthrop and Company in Chicago."

"Thank you," I said, and put down the phone.

All of a sudden, the peace and security I'd felt when I walked in the house vanished. Instead of waking up from a bad dream, it seemed that a nightmare had just begun.

Every night for more than a month, Bob had come home late, saying he'd been working on problems with Winthrop's new branch. He hadn't gone on the cruise in order to get things working smoothly out there. How was it possible there was no listing for the new office in Chicago . . . unless there really *was* no new office. And if that was true, then where was my husband?

Bob came home on Saturday, the day before the *Ocean Queen* was scheduled to dock in New York.

From the look on his face when he walked in the house and found me sitting in the living room, you'd have thought he was seeing a ghost.

"Kay!" he exclaimed. "Wh-what are *you* doing here?"

"I live here, remember?" I got up and went to kiss him, but his arms held me back.

"What's wrong? Did something happen to Tracey?"

Was that his first concern? Not that something might have happened to me, but to her?

"No, she's fine," I said. At least I hoped she was. "She'll be back tomorrow on the ship." I gave him a kiss and a hug, but got none in return. "I flew back a few days early from Caracas," I explained.

A dark, angry frown swept over his face. "What the hell did you do that for? Weren't you having a good time?"

If you only knew, I thought.

"Not really," I said. "I kept thinking about how much I missed you, and how much nicer everything would have been if you were there, too. I couldn't wait five more days to come home, so when we arrived in Caracas I asked the purser to get me a plane ticket back to New York."

"Well *that* was a hulluva waste of good money," he snapped.

"Oh, Bob. It really doesn't matter, does it? As long as Tracey's having such a good time, the money isn't being wasted. And I—I was miserable without you." I was surprised by how difficult it was to say the words. "Is that so wrong?"

His expression softened and he finally put his arms around me. "I guess not."

"Didn't you miss me, too?"

He laughed. "Well sure I did!" His arms tightened, as though to prove it. "I thought about you all the time."

"I'm glad," I said, but I wished I could believe he was telling the truth. Some strange tone in his voice made me doubt what I was hearing. "I hate being miserable by myself," I said. "It's good to know you were, too."

"Hey!" he laughed, pushing me gently away when I tried to kiss him again. "How about letting me go upstairs and unpack first, huh?"

"I'll do it for you," I said, reaching to take his suitcase.

He drew it away. "Why don't you go rustle up something for me to eat instead? I'm hungry as a bear. Is there anything in the refrigerator?"

"Of course," I said. I'd had nothing to do by myself all week but shop and clean and mark time. "It's full."

"How 'bout fixing me a sandwich then, okay? Pile it on. And if you've got some cold beer in there, too, I could down about three of them."

While he went upstairs to unpack, I made a tray for him in the kitchen. A ham and cheese sandwich, some potato chips, a big dill pickle, and a mug of beer. I thought that should take care of his appetite until I had dinner ready.

Instead of waiting for him to come down, I took the food upstairs. If he was really as hungry as he said he was, I figured he'd want to dig in right away. But he was in the shower when I brought the tray to the bedroom. His empty suitcase was on the floor beside the closet.

Why, I wondered, had he been so insistent about unpacking himself? He'd never done it before. Whenever he'd returned from previous business trips, he'd always left it to me to sort out his dirty clothes and hang up his suits.

I went over to the hamper and opened it, expecting to see it stuffed full of the usual things he took with him. Dress shirts. Socks. Underwear. Instead, I found his tennis shorts, a bathing suit, some Lacoste sport shirts, and several pairs of casual summer slacks. I stared at the pile in disbelief. It looked more like he'd just come back from a vacation than two weeks of intense work at a new office. My hands were trembling as I sorted through the clothes. Where had he been?

"What're you doing?"

The unexpected sound of Bob's voice made me jump. I turned and saw him standing in the bathroom doorway. He'd wrapped a towel around his waist, and his body was dripping wet. I suddenly felt as nervous as someone in a mystery story who's just discovered clues to a crime and been confronted by the most likely suspect.

"I'm—looking at these things you put in here."

"What's the matter? You never saw dirty laundry before?"

"Not this kind. Not after you've been on a business trip."

He padded across the bedroom to me, leaving a trail of wet footprints in the rug. "I thought you were going to fix me a snack?"

"It's over there on the dresser."

I slammed down the top of the hamper and whirled on him. I couldn't control myself any longer. I'd had a whole week of living with unanswered questions and lying awake nights with the most terrible suspicions running through my mind. I couldn't maintain a calm exterior for another second; not while my insides were churning with such fear and anxiety.

"Bob, where *were* you for the past two weeks?" I demanded.

"In Chicago, of course."

"With clothes like these?" Had he thought I wouldn't notice when I went to do the next wash? Or had he planned to run them through the machine himself, expecting that Tracey and I wouldn't be home until tomorrow and he'd have plenty of time to do it?

"Sure, why not? The office isn't officially open yet, and they're still running things on a pretty casual basis."

"They certainly *must* be," I cracked, "if you were able to wear a bathing suit to work!"

"Oh, for Christ's sake!" he said with a laugh. "I didn't spend *all* my time at the office. They've got swimming pools in Chicago, too, you know."

"Where?" I asked. "At the hotel? What hotel were you staying at, Bob?" I hoped—and at the same time didn't hope, because confirmation of my fears would have been too dreadful—that he would tell me the Regency.

"As a matter of fact," he said, "I wasn't at a hotel. I stayed with Joe Phillips and his family. He's the new manager out there, and he offered to put me up at their house in Evanston. I didn't see any reason why I shouldn't take him up on it, especially since it turned out that Joan forgot to make me a reservation at the Regency. She went on vacation herself last week, and I guess she had too much else on her mind."

"That's not like her," I said.

"No, it isn't." Then, his voice taking on an edge of annoyance, he asked, "What do you want me to do? Fire the poor girl for making a simple mistake?"

"No. Of course not."

"What's all this fuss about then?"

"One of the reasons why I came home early," I said, "was so I could fly to Chicago and spend a few days there with you, to make up for the time we've lost together."

"Yeah?" His face still gave nothing away. "That sounds like it would've been a good idea. Why didn't you?"

"I wanted to. And I tried to. But I couldn't get in touch with you. When I called information, they didn't even have a listing for Winthrop and Company in Chicago."

"They didn't?" His eyes had a puzzled look for a moment, then he started to laugh. "No, of course not! Do you know why?"

"I haven't the slightest idea."

"Those damn fools out there had everything so screwed up, they were still using the phones left behind by the last company that had the office. No one had thought to call Ma Bell and change the listing. They all figured that someone else was going to take care of it. Can you imagine that?"

Frankly, I couldn't. I found it hard to believe that any office could be run so inefficiently, but then . . . what did I know about business? And I wanted so desperately to believe Bob's explanation.

"I got everything straightened out, though," he went on. "That was the least of the problems! You should have seen what—"

I cut him short. "Do you have the number now, Bob?"

For the first time, he hesitated. "Sure I do. Somewhere."

"Are you going to write it down for me?"

"What for? You'll probably never need it. I doubt if I'll be going back there again. Phillips seems like a pretty capable guy. He should have things running smoothly from now on."

I took a deep breath before telling him, "When I called your office in New York, Bob, the girl I spoke to said there was no branch of Winthrop and Company in Chicago."

"What?" His eyebrows furrowed. "Who the hell told you a thing like that?"

"I—don't know her name. She said she was new and was just answering the phone for Miss Blair."

"Some temporary help, I'll bet, who doesn't know her ass from a hole in the ground. I'll find out who it was and raise plenty of hell when I go in Monday morning."

"*Is* there an office in Chicago, Bob?"

"Well of course there is! Where the hell do you think I've been for the past two weeks?"

I swallowed hard. "That's what I'm trying to find out. Were you really in Chicago?"

"Oh, for God's sake! What is this? I'm home ten minutes and already you're giving me the third degree!"

"*Were* you? I've got to know, Bob. If you weren't, please tell me. I'll try to understand—"

"All right!" he shouted. "You don't believe me? I'll call Joe Phillips right now; you can ask him."

He stormed across the room and picked up the bedside phone with such anger that when he pushed the buttons it looked like his fist was going to go right through the receiver.

"This is a fine welcome home, Kay. Thanks a helluva lot. It really makes me glad to be back."

"Bob . . ." I felt my heart sinking inside me. Why

206

was it always like this? No matter when I'd ever accused him of anything, he somehow found a way to turn it all around so that I wound up feeling guilty. Was I so wrong in wanting to know for sure where he'd been? Considering the evidence to the contrary, was it so unreasonable to think he hadn't been where he said he was?

"Come here!" He motioned with his hand. "The phone's ringing. When Joe answers, you talk to him. You ask him everything you want to know. Just tell him you're suspicious of God knows what, and you want to know if I'm telling the truth. Come on! Let him know you don't trust *my* word and you need him to back me up."

"Bob, please. Put down the phone."

"Come here, I said!" His face was turning scarlet with rage. "I want you to ask him! And when you're done talking to Joe, I'll call old man Winthrop and you can ask *him* whether he's got a branch in Chicago or not, since you obviously believe some three-buck-an-hour temporary help more than you do me."

My eyes were suddenly flooded with tears. I felt like such a fool now. "Stop it, Bob. Please."

"Do you want me to hang up before he answers?"

"Yes. Please."

"Do you finally believe me?"

I shook my head quickly up and down. "Yes."

"Are you sure? Maybe you'd like me to take a lie detector test?"

"I believe you, Bob," I moaned.

He slammed the receiver back onto the cradle. "Thanks a lot."

He stormed into the bathroom, and I sat down on the edge of the bed and cried.

I was home alone the next day when the telephone rang. Bob had driven into New York early that morning by himself to pick up Tracey when the *Ocean Queen* docked. It was just as well that I wouldn't have wanted to go with him anyway, because we still weren't speaking. We'd spent a miserable night together in sullen silence. I'd tried my best to make up for the incident in the bedroom, but Bob refused to forgive and forget. Even when I gave him the Dunhill lighter I'd bought in St. Thomas, he just opened the package, muttered *Thanks*, and dropped it on the coffee table. When he lit his next cigarette, he used a book of matches from his pocket.

After dinner, I'd tried to talk to him. I felt we were reaching a crisis point and we'd better get everything out in the open before it was too late to change things, but he refused to listen. When I started to tell him how I was feeling, he cut me short by turning up the volume on the TV and going out to the kitchen for another beer. When he came back, I tried again.

"Damn it, Kay, I'm not in the mood to listen to anything more you've got to say," he raged. "Not right now. I've had enough for one day."

"Please, Bob. This is so important . . ."

"I'm sure it'll keep," he muttered, as though he imagined the only thing I wanted to talk about was getting a new dishwasher or paying someone to come in and clean the windows.

When we went to bed that night, I'd hoped his anger would have cooled down enough for us to kiss and make up. In the past, many unpleasant words that had passed between us were forgotten in bed. But not this time. Bob didn't so much as peck my cheek in a good night kiss. I lay beside him in the darkness for hours after he'd started to snore, fighting back tears first and then a raging anger of my own for the way he was treating me.

By morning, nothing had changed. We got up in silence and ate breakfast like two strangers sharing a table in a public cafeteria. The first time we spoke was when he asked if I was going with him to pick up Tracey. I told him no. I'm sure he thought it was because of the bad feelings between us—and it *was* partly that—but I wouldn't have gone anyway. I didn't want to run the risk of seeing Jeff or his parents again. It would have been too embarrassing trying to explain why I'd flown back from Caracas without telling them. But more than that, especially the way I was feeling that morning, I wasn't sure what I might have done if Jeff had taken my hand and said, "Come on, Kay, let's go." I just might have gone with him.

I was in the middle of changing the sheets on Tracey's bed when the phone rang. I dashed down the hall to answer it, thinking it was probably Lorraine Thomas or one of my other friends calling to welcome me home and ask how the trip had been. I hadn't called anyone that week to let them know I'd come home early; it would have been too difficult to explain.

"Hello?" I answered on the sixth ring.

"Kay?"

I recognized his voice at once, and I had to quickly sit down. My heart made such a sudden leap in my chest that I lost my breath for a moment.

"Jeff . . ."

"Why did you *do* it, Kay?" he demanded. "Why did you run away like that, without so much as a word?"

"I—thought it was for the best, Jeff," I said.

"Why? It doesn't make sense."

"It will in time," I said softly. "I hope."

"What? What did you say?" he shouted. "I can't hear you." From the noise I heard in the background, I knew he was calling from the passenger terminal at the pier. He must have got off the ship as soon as it moored and run straight for the nearest phone.

"I said I *had* to come home, Jeff. I thought everything over and decided it was best."

He was silent for a long moment. "I've got to see you, Kay," he said. "We've got to talk."

"No, Jeff. It's impossible."

"Please? Meet me somewhere in New York tomorrow. Anywhere you say."

"I—can't." I had to struggle to say it, because I knew in my heart that I desperately wanted to see him. The week I'd spent alone in the house had been a miserable one. I'd never felt more lonely in my life. And, despite my frantic attempts to reach him, it wasn't Bob I'd been lonely for. It was Jeff. I missed him far more than I'd ever missed my husband, but I knew I just couldn't start it all over again. The break had been made, it was for the best, and it had to be a clean one.

"Then I'll come to New Jersey," he said. "I'll come to your house."

"*No!*" I gasped. That would be the most awful thing imaginable. If Bob ever found out . . .

"I've got to see you, Kay," he pleaded.

"No. It's impossible. I'm sorry, Jeff. I—I don't want to see you again," I said, forcing out the words. "And I don't want you to call here any more. *Please*. Just— leave me alone. It's over."

Before he could say anything more, I put down the phone. A few minutes later, it rang again. I'd known it would. As I went back to Tracey's room, the sound of the jangling bell cut through me like a knife. It was all I could do to keep from answering it and telling him yes, I would meet him anywhere, do anything he wanted, stay with him as long as he'd have me. But I couldn't. It was over, and it had to stay that way.

Tracey went back to Emerson early the following week, leaving Bob and me alone again. Nothing much had changed between us. We were a little more civil to each other now, but that was all. We spoke when it was necessary, and went through the formalities of being polite, but things were a far cry from the way I'd hoped they would be.

I made no further attempt to talk to him about how I was feeling. I sensed that the time still wasn't right. Perhaps, I thought, if I just let things run their natural course we would make the adjustment to being alone together in the house and start loving one another the way we used to. Though to tell the truth, in the dark hours of the night when I was lying awake with my innermost thoughts, I rather doubted it. We seemed to have gone too far in the other direction ever to turn back.

On Thursday, a little package arrived in the morning's mail. It was addressed to me, and came from a place in Vermont called the Lakeview Lodge. I couldn't imagine what it might be, and was even more confused when I opened the tiny box and found a single gold earring inside. It was in the shape of a heart, with a small ruby in the center, and it was for a pierced ear. I sat down and unfolded the accompanying letter. As I read it, I felt my heartbeat quickening and the palms of my hands starting to sweat. It didn't make sense.

"*Dear Mrs. Lawrence*," it began. "*While one of*

our maids was cleaning the room you occupied during your recent stay with us, she discovered the enclosed earring on the floor under the dresser. As we're sure you're concerned over its loss and will be anxious to have it back, we're returning it to you herewith. We sincerely hope that you and your husband enjoyed your two-week stay with us, and that you'll think of the Lakeview Lodge with pleasant memories when you're planning your next vacation." The letter was signed by the assistant manager.

"This has got to be a mistake," I murmured aloud. I picked up the letter and read it through again, but the words were exactly the same. What were they talking about? I'd never *heard* of the Lakeview Lodge, let alone spent any time there with Bob. I'd never been to Vermont in my life. I didn't even have pierced ears!

They had to have made a mistake. It must be some *other* Mrs. Robert Lawrence's earring. But how in the world, out of all the possible Lawrences in the country to choose from, had they picked our address? Surely they must keep records of where their guests lived. I stared at the address on the package and the letter again. *We sincerely hope that you and your husband enjoyed your two-week stay with us.*

Two-week stay . . .

My hands began to tremble and my stomach lurched so violently that it was all I could do to hold down the rush of bile in my throat. My head began to spin, and for a moment I thought I was going to faint.

There was no mistake. Maybe I had never been to the Lakeview Lodge in Vermont, but Bob had. The tennis shorts. The bathing suit. The sport clothes. *They're still running things on a pretty casual basis . . .*

"Oh, you bastard!" I groaned. "You dirty, rotten bastard!"

If he'd been there at that moment, I think I would have killed him. All that cock-and-bull nonsense about the phones not being listed under the Winthrop name and staying with somebody named Joe Phillips in Evanston! I bet there wasn't anybody by that name at all, no more than there was a branch office of Bob's company in Chicago. When he picked up the bedroom phone that terrible Saturday afternoon, he'd probably punched buttons at random, or dialled the time or weather information, knowing I would never come to the phone and find out the truth.

That was the part that hurt the most. Knowing what a fool he'd made of me! And then turning the whole situation around, so that *I* felt guilty while *he* went through the house with his nose in the air like the injured party.

"Damn you!" I swore, crumpling the letter in my fist. "Damn you to hell, Bob Lawrence!"

He'd never planned to come on the cruise with me at all. There'd never been any emergency in Chicago he had to fix at the last minute. The cruise was just a means of getting me out of the way, so he could cavort at the Lakeview Lodge for two weeks. A five thousand dollar excuse to get rid of me, so he could have a fling with . . . who? Who could possibly be worth that much money to him? Who had dropped the gold heart with the ruby?

I picked up the earring and turned it over. There was something engraved on the back, but I couldn't read it at first. My eyes were burning, and the letters were very small. I switched on the lamp beside me and held the earring up to the light. *To JB from BL*, it read. My stomach twisted and I thought once again I'd be sick.

BL. Bob Lawrence. And *JB* couldn't be anyone else but Joan Blair, his secretary. *Joan's on vacation this week, Mrs. Lawrence.*

"Oh, God!" I moaned. I covered my face and began to cry. Not so much for Bob's betrayal, nor even from a sense of jealousy that he'd been cheating with another woman. My tears were for myself. I cried because I felt like such an idiot. Such a stupid, trusting fool. I had never suspected a thing, though now it seemed that so many of Bob's excuses for coming home late and making out-of-town trips had been so transparent that even a child could have seen through them. I had closed my eyes to reality, even when it was staring me right in the face, because I couldn't believe that Bob would ever love anyone but me. I had given up Jeff for the same reason. Because I had felt guilty and ashamed for giving myself to someone else, thinking that Bob never would. I had thrown away what might have been my last chance for real happiness . . . for nothing.

When I'd finally cried all the tears that were left in me, I wiped my eyes and went upstairs to dress. It was just a little past ten. If I hurried, I could catch the next train to New York and be at Bob's office by noon.

I had never met Joan Blair and had no idea what to expect. I'd talked to her on the phone a few times, but the image you get in your mind from hearing a person's voice is often quite different from the physical reality. It certainly was in her case. She sounded so cool, crisp, and efficient when she answered Bob's telephone, that I'd pictured someone who wore high-necked blouses, pulled her hair back in a severe bun, and possibly had horn-rimmed glasses. But the person I found sitting at the desk outside Bob's office looked more like a *Vogue* model than a secretary.

Her hair was long and auburn, cut in a full, wind-blown style like one of the famous actresses on television. Her face was disarmingly beautiful. Fresh and natural, she didn't need much make-up to enhance the loveliness nature had given her. And judging by what I could see from the open neckline of her dress, nature had been more than generous to her elsewhere, too. She had a stunning figure.

I had to hand it to Bob. His taste in women was impeccable. Any man who had the money to spend would gladly pay five thousand dollars to get his wife out of the way so he could have two weeks in Vermont with a girl like that.

When I approached her desk, she looked up and smiled the kind of smile that toothpaste makers dream of finding to advertise their products. "Yes? Can I help you?"

I tried my best to return her smile, but it was rather like a candle trying to outshine a lighthouse beacon. "Hello," I said. "You must be Miss Blair."

"Yes . . . ?"

"I'm Mrs. Lawrence. Bob's wife."

For just an instant, a flicker of unease passed over her perfect composure, but it was quickly gone. "Oh, hello, Mrs. Lawrence. It's nice to meet you. We've talked a few times on the phone, haven't we?"

"Yes. And I had no idea you were so lovely."

"Thank you." She didn't take it so much as a compliment as an acknowledgement of fact.

"Is Bob in?" I asked. "I decided to do some shopping in the city today, and I thought if he was free we might have lunch."

"Gee, I'm sorry, Mrs. Lawrence," she said. "He's

at a board meeting right now, and I believe they'll all be having lunch with Mr. Winthrop afterwards."

"Oh, what a shame," I said, but I already knew about the meeting. Bob had mentioned it that morning when I asked why he was wearing his best suit. "Do you think it would be all right if I used his phone for a minute?" I asked. "Maybe I can catch one of my friends who works in New York before she goes out to lunch."

"Of course," she said, beaming that smile again. "Go right into his office, Mrs. Lawrence."

I went past her desk and closed the door. I'd never seen Bob's office before, and it was a little like walking into a stranger's home when he wasn't there. In a way, that room *was* Bob's home now. It was where his real life was centered and where all his hopes and dreams got their start. He even had his woman right outside.

There was a picture of Tracey on top of Bob's desk, but none of me. That hurt, but not as much as it should have. Already I was finding it easier not to care.

I picked up the phone and dialled weather information. Just in case Miss Blair was listening through the door, I asked the weather lady if she'd like to have lunch with me, but her recorded voice just rambled on about the day's highs and lows and expected forecasts. I told her I'd meet her at one o'clock at the Taft, but I don't know if she heard me. When I hung up, she was still talking about the relative humidity. I opened my purse, took out the gold pierced earring, and took a deep breath.

"Make your date?" Miss Blair asked when I came out of the office.

"Yes, thanks. I hate to have lunch alone, you know."

"Oh, yes," she agreed. "I do, too. It's such an uncomfortable feeling, when everyone else around you is

216

eating with someone."

I wondered how she would ever know. For the life of me, I couldn't imagine a girl like that ordering a hot dog from a corner pushcart without drawing a crowd.

"While I was talking to my friend," I said, "I noticed something on the floor in under the couch in there. It's an earring." I held it out to her in my open palm. "Does it belong to you?"

Her big, blue eyes brightened with instant relief. "Oh, yes! It does! Thank you so much for finding it, Mrs. Lawrence. You know, I hunted all over my apartment for it the other night. Tore the place apart like a cyclone had gone through it! I just couldn't imagine where I'd lost it."

I could. But I'd just wanted to be sure.

As soon as I went down to the lobby, I stepped into a telephone booth and closed the door. "Operator?" I said. "I'd like to place a long distance call to the registrar's office at the Harvard Law School in Boston."

Chapter 11

"Happy, darling?"

I snuggled closer to Jeff in the bed and ran my fingertips lightly down the smooth skin of his chest. His body was still as moist from the passion of lovemaking as my own.

"Mmmmmm," I murmured in reply. "More than I've ever been before."

It was the third weekend in a row that we'd taken a room at the Plaza. This time I'd told Bob that I was going to Pennsylvania to spend some time with my parents, but it didn't really matter what excuse I gave him. He barely listened and hardly seemed to care. I had little doubt that he was grateful for the chance to make plans of his own while I was away. The situation suited us both.

"You know," Jeff said, "the more I see you, the more I love you, Kay."

"That makes two of us then." I kissed his cheek and he turned his head on the pillow so my lips would touch his mouth instead. We had kissed so furiously in the wild throes of joy just a few minutes earlier that my lips were tender, almost sore, but his touch was light and the little bit of pain I felt was beautiful, too. I let his tongue slide into my mouth and we kissed lazily for several minutes. It was the kind of kiss that only two people who are very much in love can give. A kiss that comes not so much from passion or desire, but the insatiable need to be close. A sort of reassurance to each other that you're there and always will be.

When our lips drew apart, Jeff smiled and then started to laugh.

"What's so funny?"

"I still can't believe it!" he said, giving me a strong hug. "This is too wonderful to really be happening! I've got to be dreaming it!"

I gave him a playful pinch on the thigh.

"Ouch!"

"Still think you're dreaming?" I laughed.

"God, you're wonderful," he sighed.

"Even when I pinch you?"

"Even then." His arm tightened still further around me and he turned to kiss my hair. "I thought I'd lost you, Kay. I thought for sure we'd never know happiness like this. When I came to your cabin that day in Caracas and Tracey told me you'd gone, I thought I'd lose my mind."

"Let's not talk about the past any more, Jeff," I said softly. "Except for the good parts."

"Like that night on the beach in St. Thomas?"

"Mmmm-hmmm."

"Have you forgiven me yet for taking you there?"

"Well. . ." I teased. "Almost."

"Almost. . .?"

"I still would like to see a fire dance!" I laughed.

"Okay! Let me up and I'll do one for you! You can throw lit matches at me while I hop around the room!"

"Oh, you!" I squeezed him so tightly that I made him grunt.

"I'll do anything for you, Kay," he swore, suddenly

serious. "A fire dance, an Irish jig, anything. You name it, and it's yours."

"Just love me," I whispered. "That will be enough."

"That'll be easy," he said. "It comes naturally."

We kissed again, a long slow kiss, and then lay silent in each other's arms for several minutes. We didn't need to speak. We both knew what was in each other's mind and heart, and it was the same thing. I'd never felt so close to anyone in all my life. It seemed like I'd known and loved Jeff forever, and he me.

"What made you call me that day?" he asked, his hand softly stroking my shoulders. "I'd still like to know. What made you change your mind, Kay?"

I'd never told Jeff about Bob and Miss Blair. I didn't want him to think that I'd run to him just to spite my husband, or from some twisted anything-you-can-do idea of revenge. Because, in the back of my mind, I guess I still wasn't entirely sure myself that it wasn't my motive.

"Let's just say I opened my eyes and finally came to my senses," I said.

"I hope you'll never close them on me again."

"Don't worry. I doubt that I'll ever want to stop looking at you."

"Even when I'm old and wrinkled?" he teased.

"Not even then. Provided, of course," I said, as a flutter of uneasiness rippled through me, "that it's an even exchange. Don't forget: I'm going to be old and wrinkled long before you are."

"Not in my eyes, you won't," he swore. "To me, you'll always be as beautiful as you are right now."

It was exactly what I wanted and needed to hear. It would still take a while before I was able to stop thinking of the difference in our ages and realized that, where love is concerned, time is of no consequence.

"Want some more wine?" he asked. We had brought a bottle of sparkling burgundy to the hotel room with us, and been sipping from it on and off all afternoon.

"If you do."

"We might as well kill the bottle," he said.

We both knew, without saying it, that the hour was growing late and it would soon be time for me to leave. Those last moments of our weekends together were always the worst. It felt like tearing off part of myself when I said goodbye to Jeff and walked away. The pain always stayed with me until the next time I saw him, when it instantly vanished.

Without letting go of me, he reached for the burgundy bottle on the table beside him. "Where's your glass?" he asked. I reached for it on the opposite table, but we were in an awkward position for pouring wine and when he tried to fill my glass, some of it spilled out and dribbled down on my breasts. I squealed from the sudden wet feeling running down my skin and started to pull away from him to dry myself on the sheet. Instead of letting me, Jeff suddenly put down the bottle and quickly bent his head. He started to lap the wine off my breasts with his tongue, like a hungry kitten going after spilled cream.

"Jeff! That *tickles!*"

He looked up and winked at me. "Maybe so, but it tastes damn good! I think I'll have some more!" Before I could stop him, he'd turned the bottle and let more of the cool red wine slosh down on me. He burrowed his face in the cleft between my breasts and made little smacking noises with his lips while he cleaned it off.

"*Stop* it!" I squealed.

"Doesn't it feel good?"

"Well. . ." I had to admit that it did.

"The stuff's gone too flat to drink any other way by

now," he said. "Let's kill the bottle like this!"

"Oh! Jeff! No!" I laughed helplessly as he suddenly covered my belly with a thin film of wine. It collected in the indentation of my navel, and he wasted no time in filling it again as soon as he'd tongued it dry.

Slowly and insidiously, he eased himself between my legs and began to dribble the wine lower and lower. I knew what he was going to do, but I didn't try to stop him. In the weekends we'd been together, I'd learned a lot more about lovemaking than Bob had ever taught me. I felt no guilt or shame in doing anything with Jeff now. It seemed that it was right for our bodies to be together in any position, any action. When he made love to me with his mouth, it was as tender and beautiful as any other way I'd known in all the years I'd been married. Perhaps more so, since the discovery had been made with Jeff and it seemed like something special just the two of us knew.

I stroked his hair softly and ran my fingers over the back of his head and he followed the trail of wine. I sighed with complete rapture when he found me, and surrendered myself to him in joyous abandon. I had never dreamed that love had so many facets, like a glittering diamond that he'd polished and set before my eyes.

When he came back up to me some time later, I felt limp with total pleasure. I hugged him tightly to my breast and kissed his head again and again. I had tears of happiness brimming in my eyes.

"Thank you," I whispered. "Thank you, thank you, darling."

He sucked gently on my breasts, telling me without words that thanks weren't necessary. A little while later, he drew away and asked if I'd like a cigarette.

I looked at him and smiled. "I haven't had *my* wine yet."

"Gee, I'm sorry. The bottle's empty. . ."

"My glass isn't." We exchanged looks and started to laugh at the same time. He knew what I was going to do, but since I never had before, he was surprised.

"Are you sure?"

"Mmm-hmmm." I rolled him over on his back and reached for my glass.

"You don't have to," he said.

"I know that," I said, as I started to slowly spill the wine. "I want to."

When it was time for us to dress and go, Jeff held me back. I knew by the look in his eyes that he was thinking the same thing I was. Neither of us wanted to leave. If we could have somehow made all the clocks in the world stop ticking and frozen time in its tracks, we would have done so. But since we couldn't, we had to face the realization that another of our weekends was over.

"Kay," he said, "I hate this."

"I know. So do I, believe me." I tenderly touched his cheek. "But let's not think about it. Let's only think about the next time we'll be together. Next weekend's not that far away. You can make it, can't you? Or should I take a plane up to Boston?"

"No," he said. "I'll come down."

I was relieved that he wanted to. Since Tracey was also in Boston, there was always the chance that she might see us there together, and the results would be more disastrous than I cared to imagine. New York was safer. It was easier for us to get lost in the crowd.

"I'd better go then," I said. "I'll see you next week." I went to kiss him, but he pulled back.

"Damn it! It just isn't fair! I want more of you than

this, Kay."

"I know, but it just isn't possible."

"He has you all week, and he doesn't even want you. I'm desperately in love and need you every minute we can be together, and all I get is a stolen weekend."

We'd discussed my marriage a number of times before, and I'd tried to make Jeff see that I wasn't ready for divorce. Not yet. I was sure of my love for him and equally sure that I no longer loved Bob but there was too much else involved in such a drastic step. I said I needed time before I could take it, and Jeff had agreed to give it to me. But once again I could see that he was anxious for me to make up my mind.

"I'm going to come to New York," he announced. "For good."

"What. . .?"

"I've been thinking about it a lot," he said, "and I've made up my mind. I need to be as close to you as possible, as often as I can. If you won't leave your husband, then I'll come to you. I'm going to transfer from Harvard Law to NYU. They've got a good law school down here, too, and I'll take a cheap apartment somewhere so you can stay with me whenever it's possible."

"Jeff, are you sure?"

"I'm sure that I love you and that I need you," he said. "What else is there to be sure about?"

"Please don't," I said. "Not yet." Somehow, the idea of sneaking in to see Jeff while Bob was at work, having what some of my friends slyly referred to as a "matinee afternoon," seemed so sordid to me. Much more so than the past weekends we'd spent entirely together, as though in another world. "Give me just a little more time," I asked.

"You're still not sure whether it's going to be him or me in the end, are you, Kay?" he asked, and his eyes held such sadness that it made my heart ache to look into them.

"I just need a little more time."

He shrugged, resigning himself to the situation. "Okay. I'm not going to force you to do anything you don't want yourself."

I kissed him tenderly and squeezed his hand with all my strength. "Thank you, Jeff. It's going to be all right. You'll see."

"I hope so."

I kissed him again and quickly left the room. As I went down to the hotel lobby in the elevator, I hoped no one would notice I was wiping tears from my eyes.

I got home a little after ten. I heard the sound of the television blaring in the living room when I closed the front door, but I didn't bother to go in. I headed straight for the stairs. I was in no mood to confront Bob. I needed to get out of my clothes as quickly as possible and into a hot tub. My nerves felt as if a troop of Boy Scouts had been practicing knots on them.

I undressed in the bathroom while I ran a tub full of hot water. Too hot, in fact. I needed to relax, not boil myself like a lobster. While I was waiting for the water to cool a little, I went out to the bedroom to collect my curlers and nightgown. I planned to get under the covers as soon as I'd calmed down, and sleep for at least five days. Until it was time to go back to New York and be with Jeff again, like a dream in reverse, when only the waking parts are wonderful.

Bob was sitting on the edge of the bed. I hadn't heard him come upstairs, and suddenly seeing him there was such a surprise that it made me squeal and give a little jump.

"You startled me!" I said.

"Guilty conscience?" he asked. Something in his eyes made me instantly wary as he stood up and confronted me.

"Of course not. You just surprised me, that's all."

"Have a good time in Pennsylvania?"

I shrugged as I took my box of curlers from the dresser drawer. "It was all right. How much fun can you have in Pennsylvania?"

"Not as much as you can at the Plaza Hotel, I'll bet."

I froze instantly. My heart began to thump like a drum and such a shiver went down my back that it felt like I'd stepped into a block of ice.

"Wh-what do you mean?"

"You thought you were being pretty damn clever, didn't you?" he said. "Thought I wouldn't find out about your little escapades, huh?" His big, meaty hands were opening and closing like claws as he came slowly toward me.

"I—don't know what you're talking about."

"Remember Lou Moran?" he said. "Tall guy? Blond hair? Works with me?"

What was he getting at? "I don't think so."

"No, I guess not," he said. His face was grim. His left eye was starting to twitch, the way it always did when he was worked up about something. "He wondered why you didn't say hello to him in the Oak Room last night. He was sitting at the table right across from you."

Oh, my God! I'd told Jeff that we shouldn't go down to dinner; that it was safer to order from room service and eat in the room. But he'd insisted. Now the bottom had dropped out of everything. I felt like all those happy, unsuspecting people on the *Titanic* must have felt the night it hit an iceberg and, incredibly, without a moment's warning, their dream world had become a nightmare.

I backed up against the dresser. I needed to lean on something, or collapse.

"Lou wondered who the guy you were with was, too," Bob said, as he advanced on me. "He said he thought it was me at first, the way you were kissing and holding hands and making lovey-dovey, 'til he noticed the moustache."

There was nothing I could say. Nothing I could do, except lower my eyes and pray that somehow I would wake up in a minute and find this wasn't really happening.

"And then Lou wondered why you went upstairs to this guy's room, and why it seemed like you were planning to bed down for the night in there. When he called this morning, I didn't know what to tell him. Maybe you could give me a few ideas, Kay. Huh? Should I have told him he's a liar?"

I swallowed hard. "Of course. It—must have been some woman who just looked like me."

"Yeah, that's what I thought, too." His eyes were glistening like they had fire inside them. "That's why I called your folks in Pennsylvania, right after I hung up from Lou. Funny thing, though, Kay. They didn't have any more idea where you were than I did. Your old lady said she hadn't heard from you in more than a month."

I squeezed my eyes tightly shut. *Wake up! Wake up!* a voice inside me screamed. This isn't really happening! You're asleep and having a bad dream! Wake up, and you'll be back in Jeff's arms, safe and sound!

"Where the hell *were* you?" Bob demanded. He

grabbed me by my upper arms and shook me so violently that I heard my teeth rattle as my head snapped back and forth like a child's toy on a string.

"You *were* screwing around with some other guy, weren't you?" he raged. "That *was* you Lou saw in the hotel, wasn't it?"

Something inside me suddenly snapped, like Bob had just shaken it loose, and I couldn't control myself. I started to scream back at him. "Yes! Yes! Yes!"

He slapped me so hard that for a moment everything in the room went black. When the lights flashed on again, I was on the floor. He reached down and grabbed a handful of my hair, pulling me to my feet with such brute force that it felt like he was going to rip off my scalp.

"You whore! You goddamn, stinking little *whore!*" he bellowed. He shoved me backwards and I hit the dresser so hard that every bottle on its top rattled. "Who was he? Tell me his name! I'll find the son-of-a-bitch and I'll kill him with my bare hands!" From the look on his face, I hadn't a doubt that he'd do it.

"I don't know," I cried.

His face went blank. For a moment it looked like he hadn't heard me. His eyes rolled with confusion, then darkened again. "You don't *know?* You don't *know!* You mean you just let some guy on the street pick you up and take you to a hotel, and you didn't even bother to find out his *name?*"

I couldn't involve Jeff in this. It was my problem, not his, and I had to solve it.

"Yes."

Bob raised a clenched fist and if I hadn't pushed him away I know he would have smashed it straight into my face. I ran from him, putting the distance of the bed between us. If I hadn't been naked, I would have run for the door and kept on running, straight out of that house and never looking back.

"I'll kill you," he snarled. "I swear to God, Kay, I'm going to catch you and kill you. And then I'm going to find out who that bastard was you were with and kill him, too."

"Why?" I screamed, as he moved to come around the bed and trap me. "Why should you care if any other man puts his hands on me? *You* don't want to!"

"You're my wife!" he stormed. "You belong to me! I'll touch you when I damn well feel like it!"

"I don't belong to you!" I screamed back at him. "I belong to myself! You don't own me, Bob! A marriage license and a ring on my finger doesn't make me your slave! I'm a person, too! I've got rights of my own. Needs of my own. If you can't fill them, then I have to find someone else who can."

"I'll show you what rights you've got," he snarled.

"Stay away from me! I swear if you hit me again, I'll call the police!"

"Oh no you won't." He laughed a maniac's laugh. The look on his face sent shivers racing down my back. "Because dead women can't make phone calls. And that's just what you're going to be when I get through with you, you frigging little whore. *Dead!*"

"You're too late!" I shouted back at him. Though I was terrified to the very marrow of my bones, something inside me gave me the courage finally to say all the things I'd been holding back for so long. All the things that had been eating me alive for so many months. Years.

"I'm already dead, Bob! I've been dead for twenty years! Ever since I married you! Twenty years ago I killed myself, but I didn't even know it until a little while ago. Until I found out what it means to be alive again. I've been a zombie, part of the living dead, for longer than you know."

"You're nuts!" he said with a bitter laugh. "You're not only a whore, you're a *crazy* whore!"

"I don't expect you to understand," I cried. "Why should you? You've never tried to understand anything else about me; why should you start now? The worst part is, I let you do it."

"What the hell are you talking about?"

"All these years you've been ignoring me, like I was some kind of machine you could turn on and off when you needed something done," I said. "That's what I'm talking about. When's the last time you've thought of me as a person, Bob? As someone more than just your wife—whatever that's supposed to be? When's the last time you really listened to anything I had to say?"

His mouth twisted in a cruel smirk. "When's the last time you said anything worth listening to?"

It hit me like a punch in the stomach, because the words had the weight of truth in them. Of course he was right. I'd made no effort in all those twenty years to be anything else but a wife to him, so how could I really say he was to blame for treating me as he did? I'd let him. The process hadn't happened overnight. It had built up slowly, and I'd helped pile the stones. I hadn't thought of myself as a person. I'd always been dependent on him for everything. Food, clothes, furniture, the house, money, and whatever I was inside. My ideas, my values, my thoughts were all reflections of Bob's. Mirror images of his. I'd never had the desire or courage to form any of my own, because I'd always been afraid they'd be wrong.

He'd once told me that I always let people walk all over me, and he was right. I did. But it was far worse than that. Not only had I let him and everyone else walk on me, I'd got down on my belly to make it easier for them to do it. But no more. No matter what might happen between us before that night was through, I vowed, I would never willingly let myself be stepped on and squashed again. I had as much right to stand tall as anyone else.

"You think you're going to get out of it by changing the subject?" he snarled. "You think I'm going to let you go if you confuse the issue?"

"You can't hurt me, Bob," I said, though my voice was shaking as I said it.

"You wanna bet?" He slammed one fist into the palm of his other hand.

"You can beat me, if that's what you really want to do, but you can't hurt me. You lost that power the day I found out about you and Miss Blair."

He stopped cold in his tracks, like an engine that suddenly ran out of steam. His eyes screwed up in a look of half-belief. "What?"

Now it was my turn. At last.

"It's a shame you didn't look a little harder for that earring," I said. "Or didn't she know it was missing 'til you got home?"

"What earring? What the hell are you talking about?"

"I'm talking about the gold earring shaped like a heart," I said, my eyes level with his. "The one with the little ruby in the center and the engraved inscription on the back that reads: *To JB from BL*. The one Miss Blair lost at the Lakeview Lodge in Vermont. They sent it to me a few weeks ago. The maid found it under the dresser and they thought it was mine. The package was addressed to Mrs. Lawrence, and the letter that came with it said they hoped my husband and I had enjoyed our two-week stay up there. It's too bad they didn't realize that JB and Mrs. Lawrence aren't the same person. Too bad for you, that is. I probably never would have known about it any other way, Bob. I actually believed that crock of bull you told me about Chicago."

His hands unclenched their fists and his arms dropped limply at his sides.

"It cost you five thousand dollars to get me off on that cruise for two weeks," I continued. "Couldn't you at least have registered under a phony name, like every other husband who cheats on his wife with his secretary? Or didn't you want to do that? No, I'll bet not. Knowing you, you probably put the whole thing on your American Express card and even planned to deduct it from your income tax this year as a business expense. I'll say it was! A *monkey* business expense!"

For a moment it looked like he was actually suppressing the urge to smile. That, more than anything else, made me hate him as I never dreamed I could.

"All right," he said, "I guess that makes us even, doesn't it?"

"Even. . .?" I stared at him with absolute incredulity. Did he think of it as some sort of game? One for you, one for me, score tied?

"Not by a long shot it doesn't," I swore.

"What do you want me to do?" he demanded. "Tell you I'm sorry?"

"No, please don't. Save your breath, because I wouldn't believe you if you did. The only thing you could possibly be sorry for is getting caught. And I could never tell you that I'm sorry in return, because

I'm not." I brushed past him and picked up the clothes I'd brought from the bathroom.

"What're you doing?"

"I'm getting dressed. What does it look like?"

"I thought you were going to take a bath?"

"That was ten years ago," I sighed. "The water's cold by now."

"You going to him?"

"Who?" I really hadn't much of an idea where I was going, only that I couldn't stay under the same roof with Bob another night. It was finished now. Finally and at last, it was over. In ten minutes' time, something that I'd worked twenty years to salvage suddenly didn't seem worth the effort. I could walk away and feel I'd left nothing, absolutely nothing, behind. Except twenty wasted years of my life.

"You know who I'm talking about. That guy. The one you were with."

"How could I be going to him?" I said, and it was my turn to suppress a smile. "I don't even know his name, remember?"

It was the wrong thing to have said. I'd taken one step too many over the line and found myself once again in dangerous territory. He grabbed me by the arm and pulled me up against him. He ripped the dress from my hand and threw it on the floor.

"Is *this* what you're after?" he snarled, thrusting his hand between my legs and squeezing hard. "Huh? Is that what you need, bitch?"

I winced in pain and tried to push him back. "Let go of me, Bob!"

"You want some fun, huh? You're jealous of Joan, 'cause she was getting it and you weren't. That's it, Kay, huh?"

"I don't care if you sleep with Miss Blair for the rest of your life, Bob," I cried. "I just don't want you to touch me again."

His fingers dug deeper, making me cry in agony.

"You think some other guy does it better than me? Is that it? You think I can't give it to you just as good as any guy on the street?" With his free hand, he ripped open the front of his shirt, tearing the last three buttons as he pulled it off his body. His hairy, sweating chest was heaving like a wild animal's.

"Let me go! I don't want you to touch me!"

"We'll see about that!" he muttered. "Once you're getting it, we'll see whether you want it or not. Once upon a time I could make you scream for more, and I can do it again."

"Once upon a time I *loved* you!" I cried. "But I don't love you any more! I don't!"

While I squirmed against him and tried to break loose, he jerked open his belt and dropped his pants. He pushed me backwards, onto the bed, and quickly stepped out of his shorts. We were both naked now, like two beasts confronting each other in the darkness of a cave.

"Stop it, Bob!" I screamed. "Get away from me! I don't want this!"

"Like hell you don't!" He laughed savagely and dropped down on me. His mouth sought mine, but I turned my head away. "I'll have you whimpering for it in a minute!" he vowed. "I'll make you *beg* me for it, you whore!"

"Let go of me! Let *go* of me!"

His sweaty hand thrust between my legs and pushed them apart. He held me down as he scrambled into position. "I'll make you *beg!*" he muttered again.

Dear God, please make him stop! I prayed. This was

too horrible to be happening. I'd wanted him for so long, but not like this! He was like a ruthless beast on top of me, determined to have his own way.

I thrashed my legs, trying to keep them closed. His eyes burned down at me, but not with love. Far from it. What I saw in those flaming sockets wasn't even lust or desire. It was a hard, grim need for possession. As though I had challenged his authority to take me—dared to question his very ownership of me—and he was determined to prove I still belonged to him.

"*Stop it!*" I screamed, as I felt the first probe. I started to lift my knee to thrust him off and protect myself, but his arm suddenly swung up and for a terrifying instant I thought he was going to hit me again. Beat me until I lay beneath him in unconscious submission. I froze.

"That's better," he muttered. "What the hell are you making such a fuss about? When I couldn't do it, you were all over me like a rabbit in heat. Now that I want it, you're fighting me."

"Because *I* don't want it!" I sobbed. "It's *my* body, and I don't want any part of you in it."

"Yeah? Well ain't that just . . . too . . . bad."

He made a loud, grunting noise and I screamed as he entered me. When he began to move, I squeezed my eyes tightly shut and prayed that since I couldn't stop it from happening, at least it would be over soon. But he battered me for what seemed an eternity, until I saw raw with pain and certain that I was bleeding. It was like a struggle to the death, and he was determined to be the victor.

I had never fully understood the horror of rape until that night. I'd never known what it was like to be taken by a man against your will. To be used like a *thing* that existed solely for his pleasure. When it was finally over and Bob pulled off me, I vowed that no man would ever use me like that again. I would sooner die.

As soon as he let me go, I struggled off the bed. When I tried to stand up, my legs buckled in under me and I had to clutch the edge of the dresser for support. It felt as though a knife had ripped straight through my insides and the wound was still gaping wide with pain.

"Where you going?" he grunted.

"To the bathroom." The words hurt my throat. "Do you mind?"

"You can go to hell, for all I care," he muttered.

"I've already been there," I said. "Thanks to you."

I went into the bathroom and locked the door. I sat on the toilet seat and cried until it seemed there were no more tears left for me to ever cry again. Then, slowly and gently, because it hurt just to touch myself, I eased into the tub of cool water and tried to wash away every last trace of him.

He was asleep when I came out. Still naked, he lay sprawled across the bed like a well-fed animal home from the kill, snoring with self-satisfied contentment.

I carefully opened the closet door, not wanting to wake him, and took down my suitcase. As quickly as I could, I packed as many necessary clothes as would fit inside. I dressed and carried the suitcase from the bedroom, down the stairs, and out of the house. When I closed the front door behind me, it felt I was shutting the door on a prison cell and for the first time in my life, not just since I'd married Bob, but ever, I was finally free.

Chapter 12

I never told Jeff what happened that night. If I had, I know he would have gone for Bob and killed him. Instead, I said that I'd finally made up my mind and realized I couldn't live any longer in a loveless marriage, no matter what price I might have to pay to escape it. Since it was the truth—at least part of it—I saw no reason for telling him any more. It was better for him to think that nothing else but my love for him had made the final decision.

I called him in Boston the day after I walked out on Bob and told him what I'd done. He wanted to fly down immediately to be with me, but I insisted that he stay in school. It was bad enough, I said, that he was sacrificing every weekend when he ought to be studying; I didn't want to be responsible for nipping a promising law career in the bud.

I took a room in a small, inexpensive residence hotel on lower Madison Avenue and went to see a lawyer about filing divorce papers. I had plenty of grounds. Mental cruelty. Physical cruelty. Infidelity. Incompatibility. I felt like I was ordering from a Chinese menu. One from column A; two from column B. The lawyer served Bob with papers that week and, to my surprise, when the reply came through his attorney, it seemed he wasn't going to contest the divorce. Perhaps he was as anxious and relieved to finally be rid of me as I was of him.

Surprising, too, was the fact that Bob agreed to make a full property settlement with me. Knowing how he valued money and possessions, I hadn't expected him to give in so easily. Though my lawyer said I was entitled to half of everything we jointly owned, and though I felt I deserved my share after all the years I'd spent with him, I wouldn't have fought Bob in court if he hadn't wanted to split our holdings down the middle. I didn't want his money, just my freedom.

After a few weeks, I found a small apartment in the West Village at a reasonable rent, and moved out of the hotel. Jeff had applied to NYU for transfer to the law school from Harvard, and when he was accepted, as neither of us had really doubted he would be, it was convenient for him to walk to classes from the apartment.

It was a lovely little place I'd found on Ninth Street. The fourth floor of a small, walk-up brownstone. It was nothing fancy, but it had more charm than I'd ever imagined could be found in New York apartments. The living room and the bedroom both had exposed brick walls, there was a fireplace in the living room that burned logs and coal, and a skylight in the bedroom that spilled sunlight in on us each morning and let us look up at the stars each night.

I had a wonderful time decorating. Until the divorce was final and I received my share of our joint bank account and the sale of the house and furnishings, I had to make do on the little amount of money I'd tucked away over the years in a personal savings account. But that, and the money Jeff got from his parents, was enough to make do. I felt like a new bride all over again, making ends meet on a shoestring.

While Jeff was at class, or home studying, I scoured the second-hand furniture stores and antique shops in the Village and turned up some lovely, inexpensive things to give our place a warm, cozy air. Our furniture wasn't at all like the made-to-order pieces I'd once picked out at Sloane's, but we had so much fun fixing things up and buying them together that it made all the difference. I don't think Bob even noticed when I brought anything new into the house, unless I first brought it to his attention. Then, all he usually did was mutter, "Oh, yeah. That's nice." and I knew he didn't care one way or the other.

The most expensive item Jeff and I bought was an antique brass bed. I fell in love with it as soon as I saw it. The brass was tarnished and it would take many hours of hard rubbing before it was back in its original condition, but it was a one-of-a-kind piece and I wanted it more than anything. "Then you'll have it!" Jeff swore. When I told him we couldn't possibly afford the bed and still buy the oak table and chairs we also liked, he said, "So what? We'll have breakfast, lunch, and dinner in bed! Buy it!"

I spent many happy weeks making everything just the way I wanted it, but once the apartment was finished an unexpected problem developed. There was nothing more for me to do. Jeff still had his classes and his studying, but I only had time on my hands. And after a while, when there no longer were trips to be made in search of things we needed, I felt I was getting in his way. He never said anything about it, but I sensed it. Sometimes while I was puttering around the apartment I'd catch him looking up from a book with an expression on his face that seemed to say: "Can't you make a little less noise? I'm trying to study here." Other times, when I was so bored I had nothing else to do but turn on the afternoon movie on television, he would get up and say he was going over to the NYU library to do some research. I knew that what he really was doing was escaping from me for a while. My constant presence hovering over him, waiting until he was finished with his work so we could do something together, was starting to drive him up the wall.

One night, just after his mid-term exams were through and he'd passed everything with flying colors, we decided to order in a pizza for supper and catch the late show at the Waverly. Jeff was in the shower and I was changing my clothes for the movie, when the doorbell rang. I zipped up my dress in a hurry, thinking that Gino must have bought a mobile pizza oven to explain the speedy delivery, and went to answer the door. When I opened it, though, my heart jumped into my throat.

"Tracey . . . !" I stared at my daughter in stunned disbelief. It had been months since I'd last seen her, or had any communication with her at all, for that matter. Just after I'd left Bob, I wrote her at Emerson and tried to explain why I was getting a divorce. I never mentioned a word about Jeff, of course, but cited general incompatibility with her father as the reason. I hadn't expected her to understand, and she hadn't. She'd never answered my letter, nor the two I wrote after it. I'd finally decided that in time she would sort things out in her head and write back. But I had never dreamed she would just appear on the doorstep like that.

"Can I come in, Mother?" she asked.

I hesitated. The sound of the running shower was a clear indication that I wasn't alone, but I had no idea how she would handle the situation when Jeff came out of the bathroom.

"If you'd rather not see me . . ." she said, starting to turn away.

"No, oh honey, I didn't mean that. Come in. Please. I'm just so surprised to see you here, that's all." I held open the door for her. "Come in, honey, and sit down."

"I'm not going to stay long, Mother," she said. "In fact, I'm really just here as a messenger for Daddy."

"Oh?" I felt my palms starting to sweat a little.

"He's downstairs, waiting in the car. He'd like to come up and talk to you for a while, but he didn't want to come alone."

"So he sent you as a scouting party, to see if the coast was clear?"

"Something like that." She smiled uneasily. "Could I tell him it's all right to come up?"

"No." I said it flatly and firmly, without the slightest hesitation in my mind. "Your father and I have nothing to say to each other that hasn't already been said—or is too late to *be* said. I don't want to see him again."

Her eyes were starting to water. "Mother, please? Please see him? These past few months he's been miserable without you. He misses you so much, and wishes you'd come back home."

"We don't have a home any more, honey."

"Oh, Mother. Don't be like this. If you'd only hear him out, I'm sure you'd change your mind."

"I doubt it, Tracey. Maybe once I would have, but not now. It's gone too far. Your father and I are strangers to each other now. It would be like starting all over with a man I've never known."

She started to say something more, but at just that moment the sound of the shower stopped in the bathroom. Her ears perked as though she'd just realized someone else was in the apartment. Perhaps she'd heard the running water and assumed I was getting it hot for myself. "Who's here, Mother?" she asked, giving me a strange look.

I didn't have to answer. Jeff's voice did it for me.

"Hey, Kay, was that the pizza boy I heard pushing the bell? Geez, that was fast!"

He came out of the bathroom, wearing only a towel around his waist, and stopped dead in his tracks the moment he saw Tracey. His face looked as surprised as hers.

"Jeff . . . !" she gasped. She turned to me, her eyes wildly darting in absolute confusion. "Mother, what's *he* doing here?" Then, turning back to Jeff, she asked the same question. "What are *you* doing here?"

"He lives here, Tracey," I said softly.

"He—*lives* here?"

"We share this apartment."

"Oh, no." Her head started to shake. "I don't believe it. This must be some kind of a joke." Her eyes darted back to Jeff, who was just standing there, waiting, not knowing what to do himself. "He *lives* here . . . ? " With *you* . . . ?" She started to get up, but I took her hand and made her stay.

"Jeff, please get some clothes on and go outside for a walk for a while, will you? I'd like to talk to Tracey in private."

"Sure, hon," he said.

"Oh, don't bother on *my* account!" she exclaimed. "Don't let *me* disturb your little love nest! Heaven forbid!" Her cheeks were running with tears.

"Tracey, please don't cry. I wish there'd been some other way of breaking this to you, but I never expected you to—just show up here."

She turned away from me when I tried to touch her, and started to cry. Jeff came out of the bedroom in a sport shirt and a pair of slacks he'd hurriedly slipped on.

"I'll be back later," he said. "Take all the time you need."

When he was gone, I tried to make Tracey turn and look at me. "Honey, please try to understand—"

"I *do* understand!" she spat. "Boy, do I ever! All the time I thought he was gay! That's a laugh! He's not gay, he's *sick!* You were probably carrying on with each other on the ship, too. Weren't you? I'll bet that's why you flew back early. He got too much for you to handle."

"Tracey, it's not like that at all."

"How *is* it, Mother? Give me the *nice* explanation for a woman like you and a boy like him. Please. I'd love to hear it. Because as far as I'm concerned, the whole thing's just disgusting."

"You don't know what it was like being married to your father," I said. "A woman has certain needs, and he—"

"You're not just a woman," she cried, "you're my *mother!*"

"Don't you think I still feel a woman's needs, in spite of that?" I said with a tender smile.

"Not like .. *that*."

"Tracey, that night we had our talk on the ship about sex, you expected me to accept the way you felt about sex and love without question. Why can't you do the same for me? Why is it so hard for you to understand that *I* have needs, too, as you do?" But even as I asked her to understand, I knew why it was so difficult. If I had been in her place, and it was *my* mother I'd just

245

found with another man—and a man close to my own age, at that—I'd have been just as sick with shock and disappointment. Children never fully believe that their parents are human beings, too, with wants and needs exactly like their own.

She pulled away again when I tried to touch her. "Is he *good*, Mother?" she said, her voice riddled with hurt, angry venom. "In bed, I mean. Is he really *good*?"

"Please don't," I said. "I know how difficult—"

"Boy, he sure *must* be, for you to make a laughing stock of yourself like this! Because that's what you'll be, you know, once people find out about this. A laughing stock! A woman your age with someone like Jeff! Wow! You really must have needed it *bad*, Mother! You had to find the youngest stud in the barn to take care of you!"

It was all I could do to keep from slapping her. I knew she didn't mean what she was saying, that her words were only trying to give back some of the hurt she felt inside herself, but it didn't make it any easier for me to sit there and let her say them to me.

"Jeff and I love each other," I said.

"Oh, yeah! Sure! I'll just *bet!* But what're you going to do when he's had enough, Mother? Where will you be when he gets over the novelty and starts looking around for someone *else's* mother to seduce?"

"That's not going to happen."

"Of course it is! Even *I* know that much! For Heaven's sake, Mother, don't you understand that he's just got a schoolboy's crush on you? Who knows? Maybe you're the first woman he's ever had—"

"I *am* the first woman he's had," I snapped. "Or maybe the second. But he's had lots of other *girls* before, believe me. And whether you know it or not, there's a big difference between a girl and a woman."

"Sure there is. It's spelled a-g-e. A woman is *older* than a girl, that's all."

"Someday you'll realize what a ridiculous remark that is," I said. "When you're my age—"

"When I'm your age," she said, cutting me short, "I hope I have more sense than you do. I hope that by then I'll have stopped believing in fairy tales." She gave me a malicious smirk and added, "No offense toward your beloved."

"I think maybe you should leave, Tracey," I said. "I don't see any point in carrying this any further. You're very upset right now, and I can understand why. You're only going to say more things that you'll be sorry for later. When you've had a chance to think about it, call me. We'll get together and talk some more."

She picked up her purse and started for the door. "Don't hold your breath waiting for the phone to ring, Mother," she snapped on her way out.

I stared at the closed door for a long while before I was able to bring myself back to reality. My hands were shaking when I reached for a cigarette and lit it, but there were no tears in my eyes. A few months ago I would have been sobbing my heart out at that point. Probably running down the stairs after Tracey and begging her to forgive me, promising I'd leave Jeff and never think of doing anything to hurt her like that again. But a few months ago I was a different person, and no such thought was in my mind now.

I knew Tracey was hurt, and I was sorry for it. But it was *her* problem, not mine. If I'd learned only one thing through all this, it was that each of us must live our own life according to the way we see best, and not feel guilty or responsible for someone else's disapproval.

I hoped that in time she would realize I had to find my own happiness, and feel glad that I'd done so with Jeff. I hoped she would accept us one day as a couple, and learn to love him, if only because *I* loved him and he made me happy. If she couldn't do that, though, I wasn't going to waste any more of my life trying to win her approval. She certainly wouldn't have done the same for me.

"Was it pretty bad?" Jeff asked when he came back a while later. The pizza had been delivered and was getting cold in the box, but neither of us had an appetite now to eat it. Nor did we feel much in the mood for a movie. He sat down beside me and held me close, knowing that was what I needed most at that moment. most at that moment.

"It was bad enough," I said.

"She'll get over it," he said. "I think the thing that bugs her the most is that I never made a play for *her*. She's just jealous I preferred you instead."

"Oh?" I laughed and squeezed his hand. "And what makes you think that *you're* such an irresistable prize?"

"You do," he said. "Anyone that *you* can love has got to be somebody special."

Later that night, while we lay side-by-side in bed after making more intense love than we had for some time, I told Jeff that I wanted him to start looking for a place of his own and move out for a while. He turned his head, blew a billow of smoke toward the ceiling, and laughed.

"Okay. First thing in the morning. Who've you got moving in instead?"

"I'm serious, Jeff," I said. "I think we should be apart for a while."

His eyes suddenly registered a look of intense hurt.

"Why? What'd I do?"

"It's nothing you did. That's not the reason."

"Is it because of Tracey? Something she said to you?"

Where will you be when he gets over the novelty and starts looking around for someone else's mother to seduce?

"Partly, yes," I admitted. "Something she said stuck in my head and I can't shake it."

"The little bitch," he muttered. "I'd like to shake *her*! I should have wrung her neck while I had the chance."

"It's not just what she said, Jeff. It's something I've had in the back of my mind for some time now. She only made me realize what it is."

"Do you want to tell me about it?"

I took a deep breath and put out my cigarette. "It's *me*, Jeff. That's what the problem is. I'm starting to do the same thing with you that I did with Bob. I'm getting too dependent on you."

"I don't follow."

"Don't you see? Ever since the apartment's been finished, I haven't had anything to do with myself. I've fallen back into the same old routine. The cast has changed, and the setting, too, but the play's the same. I get up, I fix your meals, I clean the apartment, I wash your clothes, but I never do anything for *me*. Not in any fulfilling way, I mean. You're got your studying, but all I've got is you. I'm not growing beyond the limits of this apartment and our life here together. It's exactly where Bob and I went wrong. In the beginning, when we were both still kids, we were pretty much alike. We got married because we had to, and we thought our love would be enough for us to make a go of it. But then Bob started to grow. He went out and made something of himself, while all I did was what my mother had done before me. I kept house for Bob, but I never grew with him. And now it's happening with you. In another couple of years, you'll be a lawyer. You'll have a wonderful career ahead of you, with all kinds of exciting things to do, but all I'll still have is you."

"Thanks a lot," he muttered.

I took his hand and squeezed it. "You know I didn't mean it like that. You're all I'll ever want in a man, but not everything I'll ever need from life. There's a big difference. Can't you see it? If you ever left me—"

"You know I never will!"

"Maybe not. But maybe you won't have any choice in the matter. Maybe one day when you're crossing the street you'll have your mind on something else and—God forbid—you'll be hit by a car and killed."

"That's a cheerful thought."

"Please try to understand, Jeff. I'm just asking where *I'll* be if the time ever comes when I don't have you, for whatever reason."

"I guess I can see what you're getting at."

"I knew you would. I've got to make something of myself. Something that's completely independent of you. If I'm not able to survive by myself, then *we* can't survive as a couple, either."

"I think you've lost me again."

I tried to explain. "Do you remember back on the beach in St. Thomas, when you told me about Ellen Ramsey? How she made you feel that you could do anything in the world, because you wanted to do it for her?"

"Yes . . ."

"Well, I think I understand why she went away now.

I think she knew that if you never learned to do things for yourself first, you'd never amount to anything. No matter what you did, it would be for the wrong reason.

"You also said that two people in love have got to give *and* take from each other, in order for their love to stay vital. You were right. I know that now. And that's why Bob and I went wrong. All the things I had to give him were things he could have got from anyone. From machines, if necessary. You wouldn't want that to happen to us, would you? To suddenly look at me one day and wonder to yourself: why do I need her?"

"Of course not."

"And I don't want you to stay with me from a sense of obligation, either. Because you feel you have to. I want us to be together because we both want it. Because we really do need each other."

He was silent for a long while before asking, "What are you going to do, Kay? What are your plans?"

"I'm not sure yet. I've really only started to think about it. But I may try to write that book."

"Really?"

I smiled and squeezed his hand. "Do you remember when we talked outside the museum in Saint-Pierre, about what it must have been like there before the volcano erupted?"

"Sure."

"I think I'd like to do a lot more research about it, and see if I can't put together a story."

"That sounds like a great idea!" he said. "But why do I have to move out? Why can't I stay here with you, while you write it?"

"Because I've got to see if I can do it on my own. I've never been alone before, Jeff, and I've got to find out if I can stand on my own two feet. You can't build a solid

251

foundation if half of it is stronger than the other. When I've finished my book and I know I can make it by myself, then nothing in the world will be able to destroy us."

"Can I see you now and then while you're writing it?"

"Of course you can, silly!" I laughed.

"And afterwards . . . ?"

"We'll see how we both feel then," I said. "Let's not make any promises right now that either of us will feel bound to later on, in case things change."

"Okay," he said. "If that's how you want it."

"It's not just how I want it," I said softly, "it's how it's got to be."

Time and memory . . .

It seemed so long ago I said those words to Jeff, and yet it could have been only yesterday. I put down the paper and glanced at my watch. I'd been sitting and thinking for so long that I'd lost all track of the hour. I gulped down the last of my second cup of coffee, wincing at the unexpectedly cold taste in my mouth. I had to get a move on. There were so many things I had to do that day.

There were galleys to deliver to my publisher, first. I'd spent all weekend correcting them, and finally the job was finished. In another month or so I'd be able to walk into any bookstore and pick up the most beautiful novel ever written. At least *I* thought so, and I ought to know. It would have my name on it.

Then I had to dash to the post office to mail Tracey a sweater I'd bought for her birthday. The last time she was in New York and we went shopping together, she'd seen it and loved it.

And finally I had to meet Jeff at Forty-Seventh Street at noon. Today was the day we were going to pick out our rings.

THE CHANNINGS OF EVERLEIGH
Margaret Maitland

BT51199 $1.95
Novel

They rose from prisons... Marcus Channing from an English jail, she from the New Orleans slum district known as "The Irish Channel". Together they would build an empire amid Louisiana sugar cane. At first the "old families" shunned them and their vulgar display of wealth, the lavish parties. But soon the Channings of Everleigh were too powerful to ignore. A BT Original.

SUPERSTAR
Barry Mazer

BT51200 $1.50
Novel

This is the story of Rick Lathem, a hard rock star who was born to lose. He was a superstar who relished in excesses—of groupies, money, drugs. There were those who hated him, those who used him, and those who would profit by his death. From wild parties at Malibu to the cocaine crash pads of Manhattan, this is the story of a superstar about to fall. A BT Original.

KATHLEEN
Amanda Hart Douglass

BT51201 $1.95
Novel

Kathleen Holliday was the most famous actress in America, but few knew her as Katie O'Dowd, daughter of a drunken thief and dying prostitute, waif of New York's most notorious slum. By brains, beauty, and ruthless ambition she rose to the pinnacle of success but carried the memories of her hellish childhood. She was attended by men of wealth and power who wished to possess her body and soul. But Kathleen could never be theirs. There was a part of her that no one could own. A BT Original.

RIDE THE WILD COUNTRY BT51205 $1.50
Wade Hamilton   Western

He found himself accused of bushwhacking and stealing. He had to clear his name. But out on the prairie every man's hand was turned against him and only his quick wits and fast gun would keep him alive.

CALLAHAN RIDES ALONE BT51206 $1.50
Lee Floren   Western

An ex-Texas Ranger takes up ranching with a female partner and soon learns to take up his six gun as well. Rustling, murder, and robbery are about him and he wishes he was back in Texas. But he's in a new state and without his badge so he'll have to go outside the law.

FROM HELL TO TEXAS BT51207 $1.50
Dwight Bruckner   Western

Kincaid would have to battle a savage Mexican outlaw and his band of desperados to rescue his brother.

GUN BLAST BT51208 $1.25
Steven C. Lawrence   Western

A western family man was forced to pick up a badge and prepare himself to shoot faster and straighter than anyone in bloody Yellowstone City.

SEND TO: BELMONT TOWER BOOKS
P.O. Box 270
Norwalk, Connecticut 06852

Please send me the following titles:

Quantity	Book Number	Price
_____	_____	_____
_____	_____	_____
_____	_____	_____
_____	_____	_____
_____	_____	_____

In the event we are out of stock on any of your selections, please list alternate titles below.

_____	_____	_____
_____	_____	_____
_____	_____	_____
_____	_____	_____

Postage/Handling _____

I enclose . . . . . . _____

FOR U.S. ORDERS, add 35¢ per book to cover cost of postage and handling. Buy five or more copies and we will pay for shipping. Sorry no C.O.D.'s.

FOR ORDERS SENT OUTSIDE THE U.S.A.
Add $1.00 for the first book and 25¢ for each additional book. PAY BY foreign draft or money order drawn on a U.S. bank, payable in U.S. ($) dollars.

☐ Please send me a free catalog.

NAME_____
(Please print)

ADDRESS_____

CITY _____ STATE _____ ZIP _____

Allow Four Weeks for Delivery